Witches of Watson

A Novel

CONNOR MARSHALL

AngellStreetBooks
Frederick, Maryland

This is a work of fiction. All names, characters, and incidents are the product of the author's imagination. Watson High School and Slide County are fictitious. Any resemblance to actual persons, living or dead, or events is purely coincidental. The academic studies cited and the medical advice columns quoted are also fictitious, as is the poet Dame Therasia Awstin. The brief quotations from literature are accurately attributed and in the public domain.

WITCHES OF WATSON
Copyright © Connor Marshall 2015

Printed in the United States of America
Published by AngellStreetBooks, Frederick, Maryland
Library of Congress Control Number 2015948943
ISBN 9780692504925

For Sara and Neil
who are close to perfect

WITCHES OF WATSON

CHRISTOPHER

Annus 1993

The Queen. Of England. I read that last year she looked back on the year before, the one with Princess Diana and Charles separating, the fire and stuff, and said it was her "annus horribilis." I like that because it not only sounds somewhat anatomically funny but it describes precisely in perfect Latin my annus horribilis. This year. This annus, which has not been funny at all.

The horribilis that happened was partly my fault, I guess. I should have been more perceptive regarding Mom. I still wonder if there wasn't something more we could have done. Especially regarding her headaches, but I never thought she would do what she did. I also should have been more conscious, really conscious of my dad. My dad, as it turned out, was something of a major contributor to the horribilis of my annus. Although I'm confused on that whole issue with him. I don't think he meant to be. It just happened. I'm still trying to work that out. In the interest of my own self-improvement, I have tried not to be overly condemnatory regarding adults, but after all, they are in charge.

Certainly an exacerbating cause was and is school itself. That was where the poison was brewed.

High School! The whole gestalt. The perversesome social environment of the total place, the population of and surrounding which magnified what happened at home and exaggerated those twisted problems into even more distorted problems for me and for Miss Austin and ultimately for Mom.

School began just before Labor Day. Figure that inconvenience. Dad is still getting tomatoes out of his garden back of our nontraditional Cape Cod cottage. The baseball playoffs are over a month away, and Amy and I are piling onto the smelly, yelly, yellow bus, headed for JWWHS.

You know what I like about school? Nothing much. Or perhaps I should rephrase that. You know what I hate loathsomely about school? Everything except for that which I specifically specify otherwise, such as Amy and Miss Austin. Mr. Stetlik is okay, too, when he's sober.

I don't like the smell of the halls, the stewed food and tomatoey oregano saucey smell of the lunchroom, the sound of the lockers slamming, the endless buzz buzz of people who may or may not be talking about you, but they were in my case. I especially don't like the odor of chlorine and sweat-sogged underwear around the gym. Even the buses with their badly maintained exhaust systems make me feel slightly nauseated. I wouldn't be a bit surprised if some day they found an entire ghost school bus dead beside the road with all thirty-five passengers and the driver asphyxiated from carbon monoxide poisoning that leaked up through the floor.

Most of my teachers this first year are boringsome creepers of tediosity. Look at Mr. Beverly Beatrice Spurling. He, as they say, "means well," but he is so awesomely feeblesome in trying to explain something–probability, for instance–that he is constantly adding explanation on top of explanation. "So we see...what do we see? We see that if you have a jar, or a bowl, or any container you want—a box will do—and you fill it with black and white marbles—or any color—red and blue—or beans—it doesn't have to be marbles—so we see. Let me approach this another way...."

We move very slowly with Mr. Spurling. He wears a gold tie clasp shaped like a miniature saxophone. Do you need to know any more? I think not. You see him, right? A knit tie with a flannel shirt. Birkenstock sandals from about 1830. White sox. That teeny saxophone glittering. Advanced algebra? Dad has looked at some of the homework and he says he's afraid Mister Spurling doesn't fully understand algebra, much less advanced algebra. They say he's not married, which probably accounts for the fact that he hovers around the door to Miss Austin's room between classes on Mondays and Wednesdays to remind her that on Tuesdays and Thursdays they are supposed to be on hall duty together. She says she won't forget. She does. Forgets every time. He never understands. Yet, they put him on that faculty committee.

3

I thought debate would be interesting. I was fascinated by the last election. Amy and I watched all the debates. Watched Herbert Walker Bush watching his watch. Miss Austin talks about the "theater of politics," and she's right. If you really get into it, it's some of the best entertainment around. But Otter Olson, the debate coach, doesn't seem to have a sense of it.

The big debate question that high school teams like ours will be debating for this year, according to Mr. Olson is: "Resolved: That the United States government should significantly increase social services to homeless individuals." Now, how pointless is that? If you asked around this school I'd bet that a good share of these people would say the only reason people are homeless is they don't know any good real estate agents.

Just so you have some sympathy for me, I've been feeling more than a bit homeless myself this year. At times, I wouldn't have minded being adopted. Or running away and becoming a magician. I couldn't really make a living as a magician now, but you never can tell. Last year I got a book on sleight-of-hand and I've almost mastered the classic pass and palming a coin—well, sort of. Amy says my hands are still too small and, in her good-natured way, she says, "Your natural gift and talent is being clumsy." I work at it, though, practicing in front of my bedroom mirror. The thing that fascinates me most, I believe, is the patter–the way magicians distract you by being so verbally entertaining. I also am trying to juggle.

Uncle Bill says that if there is a God he probably started out as a juggler.

It's really not going to matter one way or another about the debate question because I won't get a chance to debate anything. The whole debate team is made up of seniors. All the boys are trying to grow mustaches. So is the one senior girl on the squad. Amy and I "add depth to the bench," Mr. Olson says. He also says we all need more "team spirit." "Team spirit?" In debate? Gurgitationsome blather, Mr. Olson.

Don't take this the wrong way. I'm not like Benjamin Gerstner who has contempt for all teachers because they don't make a ton of money. Benjamin says he wants to be a Wall Street trader so he can wear suspenders and cuff links like Michael Douglas in that movie. I regard costuming as a poor criterion for a career choice. Plus, Benjamin has no idea what Wall Street traders do except jump around yelling and pointing as the numbers change.

"PUBERTY TYPICALLY LASTS FOR FOUR OR FIVE YEARS. DURING PUBERTY THE WHOLE BODY CHANGES SHAPE AND SIZE. IN ADDITION TO THESE PHYSICAL CHANGES, PUBERTY BRINGS EMOTIONAL CHANGE. MANY TEENS FEEL ANXIOUS AND SELF-CONSCIOUS, ESPECIALLY WHEN COMPARING THEMSELVES WITH OTHERS. YOUR CHILD'S MOODS WILL ALSO CHANGE QUICKLY AND OFTEN DURING THIS TIME. MOOD SWINGS ARE NORMAL AND PROBABLY RELATED TO CHANGING HORMONE LEVELS. DO YOUR BEST TO SUPPORT AND ENCOURAGE YOUR TEEN AT THIS TIME OF HIS OR HER LIFE." -DOCTOR H.

I sometimes wonder if, for some teachers anyhow, puberty is not abnormally extended. I know many teachers must have some sort of basic adult life, but I think it's subconsciously suppressed because every day they are spending most of that day in a never-never land that, in its routine, never grows beyond their own adolescent school days. Their audience is made up of people like me and my feedback is not one-hundred percent reliable because of my intensely immature introspection. I don't mean to be overly self-critical, but there are certainly times when no other problems in the world are greater or more awful than mine. Rationally, that is total nonsensesome nonsense. Rationally we know that, don't we? But are we rational at my age? Excellent question, Chris.

This age I'm going through right now can, I'm sure, nearly ruin you for the rest of your life. Or hang you up so that you are fixated on, say, seventeen, and you never get out of it. I do think Mom was fixated on when she was about seventeen. I've heard her say, "Those were the best years of my life." I loved her, but that kind of fixation can distort your mind, your whole life. I think it did for Mom. Among other distortsome things, of course. Resolved: it can't happen to me. The days ahead of me have simply got to be better. If they aren't—well, as Uncle Bill would say, "What the hell is the point?"

Ancient Miss O' Malley teaches ancient history. She too is fixated on her own virginsome, warm and wonderful girlhood, which must have been about when World War Two was ending. Miss O'Malley identifies this golden period as "before TV," implying that most of the evil we cope with in 1993 is due to television. I think I'm going to suggest to historians, if I'm fortunate enough to meet some historians, that they make BTV, Before TV, an official era, like Before Christ or Anno Domini. Or what's the one I ran into the other day? BCE? I must look that up. I suppose you could have an infinite number of eras. Before Easter Bunny. After Santa Claus.

"Back in my day" is Miss O'Malley's favorite expression. She worries about the "deplorably lax moral standards today," but I suppose she's generally harmless, except to Miss Austin. Watching her around Miss Austin I think Miss O'Malley should have become one of those nuns who's in charge of the other younger nuns, making sure they don't sing too loud.

Worse than the teachers are the counselors. Where do these people come from? They are platitudinous blubberers of nada.

You know what Mrs. Whitestone said to me when they made me go see her? After sitting there waiting while she talked with her daughter on the phone about some girls' soccer match and would the girls like hamburgers afterward, or maybe just send out for pizza, she smiles at me and jangles her bracelets.

"Chris, Chris, Chris. Wonderful to see you. Mrs. Leitner said you needed to see me."

Not really.

"Apparently there's a problem at home?"

No kidding.

"Talk to me, Chris. You can trust me you know."

Not really.

"Don't be shy. You're not naturally shy. If there's something we need to get off our chest let's get it off our chest."

What Mrs. Whitestone needs to get off her chest is that grotesquesome twisted piece of silver hideosity that she probably made in some craft class at the Adult Education Center. It's not a necklace. It's a breast plate.

Listen to her. "I always say, when we think we feel troubled, we need to crawl out of the dark place inside and find the sunshine. We need to help you reach outside of yourself and put all this behind us. Whatever it is. With God's help, we can work together and get it right. Right?"

Sure. At least at that point she didn't seem to know what had happened. Or maybe she did. Pay attention. Her heavily Revloned mouth continues to move so she must be saying something.

"I've been thinking. What's the best thing we can have as human beings?"

Sex?

"Friends, right? You need to expand your circle of friends, Chris. You know what I think, Chris?"

I can't wait.

"I think it would be a neat idea if you had a pen pal in some far-off foreign country. Some place totally out of this school environment. Exotic. Don't

8

you think it would be a neat idea to correspond with some person your age in Denmark or Poland or the Baltic? Find out that we all share a common humanity? Exchange ideas on what's going on in your and their respective schools?"

I can't think of a neater idea. Some aquatic person who actually lives *in* the Baltic would be especially fascinating. I nod to indicate that I'm awake.

"I thought you'd like the idea. I'm going to put my feelers out with the American Field Service and find you just the right pen pal this semester."

What is this? A pen pal? Somebody in prison? This is something out of the last century, right?

And Mrs. Whitestone is my assigned counselor! I have to see her from time to time to make sure I'm taking the right classes. Right. Like she would know. She does teach one course, AP Psychology—high school psychology? A guaranteed "A," and over-flowing with cheerleaders.

"If you feel troubled, my door is always open, Chris, except on Wednesdays and Fridays. If I'm not here on the other days, be persistent. Seek me out." In addition to checking my classes, now I'm supposed to "seek her out" and talk with her when I feel troubled. That's most of the time lately, Mrs. Whitestone. I should have my own page in the Statistical Manual of Mental Disorders.

I'm kidding about that. I don't want someone thinking I am actually crazy. I just had certain very big issues that needed to be resolved.

And if you truly want to resolve something–cope with an actual issue—the whole education milieu is fundamentally against you.

I want to amend my aforestated view. Forget the teachers. I actually can relate to teaching. Socrates and all that. According to Dad, his mom was a terrific teacher. I met Dad's mother when I was very little and then last year before she died. Dad has said she was exceptionally smart. Like Dad. Like Dad was before he was struck stupid. What seemed stupid to me anyway.

And, of course, Miss Austin. Miss Theresa Austin is a real teacher. I feel like wailing every time I think about what they did to her.

No, as I reflect on this year, it's not the teaching of the teachers. It's the Educators. I mean, do you know one person who really wants to go through their life forever identified as an "educator?"

"What do you do?"

"I'm an Educator. I'm in Education.

What is an Educator? Uncle Bill says educators have gone to college and majored in Education, which according to Uncle Bill is not a real subject. They learn things like "When it's dark, turn on the classroom lights." The dumbest people he ever knew majored in Education. Education is what's wrong with education, he says. "It's all fuzzy-wuzzy."

At least Miss O'Malley knows something. Ancient history—though much of it is her own.

Doctor Harold Waltzman, the principal of Watson High, is an Educator par nauseatesomeness. He's actually beyond that category. He's an Educationist. I think he eats, sleeps and breathes Education. I've had the doubtful privilege of being in the inner sanctum of his office. He has *The Chronicles of Education* on his desk next to a glass jar full of jelly beans and a copy of his 1963 Ph.D. certificate in Education actually framed on the wall, thereby admitting to one and all that, if you believe Uncle Bill, he has not actually mastered anything more difficult than turning on the lights in a classroom. On a bookshelf behind him are titles like *The 7 Habits of Highly Effective People*. You just know that's a flakey book. Or how about *Find Your Inner Leader*. Where would I start looking? Spleen? Pancreas? Where do inner leaders usually hide?

Doctor Waltzman identifies himself as "Doctor," like he was a cardiovascular surgeon or something, and refers to himself in the third person, as in "In a Doctor Waltzman school, we do things a certain way."

One way we do things is to quickly judge people. We in Education are very good at that. We can, in fact, ruin people while, as Uncle Bill says, "We cover our own ass." I think it may be part of our job description, Doctor.

I've had eight grades of fuzzy-wuzzy. They complicated simple arithmetic so many times I'd bet that at least ten percent of the kids I sort of know in this school don't even know what ten percent of anything would be.

I thought it would be better once I got into Jason Willard Watson High School. It's highly rated.

Jason Willard Watson High—JWWHS—Slide County consolidated school, built in 1982, modeled after our latest prison architecture. 1993 student body: 1,167 students, three percent Asian, four percent African-American, Hispanic variable because of the farm workers. The rest pinkishsome white bread, blotchy acned palefaces. It's bigger than Middle School. But it isn't better. It's the same Education, only more generally unsatisfying. Over the door they should put "Abandon all hope ye who enter here."

However, let's be honest. (Don't you get ill when someone says "let's be honest?" That's the last thing they'll be, which I can assure you of, for sure.) But let's be honest anyway. Face it. As bad as the educationists who run the place are, even more appallingly rotten are a minority (let's posit the ten percent I referenced earlier) of the students who have influence way beyond their numbers in managing to create an intimidating atmosphere that actually elevates empty-headedness into a status symbol. They find ways to belittle those who don't accept it.

These students are not just ignorant. They are proud of being ignorant. "Who cares about that?" is, among them, a school motto. Ask them. I'll bet they don't know who the Vice President of the United States is. Not that Al Gore is so memorable, but Jesus, people, you ought to at least know who could be running the country.

A product of this atmosphere is a heartless devotion to gossip and petty jealoussomeness. It permeates the place. Walk these halls at your own risk. There are so many ways to mess up, so many paths to disasters big and small. Especially if some of the meddlesome (and empty-headed) mothers are involved.

Jealoussomeness? Smallmindedsomeness? Willingness to absolutely and carelessly belittle or hurt or destroy? Where do you find all that garbagey behavior? Well, one really fertile place is right over there at those girls' lunch table. Gigglesome, jigglesome keepers of the family tits. Dumb as farts in a tree house.

The prime offenders among these talentless menstrual cramps are the sophomore Witches of Watson—Stephanie, Kimberly, and Nicole—especially Stephanie and Kimberly. They started it all.

They hiss like snakes without the warning rattles. They always seem to be conspiring (and they are!), putting their heads really close together in the lunch room, quietly hissing, looking over at Amy and me and then whooping with humorlesssome laughter. Close to them, but not quite so egregiously twatsome is Lisa James. She's the only one of this gang in AP English. She has actually spoken to me and from what she's asked in class, I get the impression she's quite religious. She's not sure which way to walk sometimes. Sometimes I think she wouldn't mind sitting with Amy and me. Mostly not, though. Afraid some of the Usness of US might rub off on the Herness of HER and she'd be transformed into a permanent state of pathological weirdsomeness.

Stephanie, Kimberly, and Nicole. These stringy-blonde-haired harpies would like nothing better than for some horrible thing to happen at the school so that they could cry on television and collect teddy bears and flowers. They want dramategyness. They create it. Badly. But I'll hand this to them. If they really set their tiny minds on fucking something way up, they can do it. Not only can they do it, they did it. "Hurt" for them is not a verb, or a feeling. It is a way of life. These people give a bad name to puberty.

A small contributor to the alienation sensation is "The Man," Todd London. A tall junior with terrible posture. He slouches by the Witches' table and says something hysterically wittysome, sending them into paroxysms of shrill giggles and wowsersisms that are actually frightening. If I ran into these people in a dark alley at night, I'd be afraid

14

of what they might do just to amuse themselves. Terror lurks in their hormones.

Two exceptions to all of the above regarding the general school mise-en-scène that I have described are, of course, Amy and Miss Austin.

Amy Fowler is what you might call "cute." She has a sprinkling of little freckles across her nose, which wrinkles when she smiles, which I'm pleased to say is most of the time. Her eyes are—I'm not sure—multicolored. Hair? Kind of crinkly with little bangs. Complexion? Smooth, light tan. Clothes? Same as mine: Levis and sweatshirts. Creased-up dirty Wal-Mart sneakers. We are the sloppsy twins.

And, secretly proud of it. Sometimes.

Amy's a freshman like me, but she's already become captain of the chess team. She plays all the time with her father. I like to, as my dad says, "play at" chess, but I really don't want more teamy involvement right now. I did think that if I could get life itself straightened out, I might relent and join the club next year for Amy's sake. But now I doubt that there will be a next year.

Amy somehow got a job running errands first thing in the day for Mrs. Penny Leitner, Doctor Waltzman's secretary, so she picks up some bits of information on what's going on in the school. For that service she earns the dubious reward of free lunch prepared by the lunchroom ladies. Maria offered to make her a lunch she could carry, but Amy says her father insisted that she has to learn to eat anything because some day she'll be in college on a diet of even worse institutional food.

I'm not a fan of the "balanced meals" they have to serve, but the lunchroom ladies are actually among the nicest people in the whole school.

Amy's father, Josephus, was a Sergeant Major in the Army in the Gulf War. He's African-American and paralyzed from the waist down, on disability. But he always smiles at me and asks how things are going. We have an on-going bit of business. When I'd run over to do homework or whatever with Amy, I often seemed to be in a hurry because I frequently wanted to get out of my mom's way. Josephus would smile and say, "Christopher, do you know your sneakers are untied?" Yes, sir, I did.

"Better tie 'em or you'll trip and end up like me."

Her mother, Maria, is a flamboyantlysome Italian lady who cooks with tons of garlic and works at Talbot's where my mother used to work for a short time. "Leave the boy alone, Joe. You don't have to tie your sneakers at Harvard."

They predict that's where I'll go to college. Fat chance.

Amy's house is a double-wide about a hundred yards down Frog Pond Lane, where we also live in a double-wide. We don't know what happened to the Frog Pond because there isn't one now. No pond. No frogs. Just a lot of mud on the car path when it rains.

Dad likes the place because there's a woods behind us and room for his garden. Mom hates both the woods and the garden. "All we need is an outhouse," she says.

Our double-wide is not like some poor Appalachian-coal-miner's-holler-type-double-wide full of hippies and druggies. It's bright white with little green fake shutters. It's not dangerous like these double-wides that keep blowing away any time there's a breeze greater than six miles per hour. As Dad points out, our house is "anchored" to a cement block foundation. Dad has planted quite a few bushes around it, making it seem even more substantial. He put on a red front door and built a front porch. He's very handy when he wants to be. I call it nontraditional Cape Cod and the place looks like it might be a little cottage by a pond, if there was a pond. In my opinion, it's pretty nice. For my mom, no.

Amy and Josephus and Maria moved into their place last year when Amy and I were both in eighth grade. Mom said to my dad in her most contrived snootistic tone, "Do you know people of color are moving in down there?" He said he did and went out to his garden before further discussion could ensue. Shortly after, Maria brought over a casserole of lasagna and she and Mom talked, and pretty soon they seemed to be friends. One of Mom's few friends.

I hang out quite a bit at Amy's place. We talk and talk and talk. "Why are we here?" "How far out did the Big Bang go, and what's beyond it?" "Are people naturally good or naturally evil?" "Is there a god and if so how come all this shit?" "Can you

17

expect to be truly happy or happy at all when you are thirteen, or worse in my case, not quite yet thirteen?"

NO to this last question. All you can hope for is to somehow get through what has been described as this "awkward" stage of life. I can't emphasize enough how much I am looking forward to a more graceful stage. So is Amy. Although, Amy is physically very quick. She has excellent hand-eye coordination. Something I do not have. I am, let's say, deliberate in my reactions.

Example: last summer one hot day we were eating baloney sandwiches in her kitchen and drinking cold Snapple, when a strange cat pushed open the screen door and hopped up on the table. I pointed with my sandwich and said, "There's a cat—" Before I could say "—on the table," Amy scooped up the cat, shot to the door, and tossed the cat into the yard. I was still sitting there pointing with my sandwich at where the cat had been.

I admire this ability in Amy.

Amy hates Stephanie, Kimberly, and Nicole. As do I with good reason. But any sensible person would hate them. I truly believe that if you just met them and didn't know a thing about them, you would still be able to detect the miasma of malevolence that emanates from their pores, and you, too would hate them. And as I said before, but it bears repeating, fear them. We also hate virtually all the boys who aren't good enough to be jocks but are very good at smoking cigarettes and being swaggersome like The Man Todd London.

Amy also hates, well that's too strong—dislikes—Janet Jackson and Madonna. As do I. "Too contrived," as Dad says, although I'm not sure what that means, precisely. I think he means that it's too much like every other singer, only more so. Plus, Madonna is ugly.

Despite my mom's view that somehow I am going to be musically gifted, neither Amy nor I are exceptionally musically oriented, but we do kind of like this new group, Tag Team. And Right Said Fred. Right Said Fred is a very insightful commentator in my opinion.

"FANTASIZING ABOUT ONE'S DEATH AND HOW
MUCH ONE WILL BE MISSED IS NOT UNCOMMON
AMONG ADOLESCENTS. THIS FANTASIZING IS
NORMALLY NOT UNHEALTHY." -DOCTOR H.

My dad says Tag Team is not music to his ears, but interesting. He says all music is a generational thing. His parents couldn't stand Elvis Presley, for example. But he likes the early Elvis a great deal. The artist he really, really likes though is Stevie Ray Vaughan, who died in a helicopter crash when he was only thirty-five or thirty-six.

According to Doctor H., many people my age fantasize about going out of this life in a blaze of fire and glory. Not me. I don't like the idea of getting vaccination shots, much less the pain that must accompany actual dying. Dead. Never to eat another Twinkie. Never to open another book, never to feel wind or sleet, or see the sun. Never anything. What kind of ending is that to look forward to? Bleak, don't you think? Yet, I have serious doubts about heaven. Billions of dead people in one place with golden streets and choir music? I'm skeptical.

I'm getting so I too like Stevie Ray Vaughan. "That is a mean guitar" Dad says and I agree. I like watching Dad when he plays Stevie Ray Vaughan. He sometimes puts on this old cowboy hat that he wears in the garden and pantomimes playing a guitar, nodding to the music, as if to say, "That's right. That's right." Mom, as you might expect, is not exactly delighted. When Dad plays Stevie Ray Vaughan, Mom says things like "so this is what I married" or "don't we have enough blues of our own" or, like she suddenly screamed once so loud that if there is life in space, they heard her: "JEFFREY, I CAN'T STAND ONE MORE SECOND OF THAT CRAP!"

Over time that became more and more her normal tone.

In retrospect, Dad was blue. Bluer than I knew, if you'll pardon the rhyme. And Mom—well—she had many shades of blue ranging from inky purple to the blue intensity and menace of a hot gas flame.

Amy and I skipped third grade together at different schools, which is why we are probably the only twelve/thirteen-year-olds in the entirety of Jason Willard Watson High. I'm actually even a few months younger than Amy. Because of my birthday being in December, they started me in kindergarden early. So, if you're interested in the math, I was twelve when I started freshman year. I'm convinced that at the age of twelve, I'd be better off in some college than in high school. None of the older students in high school remembers that he or she was ever twelve.

Amy and I are both, in effect, only-children, that is "only" as in there's-just-one-of-us children. Amy's older brother, Micah, has been gone a long time in the Navy. I have no siblings. I've always wanted a dog, but Mom says a dog will screw up the vacuum cleaner.

Amy and I are both about five-feet tall and weigh in the neighborhood of a hundred-and-ten pounds, which is not the best neighborhood to be in. Needless to say, we both wear glasses. Not the sexy, stylish kind you see in the *New Yorker* ads but the kind that look like they gave them to you at the free health clinic.

Speaking of sex, and Amy and I have spoken about it at some length in our short lives. There's so much to explore on this whole issue. It's endless. And from our reading, and from TV and movies, it just seems to go on and on, in endless permutations, driving people half nuts or totally nuts. We haven't yet managed to see any of the "adult" pornography that is in all the video stores but its presence certainly contributes to the "libidinous milieu" that Doctor H. says "makes adolescence more challenging than in the past." Huck Finn never had to deal with a libidinous milieu.

Right off the bat, we agree that parts of our bodies now seem alien to us, attached but with their own separate lives and personalities. (Total understatement on my part!) We agree with Doctor H. on the matter of mood swings, but we also agree that many of our teensome acquaintances exaggerate their angst compared to real angst — like mine. We also agree that some people are early social bloomers interacting seemingly coolly and easily with their early-social-blooming peers in a mutual harmony of perfect internal emptiness.

And some are late social bloomers, so late they're almost one might say, "anti-social." We seem to fall firmly into the latter category. Not totally by choice.

Amy once asked me seriously, "What do boys want?" There are obvious carnal answers to that question. But if you want to go beyond flesh and bodily fluids, the connection between boys and girls is like a black hole that pulls everything in and never lets it out to be discovered and understood. Even when sex is not active, like a dormant volcano, its mere existence is like the energy of mass in a gravitational field, or of charge in an electrical field.

It's that potent. It sends matters spinning, even just on its speculation.

Watching Mom and Dad, I know at some point they must have felt a powerful magnetic attraction. They must have, right? But now, what intrigues me is how their complete separateness has grown and grown, their touching but not touchingness, except in their almost perpetual sad conflict over their problems. And, of course, Mom's condition.

At school there is no doubt that sex is a palpable presence in the classes, in the halls, throughout the whole day. It is overwhelmingly tantalizingsome and experientially mysterious, but, at the moment, of marginal utility to Amy and me. In fact, because it is subject to such a wide variety of interpretations, it has the potential to be devastating. And that is what happened. Total misinterpretation leading to devastation.

The more I think about it, the more I'm beginning to believe that the most devastatingsome force in life on earth as we know it is sex. Sometimes I just wish it would go away, like a bad cold. It's inefficient, to say the least. Weeds are better designed for reproduction. Furthermore, the whole thing is convoluted by thousands of years of absolute myth and, as Dad says, religious superstitions.

Still, while on one hand I say I'd like to stop thinking about sex, on the other hand I'd be dishonest if I didn't say I'm eager to read things by so-called "sex writers," like Sigmund Freud, who apparently thought a great deal about the subject. Although Dad says Sigmund Freud was really just a very good fiction writer who made a very good living simply asking the same question Chaucer did: What do women want?

"Whips!" Miss Austin said with a mischievous smile when we were doing the little section on Chaucer. She recited:

> *"Of tribulacion in mariage,*
> *Of which I am expert in al myn age*
> *This is to seyn, myself have been the whippe."*
> *--Geoffrey Chaucer*
> *The Tale of the Wyf of Bathe*

Miss Theresa Austin, as in Jane but with an "i", is absolutely, excruciatingly, breathtakinglysome beautiful. She has short dark hair that curls on her cheeks like quotation marks. Quite a few strands usually fall across one eyebrow. Amy says I'm obsessed with hair. Well, if you met Miss Austin, you would be, too. I wish I knew how to paint because I would paint her. Her hair is so dark it is almost Prussian blue, but with little glints of red when she stands against the window with sunlight forming a nimbus around her head. I love words like "nimbus."

Miss Austin wears these form-fitting sweaters and long pleated skirts that swish when she walks, and boots—sometimes cowboy boots not unlike Dad's. She has dark olive skin and eyes that Amy says are "purple as midnight." I told Amy that she is obsessed with metaphors.

We speculated on where Miss Austin was from, and with her usual bluntness, Amy said just after class, "Miss Austin, where are you from?"

"New York."

"But before that?"

"Ah, well some believe I am a distant descendant of Cleopatra."

Her father, she said, was a recklessly daring English archeologist who taught at Stony Brook University, and while he was digging around in Iran, he met her mother. They fell in love among Persian ruins, and rode off into the sunset on camels and lived in silk tents, "subsisting on jugs of wine and loaves of bread."

"Sounds like he was Indiana Jones," I said.

"That could very well be," she said. With a smile.

Amy and I are both impressed with the whiteness of her smile. I expect any day Amy will ask her what kind of toothpaste she uses.

Miss Austin went to Wells, a girls' school in upper state New York, where she, as she put it, "acquired a taste for Medieval feminists." Amy thinks that means she's a lesbian. I don't know. I would like to think she's not. However, I've read that one can practice several preferences at the same time. But I'm not familiar with the cues one should be aware of in sexual identification, having lived among people who seemed rather unadventurous. At least I thought they were. Unadventurous.

In any case, lesbian or not, it would not have made the difficulties less difficult.

Miss Austin drives a restored green 1963 Avanti Convertible, says she loves football but hates football coaches and other exploiters of the corpuscular life, and teaches advanced English and Drama. This is her first teaching job after she spent a couple of years in Africa in the Peace Corps, and Amy and I have the great good fortune, or did have, to be the only freshmen in her class, which is our last class of the day.

Miss Austin puts a great deal of emphasis on the "music of words" and she reads poetry to the class with an interesting accent.

> *"My candle burns at both ends;*
> *It will not last the night;*
> *But ah, my foes, and oh, my friends—*
> *It gives a lovely light!"*
> — Edna St. Vincent Millay

If you've ever heard Sharon Stone, but about half an octave lower, that's how Miss Austin sounds. I really don't care much for poetry, but she makes it all sound so deep. Hypnotic. I've wanted to try to write some poetry since starting this class, but let's be practical, you don't string together a bunch of clichés or arcane abstractions and call it poetry unless you have a lot of nerve. I wouldn't dare show it to her. Miss Austin, I mean. On the other hand, to be fair to myself, have you looked at some of the poetry in the *New Yorker*? I think I could certainly compete with a few of those. Miss Austin always has the latest *New Yorker* on her desk. Contrast that with Doctor

Waltzman and *The Chronicles of Education.* Which would you rather have your educator reading?

She also has a plant on the other corner of her desk that she said her elderly aunt insists she keep in the classroom to "purify the air." Miss Austin says she has named the plant Persephone, because "she keeps coming back from the dead."

Greek mythology. Amy and I looked her up. A bit spooky, but Miss Austin really admires the Greeks. Then on another day she is especially admiring of the Romans. And the French. And, of course, the English. The class is, after all, supposed to be English. I said to her one day, "Miss Austin, do you realize you seem to admire everybody?"

"I guess so, Christopher. I admire everybody who writes something that I enjoy reading. And that includes all of you in this class."

I think Miss Austin is the most gracious person I know. Josephus says that simply being "gracious" is the highest form of human behavior.

Miss Austin is also courageous.

Outside the doors to our putridsome lunchroom there is a large lounge with a pay telephone, a big Pepsi machine and plastic couches. Amy and I hurry through the area because Stephanie, Kimberly, and Nicole hang around there drinking Mountain Dew and watching The Man Todd and his friends throw pennies to an older boy they call the "Chuckster." The Chuckster is Chuck Remsley, a student with Down Syndrome. Todd and crew throw pennies to Chuck, who laughs and whoops while he scampers like a monkey after the pennies, gathering them up and putting them into a paper cup. Stephanie and friends laugh and say, "Chuckster, how much money you got there?" He laughs and answers nonsense like "A hundred money."

This happened almost every day. We'd run through the place and there would be the penny-throwing crowd and poor Chuckster. Often as not my gym teacher, Penis Breath Himoski, and sometimes Mr. Spurling were sitting there talking and indifferently watching the show.

One day Miss Austin appeared. Amy and I happened to see her heading toward the soft-drink machine and then stop. She raised her hand to her mouth like she wanted to scream, then she stepped into the middle of the room. A penny bounced and hit her shoe. She picked it up, then in the lowest, most threatening growl I've ever heard from a female of our miserable species, said, "You think this is cute? You, Stephanie Schaller! You, Kimberly Wellborn!" Pointing at the others. " You, you, all of you! Stop this barbaric, disgusting game! And you two (PB and Spurling) just what are you doing sitting there?"

PB: "Hold on, now. Don't get 'em in a bunch, Sweetie. Can't ya see he's a crip. He loves it. Don'tcha Chuckster?"

Chuckster grins.

"See. He's having fun. It don't do him any harm."

"I'm not concerned about the harm it DON'T do him! I'm concerned about the harm it does to all the rest of these kids. I'm going to Doctor Waltzman now and make sure this never, ever happens again."

And she left. The penny-throwing never did happen again that I knew of. Amy doesn't think she went to Waltzman at all. But she scared Spurling and good old PB.

Gym. Every thinking person knows that gym is way beyond the general horribillisness of school. It is a hell unto itself, presided over, in my case, by the puerile Penis Breath Himoski. I tried to get into coed folk dancing with Amy, but it was closed by the time I got to school that day. Things were fuddled up at home again and I missed the bus. Mom was throwing dishes. With food on them. (By the way, I didn't really mind that compared with later events. Matters of throwing and screaming accelerated.)

"Climb, you pussies. Climb. You, too, Mullins! (Me.) Don't be such a fairy!" PB is our football coach and teaches (the yelling theory of teaching) my required gym class where they torture us with rope climbing and dodge ball. He is also, would you believe, Acting Vice Principal which meant he helped make decisions regarding faculty, including Miss Austin.

After the penny-throwing incident, when Himoski found out I was in Miss Austin's class, he exhibited considerable curiosity. I feel that PB is not a naturally curious man, like my father. But on the subject of Miss Austin he was a veritable fountain of questionsomeness. Is she a *MusliN*? (With an N.) Who gave her that car? Does she have you reading any dirty books? Like what, Himoski? I resented his lascivious interest in Miss Austin—deeply.

One time he got real close and actually whispered to me, "Hey, short stuff, you ever look up her skirt?" I turned red, of course, and he coughed up an evil laugh like Jack Nicholson. He is so outrageously and demonically lecherous that I'm sure he has a large collection of psychopathic pornography, probably of crippled children. Another time he whispers, "Gettin' any in that pussy class?" I'm quoting him. Pussy and fairy are his two favorite words in an otherwise very limited vocabulary.

If I were a medical doctor I would want to test old potbelly Penis Breath for severe hypothyroidism. The same with Stephanie, Kimberly, Nicole and Todd, none of whom are in advanced English. However, after the penny-throwing, they all seem to have a preternatural interest in Miss Austin. And resentment. Great resentment.

"Never pet a porcupine in the dark."
-Uncle Bill

Stephanie, smiling, "Hey, Chrissy, come over here." What am I going to say? "Go to hell, I wouldn't come near your table without wearing a Hazmat suit." Don't I wish I said that! Instead I walk over. Amy follows cautiously along. Dangerous territory. They're all there smiling at us. Grinning like a clowder of Cheshire cats.

30

Stephanie: "Did you two hear about the prize for the smartest dweebs in school? We think you could win it. Don't we?"

Mock straight-faced nods.

Stephanie: "My you both look so cool today. Don't they?"

Kimberly, Nicole, and Todd, who is slouching with his legs straddling the bench sideways, like he's riding a horse, all grin and chortle and say things like "great look," "too cool," "great two-dollar haircut, Amy."

"Piss off," that's Amy, starting to walk away.

"Be nice, Amy. Blondes really are dumber." That's me, joining Amy in walking away and feeling my comment was pretty good.

Stephanie: "Oh, yeah, midgets. You think you're so smart? You didn't hear what we saw. Like, you know that stuck-up Miss Austin you suck around?"

Nicole: "Like My-Shit-Doesn't-Stink-Austin? You know what we saw? Like we saw her totally stoned on Market Street."

Kimberly: "Stoned totally. Like she could not stand."

"This big guy with snake tattoos was all over her, groping her. She loved it. Right Todd?"

"Fuckin' A."

"Like right on Market Street!"

"Go fornicate yourselves!" That's Amy again.

Lisa walked by later and said it wasn't true about Miss Austin, but the garbage spilling was already underway. I think some people can't bear the sight of perfect beauty.

I wished I had known what was wrong with my Mom. As it was, I was constantly off guard.

The furniture, for instance.

We didn't have a showroom full of it, but sometimes I'd come home and none of the few pieces we had were where they had been that morning. She'd put together arrangements that, to be nice about it, were eccentric. She put a chair in front of the hall, so you'd have to squeeze by it to get to the bathroom. Once she took the chair my dad usually sat in when he did happen to watch television and faced it in the opposite direction, toward the wall.

"Mom? What are you doing?"

"I'm trying to make this crappy dump at least a decent dump."

Memory is a tricky, murkysome thing. When Uncle Bill talked about a snowstorm in some long-ago year, he included me. "You remember the snow high as the top of the old skipper laurel." I begin to think I do remember it. Even though, if you pressed me, I couldn't possibly identify skipper laurel.

What do I really remember and what have I been told? There is no way to sort those tangled images out.

I think my Mom is in every mental picture I have of me when I'm younger and we lived in Texas. I think now that she would have been happier if I had remained little forever. A fate I devoutly wish to avoid, believe me.

I think I can see Mom kneeling down while she's making the bed, and I run into her arms. She hugs me tightly and kisses me and calls me her "precious little baby." Sometimes I'm pretty sure she'd say "my precious little upside-down baby." In later years, Mom often referred to the pain and difficulty of my breech birth. I don't remember it. I think at times she thinks I should.

Mom has reminded me how we used to play hide and seek so many times that I'm sure I do remember it.

"You'd crawl into the cabinet with the pots and pans, making all kinds of noise. I'd call, 'Where is my precious baby? Where are you?' I'd look everywhere but there. Finally, you couldn't stand it any more. You'd pop out, pointing at yourself. 'Here I am, Mommy!' Oh, how you had fooled me. Remember, I'd be so surprised and then we'd laugh and laugh. You were so cute."

I was pretty cute when I was little. Mom has a whole scrapbook devoted to me. There's a little knit cap from the hospital, a clipping from the Midland paper announcing my birth, and lots of pictures of me up to about the age of six. Then not another photo, but I have to admit, when I was real young I was adorable. Now I'm not and I don't think Mom likes the way I look now. She certainly doesn't like it that I'm sloppy, like that little "mulatto" girl. That's Amy in Momspeak when Mom is having one of her "cruelty attacks," as Uncle Bill describes them.

One cruelty attack that came on every so often had to do with Amy.

"You be careful with that girl, Chris."

At first I was stupid about such comments, saying "what do you mean? Or, "She's my best friend."

"You think so? You don't know women."

True, oh so true.

"They connive. Trap a good catch like you."

A good catch? We live in a crappy dump, don't we? But I've learned, if she's on a cruelty binge and Amy enters the picture, I just say something as non-confrontational as possible, like "don't worry." Sometimes "don't worry" is good enough. Sometimes no.

"If a hairy black baby falls out of the sky, don't expect me to catch it."

What?!

Doctor H. says that children sometimes contrive to shock their parents by saying outrageous things. In our house, I'm convinced Mom sometimes says outrageous things to shock me.

I've opened our pots and pans kitchen cabinet in this house in the spirit of research. I have a very difficult time imagining myself inside any cabinet. But I think I ought to be able to do it. What does it look like to be this lilliputian person scrunched up with pots and pans, opening the cabinet door and looking out at your mother? Probably only her legs and shoes were visible. In fact, she could have been a strange woman who happened to walk in, and I wouldn't know it. Was I frightened? Maybe I should have been—even back then.

I'm positive I remember bringing home a valentine "for your mother" that I'd made in kindergarten. I'd colored it brown and black. When she saw it, she snapped, "Is that what you think of me?" And I remember that she slapped me. I cried, of course, but explained that those were the only two paint colors left at my end of the worktable. Then I'm pretty sure she hugged me and laughed and said she was sorry. She taped it to the refrigerator where it stayed until Christmas. Mom thought my sense of color needed improving so she provided more coloring books and one of those big boxes of sixty-thousand crayons. She'd color. I'd watch.

"You try."

Okay.

"Stay in the lines, Chrissy."

Okay.

"You went out there. You don't want the picture to be all over the place, do you?"

"I'm sorry."

"Stay in the goddamn lines!"

I always had trouble staying within the lines. Still do.

I remember—I think I remember—Mom using some swear words, like "goddamn" even when I was small, but not many. Not like now. As I've gotten older she's gotten swear-ier and swear-ier.

One thing I know I remember is seeing colors when Mom would decide "we've had just enough of your father's red-neck music," and she'd decide to play her "classical" music on her old Sony CD boom box. A Beethoven symphony, the seventh, was dazzling for me. I remember reading that yellow Deutsche Grammophon label and asking her to play that one again. Sometimes she would. Sometimes she'd say, "You can't just listen to the same thing over and over again."

I don't know when those colors went away, but much as I try, I don't see them any more. To any music.

Mom said, one day after listening to the Greig piano concerto (in A minor, Op 16-Gilels), "If your father could afford to buy us a piano, you could be a concert pianist, Chrissy." She seemed convinced of this. I can't even carry a tune.

One day I came home and she had put all her CDs in the trash.

"Why are you throwing those out, Mom?"

"What's the point? Do you think we're going to go to a concert in Carnegie Hall or anywhere ever— EVER?"

Apparently her parents, the Harvins, went to fancy concerts frequently in the city and Mom liked the idea of doing that. In their living room they had an unusual grand piano called a "Bosendorfer" that had been handed down through Mom's father's family for over a hundred years and, according to Mom, her mother played it beautifully. Mom referred to the Bosendorfer the way some older people refer to the Rolling Stones or one of those groups. An object of worship. If I say, "How big was this Bosendorfer?" Mom perks up, indicates an entire end of our little living room. But if I ask about the Rolling Stones or even the Beatles, she says, "Oh, I don't remember." I think she does remember, but because my dad tends to sing fragments of tunes that were popular when he was growing up, Mom has decided not to even recognize that music. She pretends that she had some sort of very lofty taste, like, maybe, opera.

But, as far as I can tell, the only opera around our house is Dad singing "Vesti la guibba" in the shower, loudly. I think it's funny. Mom did laugh about it once or twice, I remember, but not lately.

I do definitely remember that when Mom was still grocery shopping, she took me along. I was in charge of the latest list. "Don't forget to memorize the list, Chrissy."

I never knew why she bothered writing out new lists. I certainly had no trouble memorizing them. All of them were the same: bread, milk, orange juice, cold meat. But if I neglected to mention one item because I was distracted and stopped to read the peculiar ingredients of some exotic packaged good, like Hamburger Helper or Fruit Loops, she'd grab my hair and say, "I told you to memorize the list. Do you want to end up selling cars?" I didn't particularly want to sell cars, or sell anything really, but I didn't see anything wrong with it either. There were some benefits. Bigley Buick let Dad use fairly nice new cars all the time so we rode around looking pretty good, I thought.

I really wish that Mom didn't grab my hair as often as she did. In her mind I guess it was some form of discipline for my lax ways. But still — it was hard. I wish she didn't lash out that way.

Mom didn't read to me as much as Dad did, but I remember she really liked *Green Eggs and Ham.* I could read it with her, and we'd recite the words together. *"'I do not like them here. I do not like them there. I do not like them anywhere!'* That's how I feel when your father decides we need to eat more healthy food," Mom said.

Memory is unreliable, but one thing I'm sure of. Though Mom reminded me how hard we laughed over hide and seek or my brown and black valentine, or how funny some moment struck us a long time ago, ever since I could remember, if Mom wasn't angry about something, she was mostly sad. I'd find her sitting just staring out the living room window with a magazine lying unopened in her lap. She'd been crying.
"Are you mad at me, Mom?"
"No, Chrissy. I'm just thinking."
"About what?"
"How things have turned out."

I wished again and again that she would feel better or that I could do something to make her feel better. It was rare to hear it now, but when she did laugh it was a surprisingly loud and high-pitched laugh.

When we lived in Texas there were some moments, especially in summer, when Dad would be reading, as usual, and Mom, for no apparent reason would dance in from the bedroom in shorts and suddenly say, "You know what we need to do? We need to go to the amusement park!" And we would. The three of us would pile in the car and drive to this place called Joyland in Lubbock. Mom loved the rides, the scarier the better. I've always had a queasy tendency, but she'd just burst into her loud laugh and head for the next whirling machine.

Then we'd get home and often, just as suddenly she'd look sad again. I'd ask her if I'd done something wrong at Joyland because I did throw up there one time. Sometimes when I'd ask her questions like that she'd smile and hug me and say "Oh, no, Chrissy. I'm just tired." Then other times she'd just look at me and not answer at all.

She'd often tell me—and especially my dad— how poor we were compared with how nicely-off her family was when she was growing up. Mom always wanted "nice things." I wasn't sure exactly what but not what we had. Compared with her growing up we were right down there near the poverty line tending toward the homeless level that Olson's affirmative debaters at school thought the government should be helping out.

"We weren't rich, you know. Oh, my goodness no. But we had very nice things, and, I must say, Martha and I had some of the most beautiful clothes of anyone at our school. The other girls were very jealous. Daddy thought it was important for a girl to have confidence in how she looked. Your father is indifferent to such things, aren't you, Jeffrey?"

My dad would be sitting right there, reading. He wouldn't say a word if he could help it. If he knew what was good for him.

"Daddy was a professional and Mother was quite active in civic groups, the women's clubs and our Episcopal church. All the best people were Episcopalian. She did volunteer work. She didn't approve of women working. Not that I mind. Talbot's is a lovely place to work, if you have to work. The customers are reasonably nice, though they naturally look down on me."

Mom felt that most people looked down on us and felt sorry for us. Dad didn't think so, but his opinion hadn't counted for some time.

I asked Mom why, since we came back here from Texas, she didn't go back to that Episcopalian church, see the old friends who were in her wedding.

She looked at me like I was out of my mind. Like I had suggested she go off and climb Mount Everest or fly to Mars.

"Don't you understand anything? Do you or your father have any idea what I've had to put up with? How could I go into that church? Can't you just hear them? 'She lives in a crappy old trailer on Shit House Road.' I don't ever want to see them anyway."

Dad said that when he first met Mom there was a slam war going on with Mom and those three girls who were her best friends one day and then not friends the next and then some were friends again but others weren't. He said that for a long time he was convinced they all hated each other, then they didn't, and then, lo and behold, they were what Dad called "the Ditzy Dips," the bridesmaids in the wedding. Then something went wrong and everyone was on non-speaking terms with everyone else. Or at least Mom wasn't speaking to anyone. Uncle Bill says he's not too sure we should have armed women in combat. "War is violent enough as it is," he says.

Things with Mom kept getting edgier. One day she told us about some lady who came into the store, snapped her fingers and said 'I'm looking for some casual clothes you could still wear out to dinner.'" She didn't say "casual" Mom said. She said "cazhee." Dad made the mistake of enjoying this and saying, "I don't want to go to a place where I'd have to be 'cazhee.'"

"McDonald's, Jeffrey. How would that be?"

41

She disappeared into the bedroom and came out about fifteen minutes later in this light brown-colored silk dress I'd never seen with a surprisingly low neck line and wearing lots of make up. "I'm going to dinner at Adrian's. Anyone coming with me?" Well, we hustled into some "cazhee" clothes (Dad always looked great by the way, in my opinion.) And we trundled off to Adrian's. I'd never been there. It looked pretty fancy to me. Lots of glasses on the tables, waiters in white shirts and black string ties.

So we're seated by Dieter, this maitre'd who looked and sounded like an ex-Nazi. He gave us these menus. Mine had no prices in it. "Dad, there're no prices in my menu."

He started to explain this nicety, when Mom swept her arm across the table, breaking a number of glasses. "Let's go," she said, getting up. We followed her out toward the door. As Dad passed the Nazi he said, "I'll drop by and pay for the glasses tomorrow."

"Think nothing of it, sir," said Dieter.

In the car Mom said nothing. Not a word.

"What was wrong, Honey?" Dad said.

"I wasn't hungry!"

I was, but I figured this was not the time to mention it.

Finally, we get home. Mom stalks off to the bedroom and comes back with her make up wiped off, wearing this really ratty old, pink housecoat.

She looks through us like we're not there and goes to the refrigerator, pulling out this KFC bucket of leftover fried chicken. She slams it down, opens the silverware drawer and grabs a handful of forks and knives. She throws them down next to the chicken. Ring, ding, pling. "There. Eat!"

Dad pleads, "Mary, come on—"

"We don't belong at Adrian's, Jeffrey. We can't afford it and everyone there knows it. You saw them. Looking at us. Wake up! Look how they LOOK at us!

"That's 'cause you broke a bunch of glasses!" I unwisely noted.

"Before that, you smart aleck little shit!"

She hit me. Hard. I started to cry.

"God, you're a crybaby."

Then she left the room and went to bed.

As I got older, it seemed to me that Mom was more and more aggressively unhappy with just about everything involved with Dad. If he gave her something for her birthday—a watch for instance—she'd say, "Take that back. We can't afford it."

He'd say we can. She'd say he was a fool. He'd walk away. She'd say don't walk away from me when I'm talking to you. She'd throw something. The watch, for instance, if that was the issue. He'd pick it up, see if it was damaged. That made her even madder.

You see how it goes, right? Dysfunctionness all over the place.

But bearable. Tolerable. That was just Mom. Happy in some few memories. Unhappy in most. Now? Unhappy and seemed like she would always be unhappy, as far as I could see.

Dad bore the brunt of it, of course. I have no idea what they must have said to each other when I couldn't hear or wasn't there. I don't know how Dad really felt. I certainly was aware that he began to spend more and more time at Bigley.

Or in the vegetable garden. Mom not only hated the garden, as I said, but every so often she singled it out for an extra dose of contempt, as when Dad came in with a whole bunch of tomatoes. He'd lay them out on the kitchen counter and admire them. That was especially offensive. "If you think I'm going to take up canning like your grandmother, you've got another guess coming, Jeffrey."

Somehow the very idea of raising something to eat offended her sensibilities, emphasizing the fact of what she viewed as our "Red-neck poverty. We might as well keep chickens like that old fool uncle of yours."

I asked Dad if Mom had ever been happy. "Yes, for nearly twenty years, we both were very happy. Then we got married. Ha. That's Rodney Dangerfield."

For a long time, I felt he just dismissed the situation. He seemed rather cheerfully resigned, even if she kicked him, which I saw her do. So hard I winced. He said, "Now, now."

You can get used to anything, right? Look at those prisoners of some war, like the big World War Two. Their daily lives were nothing but torture and starvation and rats and typhoid. We didn't have it so bad. Mom's constant miseryness was just the ordinary underlying accompaniment of our lives. It just was.

Even if she started out with a sunny disposition I could pretty much count on the fact that something would bring on a dark cloud.

However, beginning one night in November, when Dad got home rather late from Bigley, what I thought was merely a bad situation, deteriorated. Rather sharply.

He'd brought Chinese food. We all agreed that we liked Chinese food, even Mom and especially what Dad had brought—Egg Rolls and Sweet and Sour Chicken from China Garden. But it didn't work out well.

When he came in, she walked up to him, sweetly saying, "I stopped by Bigley on my way home this afternoon. You weren't there."

"I guess I must have been out showing someone a car."

She kissed him nice as could be. Then she threw such a hard right to his cheek that she knocked him into the chair. She picked up the cartons of Chinese food, threw them in the garbage can, and went into the bedroom, slamming the door after her.

Dad scrambled us some eggs. By the time we finished, he was beginning to develop a bruise on his face.

After that, day-to-day existence got even more precarious. You never quite knew what was going to explode in what direction. I was what some dingbatty counselor like Mrs. Whitestone might call "insecure."

I was also becoming frightened about what might happen.

Dad's old Uncle Bill, came by out of the blue every now and then. His rusty LUV truck would rattle in one day, and there he'd be standing at the door wearing his U.S.-Air Force-Retired cap.

"I was in the neighborhood. Thought I'd drop by. See if the Missus killed you yet."

I didn't think that was funny.

Sometimes he brought a few eggs. As Mom noted contemptuously, Bill committed the extremely déclassé sin of keeping chickens around this unpainted tumbled-down house he lived in out on Sandy Spring Road. The savanna of weeds around his house was also cluttered with several old cars in varying states of restoration. He was, according to

46

Dad, "A DaVinci mechanic. Many of his works are unfinished."

Uncle Bill had a cowardly one-legged rooster that he'd named Mildred. "Mildred," said Uncle Bill, "fell out of God's ugly tree and hit every branch on the way down." Mildred was ugly, with a strangely long neck and the one leg. But, for some reason, the hens tolerated him. Uncle Bill said, "Mildred is proof that if you're male, you can look like shit, and some female somewhere will love you."

I said, "I hope that's true 'cause I don't look like much at this point. Mom says so."

"Don't you worry, Chris. Look at Henry Kissinger. Look at Alan Greenspan. Look at Cal Findley. You've got a terrific future. Your problem is you're not ugly enough."

I really enjoyed Uncle Bill. By the way, Cal Findley, the father of one of the Witches, Nicole, was apparently quite rich. I saw him at the Book Fair. Uncle Bill was right. Ugly. He looked just like Hagar the Horrible.

When Uncle Bill wasn't dropping in on us, Dad and I went up to visit him every so often, mainly when Dad took a day off. "Come on, it's a beautiful day for a little drive, let's go see Uncle Bill."

Mom wouldn't go. Are you serious? Go to that place? The big old house was dirty and dangerous, she said. It's true, Uncle Bill had fallen through the floor boards on the front porch, but he put a piece of plywood down, and that seemed to work. When we did visit him, he'd always say, with a laugh and a wonderfully expansivesome gesture, like he was encompassing thousands of acres, "Just think, Jeffrey, some day all of this will be yours." Dad said Uncle Bill had just an acre shy of an acre-and-a-half. On a tiny part of it he had a few cannabis plants.

Uncle Bill was full of odd sayings, which he would deliver to me in great seriousness.

> "Never kiss a pig on the ass unless you mean it."
> —Uncle Bill

Mom didn't like him at all. She regarded him as crude and boring. But there he would appear, for no particular reason that I could tell, having a beer with Dad and talking away. He'd talk about way back when Kennedy was President and cars had crank windows, and the family went here or there to picnic or fish. Snowstorms, weather of all kinds was of interest. Fishing was a big topic. Or how Aunt Helen always won at poker. Or which car they drove to Chicago. Was it the Dodge? No, it was the tan Oldsmobile with the black simcon top. Yes, that was it. Some of these quite pointless discussions mesmerized me, intimately included me as a passenger in that Oldsmobile, and I was transported there with Bill—watching those incredible trick dogs in Las Vegas with him, repairing a chain saw, seeing the sunset in Key West and petting Hemingway's five-toed cats.

"Ever see anything like them cats?"

Never.

Uncle Bill Davlin was Dad's mother's brother. He'd been a pilot in Vietnam and married Miyako, a Japanese woman who died from cancer, which Dad said took all his money. He always seemed concerned about Dad and Mom and later was, I guess, somewhat helpful with the Sheriff.

One time Mom appeared at the door, looked at Dad and Uncle Bill, and said "Goddamned trash!" and went back in. Uncle Bill said, "Looking at options, I think if I was you, Jeff, I'd definitely have divorce on the table."

Dad said, "I'm responsible for her, Bill."

"Suit yourself."

I'm convinced you can never really know your parents. They appear in your life, full-formed out of a void from which there are occasional releases of old photographs and scraps of incomplete stories, fragments of some hazy past floating by from time to time—pearl earrings—a baseball signed by Eddie Murray—crocheted Christmas ornaments—a prayer book in old German script that belonged, apparently, to my mother's grandmother's grandmother's mother.

I could get the black and white of the big portrait of my parents pretty well sketched in terms of the broad outlines of who my parents had been, who they were and who they thought they were. Dad was a Mullins, smart, good-looking, but essentially, in Mom's eyes, "not one of us." Not trash, like Uncle Bill, but a cut below the Harvin standard. Mom was fairly smart, but especially good-looking, and, in

Dad's eyes, part of the local aristocracy. This picture was drawn and redrawn all the time in America, right? Some of us are upwardly mobile. Some downwardly. However, the whole lifelong process makes for a lot of worrisome turmoilness in some families. Like ours. Especially ours.

"Mrs. Bennet in *Pride and Prejudice*" said Miss Austin, "reminds everyone a bit of their own mothers. How their mothers sometimes embarrassed them. But as we get older we realize that our parents just want us to have the opportunity to be happy."

"I'm not sure I agree with that," said this smart aleck little shit—me.

"Parents-in-literature is a very interesting topic, Christopher. Some are wonderful. Some dreadful. But the interesting question is why do authors write about them so often?"

"To make *their* parents mad?"

"Possibly. But I think mainly...to try to understand them."

In my case my ability to stitch together more complete continuity about exactly what happened when and where with my parents was hindered by my lack of grandparents. Both Mom's and Dad's parents were dead. There was Dad's old Uncle Bill, of course, but his memories were more personal and entertaining than informative—or even accurate.

I envied Amy because she had two grandmothers who appeared from time to time. The black one was very severe, no-nonsense, you'd better shape up. The Italian one was like a songbird, light, funny. A good combination for Amy, I thought. She learned about slavery and opera at the same time.

Dad and Mom met in an unusual and unhappy way.

Mom thought the world of her father, Frank Harvin. He was her "Daddy," a successful optometrist with, according to Mom, "a very respectable" business selling glasses and contact lenses. The Harvins lived in a fine Victorian house on Pearson that I never saw because of the fire, but there were quite a few pictures which Mom brought out from time to time. It was indeed a large handsome house, though the fussy gingerbread of Victorian architecture is not to my taste.

"Up here was a playroom. The garage had been a stable. See the corner of it there." Mom would close her eyes and go on about the house and how they lived with her grandmother's Rosenthal china and Kirk-Steiff silver.

Mom said, "I used to imagine what it must have been like to live in our house ninety or so years before I was born with lots of servants and a beautiful shiny black buggy and beautiful shiny black horses pulling up and taking us to dances and parties. Cars never fit the spirit of the place. Ever since I was a little girl, I always wanted a horse to ride in the park across the street. It would have made the house picture perfect, but Daddy never thought it was a

51

good idea. Martha said I was a hopeless romantic born in the wrong century. Maybe I was.

"But we were very happy.   Everybody was happy up there on Summit and Pearson. Martha had been editor of the Scroll, the school paper, in her senior year. I did her one better in my senior year, I was runner-up Homecoming Queen. I should have been Queen, but Louise Finch, now Schaller, beat me out. She cheated. What Louise did was she actually campaigned. Ask anyone. You didn't campaign to be Homecoming Queen. I think everyone appreciated my better character. We Harvins had character."

Mom often sounded very actressy, affected by something she'd read or seen in movies. She played Juliet in her high school play and like so much of her life at that time I don't think she ever got over it. Mom told me several times that her high school drama teacher, Mr. Lubinoff, told her that she had been the most beautiful and sensitive Juliet he had ever seen. He told her that "someday I'll be watching you in the movies."

Mom truly must have been quite romantic when she met my dad. She isn't now. I think Dad is, unfortunately, the romantic now. What Mom wants now is nice stuff we "can't afford." Nice stuff and exciting stuff happening. I feel she'd like to be the star in her own movie all the time. Like during the fire. Only she never called it "the fire." She called it "the trouble."

The trouble happened when Mom was seventeen. Dad was twenty.

Mom was in high school and her sister, Martha, four years older than Mom, was finishing up at the University. Mom said she didn't like being separated from Martha, but I guess they saw a good deal of each other in the summer and on holidays. Both girls were home for the Christmas break, and the house was, as Mom put it, "Decked out and full of Christmas cheer."

"Although," Mom said, "I wanted to go to Florida for the break like the other kids. If Daddy had listened to me, none of the trouble would have happened. If we'd been in Florida, you see, we couldn't have been in the house."

The Harvins had had a party.

Mom said they knew all the people up on Summit and Pearson and she went into great detail about who was who in that grand neighborhood and who was at the party.

As Mom inventoried these people she closed her eyes, as if she was seeing them and seemed to imply that I should know them too because many of these same names are still around the county and in my school.

In point of fact, several of these same people did us all the great disfavor of spawning the young Witches of Watson.

There were the Schallers. Their dumb son Normie later married Louise Finch, who was Mom's age and perpetually jealous of Mom. At the time of the party, Louise was in Florida. The Findleys—the "obscenely rich" Findleys—were also in Florida with their son Cal and friends. And the Wellborns were there. Their son Del was on break in Florida, too, along with the girl he ended up marrying—Mom's friend, Franny. Mom said Franny was also jealous of Mom.

However, Mom's three closest and apparently most jealous and gossipy friends at the time, Louise, Polly, and Franny, were on good enough terms to be, as Dad said, the "Ditzy Dips" at Mom and Dad's wedding. There was a wedding picture of them all in a silver frame on the little bookcase in Mom and Dad's bedroom. I thought the Ditzy Dips looked pretty grim in the picture, but Mom said that was because they resented Mom being the first to marry.

When we came back here from Texas, Mom was still not speaking to those three women, but later she was. For me and Miss Austin that wasn't a good thing.

Mom said Uncle David "gave her away," which certainly sounds not only quaint but barbaric. Amy says no one can give her away. I agree.

During the Christmas party the Harvins had a big fire in the living room fireplace, which had glass doors on it. After the party, after the couple who helped the Harvins with parties (Melody and her husband, some black man Mom couldn't remember) had cleaned up, they closed the doors on a few remaining coals in the fireplace, and everyone went to bed. According to Mom they'd done this many times. That night, however, as Mom explained it, something apparently went wrong in the chimney and a fire started where the chimney went through the hall next to Mom's parents' bedroom. By the time the fire department got there most of the upstairs was in flames.

Dad had just become the youngest fireman in the county. He's about six-two and back then he was quite strong from working construction in the summers. He still is. Strong, I mean.

Uncle Bill was with the fire department back then, too, and he said gray and black smoke was pouring out of windows, doors, everywhere. Mom's sister, Martha, was asleep in the girls' upstairs bedroom over the front door. Mom had somehow made it downstairs and was on the front steps screaming, "My sister is up there!"

"Where's Frank? Where's your mother?" Uncle Bill shouted. Uncle Bill described that night one time. He said Mom just stared at him and pointed upstairs.

Dad climbed up the ladder and broke into the girls' bedroom. The smoke was very thick and, according to Mom, Martha was unconscious in her bed.

Dad picked up Martha and carried her down. "I threw my arms around both of them," Mom said. "Martha and I were so lucky."

Their parents, Frank and Annette, never got out.

A piece of burning lath had fallen on Martha's open left hand, leaving it scarred and partially crippled. Mom said it had a deep and depressing effect on her.

The two girls went to live down the road with Annette Harvin's sister, Cheri and her husband, Uncle David. Dad began to hang out with them whenever they were home from school.

Martha was, according to Mom, nice looking enough "in a practical, no-nonsense way." Even though she was older than he was, it was Martha Dad started dating regularly. Mom said Martha was always the privileged one, the "apple of Mother's eye." Mom was closer, she said, to "Daddy."

Mom had a liquor box in her closet and from time to time, I'd see her looking at things she kept in it—old Christmas cards, old copies of the Scroll, her high school newspaper or her yearbooks from high school. She never went to college.

"Can I see?"

"Sure. It's just some old trash I ought to throw out." But she didn't throw the things out. Instead, she'd begin to talk quite a bit about this girl or that boy, and especially about Martha in a mumbly voice full of wistfulsomeness. While she mostly spoke quite harshly about how unfeeling and jealous Martha was, at other times she seemed to have very affectionate though rueful memories of Martha. Mom would say,

"I understood Martha. I'm just sorry she never understood me. I'm afraid because we were orphans she wanted to be in charge of both of our lives. I admit, I did rely on her. Up to a point she was a kind of substitute mother. Up to a point. But that's water under the bridge now.

"She could have done more for me, though. She should have come to be with me when you were born. She should have been here for my wedding."

In the box she also had a little angel Christmas ornament, blackened and melted from the fire, but you could still recognize it.

> **"AS PUBERTY CONTINUES, SPURTS OF GROWTH OCCUR AT VARIOUS AND DIFFERENT TIMES FOR DIFFERENT PEOPLE. SOME TEENS, ESPECIALLY GIRLS, HAVE ALL THEIR HEIGHT BY THE TIME THEY ARE THIRTEEN. BOYS TEND TO ACHIEVE THEIR FULL HEIGHT CONSIDERABLY LATER. SOME BOYS CONTINUE TO GROW ON INTO THEIR COLLEGE YEARS, AND, IN SOME FEW CASES, EVEN BEYOND." -DOCTOR H.**

I'm small for my age, for any age. Dad really must have been something. In pictures from back then, he has this big smile, blue eyes, and wavy black hair. Mom said he was what some called "black Irish," which, I gathered from her tone, was not Premium Grade. However, Uncle Bill said Dad had loads of girlfriends. He'd been president of everything in high school as well as quarterback of the football team. I think in general, athletes must have been smarter and nicer back in Dad's day. (I have to confess this—when I'm being totally honest with myself—I wish, I hope, Doctor H. is right and I'll grow to be Dad's size and learn somehow to throw a football, or just any damn ball, the way he does. I hope there's something to genetics.)

Dad didn't go on in college athletics—"I wasn't crazy," he said. He became a full time fireman and a part-time student at the community college. For some reason, he majored in philosophy which, as Mom continued to point out, was not a practical major. He's still not a practical man.

"I always see a lot of help-wanted ads for philosophers. Why don't you give them a call, Jeffrey?" That's Mom in one of her more amusing sarcastic moods.

I gather from Uncle Bill that Dad was very popular in the whole community.   I still get the impression that most everybody likes him.   Even Sheriff Hennessy.

Dad's mother, who had multiple sclerosis, had been forced to quit teaching and was in a wheelchair at home. Dad's father sold cars for Bigley. ("I inherited the dreaded 'car-selling' gene," Dad says).

After Mom and Dad were married, Dad said that on the first day of their honeymoon in Bermuda, for which Dad had borrowed a lot of money, Mom said she hated the wallpaper in their hotel room and the bad English food in the stuffy dining room. She wanted to leave. But she didn't want to go home. She wanted to get away from "that jerk-water place" and go someplace exciting. She was tired of her mean and jealous friends. She didn't like Dad's trashy fireman and policeman friends at all. She wanted Dad to "better himself." She asked him to do something interesting! Anything!

One of Dad's fireman friends, Brian McCauley, had gone off with an oil company in Midland, Texas. Dad called him. It turned out the company was looking for Business Development people. McCauley said the job was mainly political schmoozing and, sure, he'd introduce Dad to the executives doing the hiring

They liked Dad. Dad said Mom was really eager for him to take the job. He said, "The romance of an adventure in rough country appealed to your mother at the time." Also a membership in the Midland Country Club went with the job. So, Mom and Dad packed up the little BMW that Mom's Daddy had given her for her sixteenth birthday, and they adventured to Midland.

I was born. Dad said Mom had such trouble changing diapers that she would gag and almost throw up. She hated diapers. She hated feeding me. It turned out she also hated Midland. "Your father should have known I wouldn't like it. The people were narrow-minded and uppity," she said.

When I was almost five, we moved out of our first house in Midland because Mom had some sort of fight with Brenda, the wife of Brian McCauley, the man who helped Dad get the oil company job. The

McCauleys lived just a few houses down the street and I have a vague memory of being with them often when I was small. The two families cooked hamburgers outside a lot and the McCauley house had a small swimming pool that I played in with their two children, a girl and Brian Junior. I remember Brian Junior's name because he had the annoying habit of urinating in the pool and his sister would yell, "Ma, Brian is peeing in the pool again!"

Except for that unhygienic drawback, I remember having fun with the McCauleys. I particularly liked their dog, Lobo, a cute little dog that Dad says was a Dandie Dinmont. Mrs. McCauley told us that Lobo kept the tigers away. I remember Mrs. McCauley being pretty and laughing a lot.

But something went wrong and Mom got more upset than usual. I remember Dad saying "let's not move, oh, let's not move," but we did. They pulled me out of kindergarten and put me in another school.

I went to three schools in Texas because we moved three times. Mom said they kept making mistakes in choosing neighborhoods where the people were either jealous of Mom or looked down on us. In my memory, the last one of the houses rambled over quite a bit of space, much of it unfurnished with floors that were soft in some places. I think that's where Mom started moving furniture around in strange ways.

Out back, there was an empty swimming pool with big cracks in it that Dad kept working on. I can see him standing down in the empty pool slopping cement on the walls.

We had a maid. A nice black woman named Crystal. Crystal was replaced by Daisy. Mom said Crystal didn't know how to polish Mom's silver candleholders and she twisted them out of shape. We still have those candleholders and, sure enough, there are little clockwise ripples in them. But I really liked Crystal anyway. She hugged me a lot.

While we were in the rambling house with the pool, from somewhere Dad acquired an Audi. Dad said, "You'd never know this car was used." I remember, even then, knowing that that was the wrong thing for him to say. However, in general things were better.

Then the oil company went broke.

They fired Daisy and sold the Audi. They packed up the little BMW and were going to go to Dallas. Mom had heard that Bonnie & Clyde was made there many years ago, along with lots of TV shows. Mom thought she might have a chance to be in movies or TV or "something besides *this*," but as Dad said, "Mean-old fate intervened."

Dad's dad had a "massive myocardial infarction" and died. By that time his mother was basically helpless in the wheelchair. The only child, Dad, had to help her. Mom said Dad's mother could certainly afford to hire someone, but Dad said she couldn't and he felt responsible. He said there was no one else.

It was one of the few times I ever heard him muster much of an argument with Mom. "How would you like it," he said, "if when you're very, very old, Chris just walked out and left you to die alone?"

Somehow that touched her. Momentarily.

So, while she was being touched, we came back here just as I was going into seventh grade. Dad went to work selling cars for Bigley, and still does— much to Mom's distress and never-ending shame and embarrassment. They never got to Dallas.

I went with Dad to see his mother three or four times, and then she died. She had a nice, kind-of-crooked smile, like Dad's smile. Mom never visited her.

"That selfish old woman and her son (that's *Dad!*) ruined my life," Mom said more than once.

I have a feeling Dad's mother visited us in Texas only once. She was able to come down to Midland on a bus, I think. I was very young. I must have been a rather dour child because I remember she was forever trying to make me happy by using silly little rhymes. Some of them have stupidly stuck in my head. "Don't be a mopey dopey." "A smile is a frown upside down." "Cheer up, buttercup."

I think I've made the point that Mom wasn't fond of her. One reason might be because she taught me to sing: "I got plenty o' nuthin, and nuthin's plenty for me. I got no car, I got no mule, I got no misery."

I sang that over and over around the house, with particular emphasis on the "no misery." Until one day.

"Shut up! Shut up! You're driving me nuts." That was Mom, in case you couldn't guess.

When Mom and Dad came back from Texas it was not, Mom said, the "way I envisioned us coming back." I wasn't sure exactly how she did envision coming back but I imagine she saw herself as some kind of returning royalty coming to visit the peasants back home. If she could have ridden in on an elephant or come up the river on a jeweled barge, that would have suited her.

In their pictures together when they were young, Mom always looks like she's posing in an exaggerated, "Kodak moment" way for the camera. Martha is just smiling. Mom is turned to one side or looking over her shoulder, like in an ad. Martha is standing with her arms at her side. She looks like she doesn't care to have her picture taken. Mom really wants her picture taken.

Mom is still very pretty. Maria said, "Your mother is what I would call glamorous." I don't think I'd call her that, but she is quite good looking. Aunt Martha, now that I've met her, seems many years older, very pretty but not high Technicolor like Mom. Mom said they both were very popular with an almost uncountable number of friends. "Our house was just full of handsome, laughing boys," she said. "Handsome, laughing boys," sounds like something Mom picked up on a late-night television movie. I'm never sure if scenes Mom described actually happened, or if she saw them in some old movie.

How it happened I still don't know precisely, but from what I can piece together Mom somehow took Dad's attention away from Martha to such a degree that he ended up marrying Mom. I don't know how to say this—well, I have to say it because I did discuss it with Amy—I suspect Mom was pregnant when they got married. Either that or I was, as Mom said when I asked, "very premature."

When I asked about the wedding in the wedding picture, Mom rhapsodized about how beautiful it was and what a wonderful gown she had. But she said Martha almost ruined her, Mom's, "special day."

Even before the wedding, according to Mom, Martha soundly and roundly condemned the whole enterprise, predicted its and Dad's failure, dropped out of the University without finishing her degree, packed up and went to New York where she became something with a bank. Mom said that Martha walked out on her "In my hour of need." After that, Mom never wanted to talk to her or write her or wanted anything to do with her selfish, thoughtless sister. For all practical purposes, except for what Mom regarded as a hypocritical, empty gesture, sending us an annual Christmas card, Aunt Martha was never heard from again—until recently, that is.

The evening of the Chinese Food Fight, I quickly absented myself to Amy's, and found Maria talking very quietly to Josephus. Not the usual your-sneakers-are-untied welcome, or Maria's hug, but concernsomeness I'd not seen before.

Maria asked, "How is your mother doing this evening?"

"Oh, you know Mom. Why?"

"She's very high strung, you know, Chris. We sometimes worry about her— and your Dad."

"What happened?"

"Well, Mrs. Wellborn and her daughter Kimberly came in. Kimberly was home with a cold, and said she happened to see your father get out of a green Buick and go into a neighbor's house in the middle of the day. For some reason, that upset your mother. After they left she yelled at me, 'Did you hear that?'"

"What's the point? Josephus said.

"What happened next is the point. Mary stands there, stock still. All of a sudden she throws the clothes she was holding and screams. An eerie kind of scream. It made the hair stand up on the back of my neck. Then she knocked over a mannequin and shouted 'Get out' at the customers. I'd say she had a tantrum. Thank goodness Sandy wasn't there."

I worry about how I think. I know Mrs. Whitestone could have a point and I do look inward too much but it wouldn't be natural not to look inward and wonder why one thinks the way one does think. Or would it? I want to get over this and be more of an outgoing, jolly, "hail fellow well-met" but then people would look at me and wonder, "He's not behaving the way he usually behaves. What is *he* thinking?"

Back when this Talbot's-Wellborn-screaming issue came up, I thought and thought about how best to approach it. Should I ask Dad why he was up near Kimberly's house in the middle of the day? There could be a million reasons, but why was Mom so upset about it that she had a tantrum in public. She had mini-tantrums all the time, but this sounded like a really-over-the-top tantrum. If I asked him it would sound like I was suspicious of something, which I wasn't then, and I didn't want to be.

But Mom was even madder than usual and I wanted to know why, without actually finding out something that I didn't want to really know in the first place.

I certainly didn't dare ask Mom. I was worried, but I would have rather not pinpointed the cause of my worrisomeness in a burst of Mom's fury.

I hadn't been eating much lately. I thought I was losing weight. I mentioned it to Amy on the way to school.

"God, Chris, stop taking your temperature every fifteen minutes. You're fine. You look fine. We'll have some kind of disgusting high-calorie junky food at my house when we get home. You'll be an *obeast* by tomorrow."

I want to correct the record for Maria's sake. We never had junky food at Amy's house. We had the "Newly Popular Mediterranean Diet" as Josephus called it. He said, "My wife invented the newest fashion diet, the "Mediterranean Diet," pasta with more pasta on the side."

Dad says the Mediterranean Diet has been around since the Bronze Age.

Like Miss O'Malley.

As I indicated, it's obvious Miss O'Malley disapproves of Miss Austin. I sense that she thinks Miss Austin is much too young and somehow ethnically wrong to be teaching something as important as English and drama. She talks to Miss Austin as if Miss Austin is not far removed from being one of the "morally lax" student trouble-makers. In her class Miss O'Malley makes oblique references now and then to "The White Man's Burden." Dad says it's a poem by Rudyard Kipling written to justify British imperialism, but I think Miss O'Malley is just not happy with people who look different in general, and especially those who have too many children on welfare.

We were rehearsing the Pyramus and Thisbe scene from *A Midsummer Night's Dream*. Every English class had to take turns doing something for a monthly general assembly and Miss Austin had us do Pyramus and Thisbe. I was the Wall and really having fun hamming it up. There's this part where Pyramus is saying,

"Thou wall, O wall, O sweet and lovely wall,
Show me thy chink, to blink through with mine eyne!"

And I make a little "O" with my fingers. Pyramus is on my right. Thisbe on my left. I, the Wall, am between them and Miss Austin has the two of them moving around a lot, trying to peek and talk through my fingers. Meanwhile, I'm supposed to move this way and that, practically standing on my head as Pyramus and Thisbe try to connect through their peeking exercise. Well, there's lots of giggling and silliness in the classroom, but when Thisbe says,

"I kiss the wall's hole, not your lips at all--"

it's a laugh riot—until we're aware that Miss O'Malley has slipped in and is standing in the doorway. She gives Miss Austin her sweetest, most disapproving smile and says, "We're having a little trouble concentrating next door, dear."

Miss Austin says, " I know. I told them, 'Class, this is Shakespeare,' but they think it's funny anyway. We'll try to do better, Miss O'Malley."

I've never heard anyone on the faculty call Miss O'Malley anything other than Miss O'Malley. I don't think she has a first name.

Another school day. Spurling looked down at my paper. He said, "Good." Then he asks, "How's that new teacher in advanced English?" I say she's good. And he says "good," and goes to the next desk. There was certainly widespread interest in Miss Austin. I think she barely knows Mr. Spurling exists

68

except as someone who didn't stop the penny-throwing. And he helps hold up the wall on hall duty outside her classroom. Creepysome, really.

Once we heard her at the classroom door saying to him, "I'd love to, but I'm engaged."

Amy, ever the blurter: "Congratulations, Miss Austin. When did you get engaged?"

Miss Austin, holding a finger to her lips, "Just now."

The day plods on. I'm definitely not feeling too well. I believe it may be a psychosomatic reaction to Mom's reaction to whatever happened at the store, but I can't quite ignore the notion that I could be in the incipient stages of one of many possible serious diseases.

> "THE YOUNG BODY'S INABILITY TO ABSORB NUTRIENTS CAN ALSO MEAN THAT YOUNG PEOPLE WITH UNTREATED CELIAC DISEASE MAY NOT GROW PROPERLY AND MAY HAVE WEIGHT LOSS AND FATIGUE. IN ADDITION, PEOPLE WHO HAVE CELIAC DISEASE MAY BE PRONE TO DEVELOPING OTHER DISEASES, SUCH AS THYROID DISEASE, DIABETES, AND GASTRO-INTESTINAL CANCER." -DOCTOR H.

I spoke to PB and told him I definitely needed to skip gym, but he said today was written-test day, so I'd be all right no matter how sick I was.

It was a test of unmitigated unbelievableness. Questions: "In American football a touchdown counts for 3 pts—9 pts—6 pts—none of the above."

"In American baseball there are how many men on each team? 5—9—11—none of the above. In tennis, love is—etc."

"No laughing, you pussies. This is a test and if you don't pass you'll have to take it again and again until you do pass. No basketball, no nothing. You won't set foot back on that gym floor until you pass."

What a tantalizingsome temptation.

> "THEY SAY, 'TWO HEADS ARE BETTER THAN ONE.' STUDIES SHOW THAT THREE OR MORE HEADS ARE EVEN BETTER. WE KNOW THAT GROUP PROJECTS CAN HELP STUDENTS DEVELOP NUMEROUS SKILLS AND CAPACITIES THAT ARE INCREASINGLY IMPORTANT IN THE PROFESSIONAL AND BUSINESS WORLD."
> **BLASTIC & SCHMOOLLEY, 1977**

My next to last class occasionally employs the *Group Project*—one of the worst ideas that some educationist ever came up with. I like to think it was Schmoolley (see above reference) because it's the kind of completely unproductive, time-waster that a man named Schmoolley would come up with. I'm going to invent a Schmoolley Action Figure. Its ass will be its head and its head will be on backwards. (All right, that's completely sophomoric.)

This next to last class of mine is advanced physics taught by Mr. Ivan Stetlik. Everyone in the class looks like they're about thirty years old. I'm exaggerating, but two do have little scruffy goatees. Typical of physics boys, they have more unruly but more highly developed hirsute adornment than the mustachioed boys in debate.

Mr. Stetlik looks exactly like your stereotypical Mad Scientist and delivers his wisdom with a thick, almost unintelligible Brooklyn accent. He has a sense of humor though, which is rare among those in the employ of the school. One day I was at the blackboard writing an equation, when I dropped the blackboard eraser for the third time and said, "It's alive. It's moving. It's alive." He laughed. The only one who did, but I'm grateful for any recognition of my entertainment abilities. I also appreciate the fact that he doesn't think much of what he refers to as "our benighted overlords," meaning our Principal and especially our Acting Assistant Principal.

Mr. Stetlik frequently refers to his days spent working on his Masters at Rensselaer Polytech, which he describes as "the most selective and demanding school in the nation." He's a big fan of his school and feels that some few of us, if we continue to work as hard we can, might qualify for admission, which would be a great honor and privilege, you can be sure. Mr. Stetlik is completely indifferent to everything at Jason Willard Watson High School except his physics class. I'm convinced Mr. Stetlik smokes pot during the day.

I like the class. I'm very interested. I even like Mr. Stetlik. Except...except when he believes he needs to leave the room for quite a while. When he does this, he instructs us all to pursue some morsel of physics knowledge via a *Group Project*. He has us split up into groups of three and each group is assigned a project.

I'm in a group now with two seniors, Harvey Young and Silvia Berger. We are investigating the Mpemba effect—does hot water freeze faster than cold water. It's silly because we already know the outcome. Nevertheless, we have these trays and access to a little freezer set to its lowest temperature. There isn't much to the experiment except timing how fast a film of ice forms, and writing up notes on what we did, when.

This is a wonderful chance for Harvey to get to know Silvia better. I am, in their wily minds, the equivalent of a very young, younger brother who wears hand-me-down clothes and takes out the ashes. In addition, I fill the trays, do the timing, and write up the notes.

But guess what? We all three of us get the same "A," and the same "excellent-write-up" comment from Mr. Stetlik. This is a flagrantsome miscarriage of justice. When I get to be King I'm going to unilaterally outlaw *Group Projects* in any school in the world, with special oversight on Doctor Waltzman's school and, even-though-he-is-otherwise-a-nice-guy, Mr. Stetlik's class.

Last class. I think I'm feeling better.

Miss Austin wore a scarf draped casually across one shoulder. It served no purpose. It was just a scarf. It undulated in silky waves as she wrote on the board, "Madame Bovary."

"Madame Bovary was what?"

"French?"

"Yes, she was French, but what else?"

I thought Miss Austin looked very French today. I've never been to France, of course, but she looked the way French women should look, I thought.

"Madame Bovary—Emma—as a character was? What?"

"Discontented?"

"Yes, Amy. Very good. She is discontented. She has a romanticized view of the world. She has what she thinks of as a drab country life. But what she wants is?"

"An exciting life?"

"Absolutely. She wants wealth, beauty, social position and above all —what?"

I don't dare say anything. I'm afraid of what might come out regarding the discontented Madame Bovary.

Amy pipes up: "Love—love and passion."

"Yes, indeed Amy. You might make the case that this is great literature because it speaks to what, deep down, all women want."

A couple of girls in the class giggle. Not much. Just enough to show discomfort. Keri Quinn coughs a small disapproving cough. Miss Austin is oblivious, but instead sweeps on into the book, opening it to a marked passage. She reads.

"At the bottom of her heart, however, she was waiting for something to happen. Like shipwrecked sailors, she turned despairing eyes upon the solitude of her life, seeking afar off some white sail in the mists of the horizon. She did not know what this chance would be, what wind would bring it her, towards what shore it would drive her, if it would be a shallop or a three-decker, laden with anguish or full of bliss to the portholes. But each morning, as she awoke, she hoped it would come that day..."

--*Gustave Flaubert*

They say mothers know when their children are in trouble or danger even if they are miles away. I think this kind of telepathic communication can work the other way round. I felt something bad had happened with Mom that day about a week after the Chinese food caper. I had this feeling of dreadsome. You know the feeling of dreadsome, hanging in the air? I felt it on the bus coming home from school. I thought it might just be a touch of nausea, but I knew it was something more.

Amy and I got off the bus and walked down Frog Pond past her place.

"Wanna come in?"

"Not now. Later maybe."

I hurried on. The ancient little red BMW wasn't there. Mom was always, always home from her part-time job at Talbot's by the time the bus dropped us off. I called Dad at Bigley. He thought she was just shopping. But I had this feeling she wasn't. I went down to Amy's. Her Mom thought my Mom had left the store about three or so.

"Was Mom okay? No screaming or anything?"

"She seemed fine. For her, she seemed fine. Have a biscotti, a little coffee with cream. Don't worry. You worry too much, Chris." Maria went to the window. About six-thirty it was dark. I worry too much? Maria was glued to the window.

Finally—"There! See!"

The four little car lights were bouncing along, coming down Frog Pond Lane.

Yes, at last, there she was. I ran out to meet her.

"Where have you been, Mom? I've been really worried."

"Why? I just went for a ride."

"Where did you go for a ride?"

"I just felt like going someplace."

"Anywhere special?"

"Just looking at houses."

"Where?"

"What do you care? I like to look at the big houses on Summit and Pearson where we used to live."

"I do, too. They're very nice. I would have gone with you."

"I needed to see them in the afternoon. And now. Especially in winter like this when the lights are coming on, you can see people. They're all so happy."

"It's really hard to tell, Mom. I'll bet they're not all happy."

"I THINK THEY'RE HAPPY!"

"Okay."

"They're happy, Chris. You can see it."

"Okay."

"I have a headache."

"Okay. Want me to help start dinner? What're we having?"

"Having?"

"For dinner."

"Oh, for God's sake! How should I know? You're just like your father. Is that all you think about? *Dinner?* Dinner, for God's sake. *Dinner, dinner, dinner!"*

The outburst about dinner was not unusual. Meals with her always made me jittery because if something erupted with Dad, stuff was likely to fly. Except for snacks like Fritos, which she loved, Mom fundamentally hated food. Green Eggs and Ham and all that. But the riding around was a horse of another merry-go-round, as Uncle Bill would say.

Furthermore, it began to happen more often. I'd come home, the old BMW would be gone and Mom with it. Finally, some time after dark she'd come home.

She began to simply walk in, take off her down coat, drop it on the floor, and lie down on the couch. It was as though I wasn't even there. I'd try to talk to her.

"Looking at houses, again, Mom?"

"Yes."

I'd stand there, wondering what to do.

"Don't look at me. I have a headache. Go be a magician."

This last a reference to my practicing the Cups and Balls magic trick in the kitchen when two of the balls somehow flipped out of my hand and into one of the few cake mixes my Mom ever bothered to whip up. Not the laughing matter I thought it was, let me assure you.

Pretty soon she stopped cooking altogether and I certainly never mentioned dinner.

Always a chore, meals got weirder and weirder. Dad would come home around seven-thirty or so and fix something to eat. We had lots of scrambled eggs. Mom would pick at her eggs and sit silently staring at us for a while. She looked at us like she didn't know who or what we were. Then, as if she had an idea, she'd get up and go to bed.

Dad and I should have done something about the situation with Mom, right? We did try. He did. He made an appointment for her with Doctor Shore, our old family doctor. He suggested that Doctor Shore could just do a routine exam, a blood work-up. That sort of thing.

"Maybe a scan of some sort to try to pinpoint the cause of the headaches."

"Everybody has headaches."

"Not all the time."

"I DO NOT have headaches all the time!! Get your own head checked out, Jeffrey. Maybe you won't make an ass of yourself going calling in my old neighborhood."

Back then it seemed reasonable, to me at least, that Mom's problems could have been something physical, or maybe—probably—psychological. I mentioned this to Dad, but Dad didn't want to have another fight.

With reason, I have to say.

The storm cycle of fights was intensifying. Those fights were terrifyingsome. They were getting worse and worse. A tiny spark could set it off.

"Would you like some coffee, Honey?"

He was, for some reason, using the address "honey" more often. In and of itself it was like lighting a fuse.

"Now when did I last drink coffee, HONEY?"

"I don't know."

"I don't drink coffee any more. It gives me headaches."

"I didn't know that."

"You can't see that I'M NOT DRINKING COFFEE?"

"I just didn't know."

"You don't see anything I do, do you Jeffrey?"

"I honestly didn't know."

"What do you know, Jeffrey? What do you know? How to sell cars? They give you an up now and then. That's it. That's it. They feel sorry for you,

78

Jeffrey. I feel sorry for you. Chris is ashamed of you."

My turn. "That's not true."

A mistake. "How dare you? This is between your father and me. Did I ask you?"

"No."

"Then shut up! Read something. That's all the two of you ever do. This place is like the reading room. The damned reading room at some damn library. The reading room in Gadfield's funeral parlor."

In this matter she was right. Dad read all the time. Last summer, I sometimes biked down to Bigley Buick just to talk with him, and he'd be in his little salesman's office reading. If a customer wandered in, he'd have to hit my father over the head with a catalog to get his attention.

Dad wasn't ambitious. I don't think he was opposed to ambition or the material rewards of life. I think he was just indifferent. He should have been in an ivory tower at Cambridge or Oxford. He was a walking encyclopedia. He knew more about more things than the entire staff of educationists at Jason Willard Watson. Trivia. Who sang the Pina Colada Song? Theories. Ibn Khaldun and *The Muquaddimah*? If you picked up a piece of string, he was likely to try to explain string theory. If you mentioned turkey for Thanksgiving, which was coming up, he was likely to do a five-minute monologue on how Ataturk had modernized Turkey. If an old Marx Brothers' movie was on TV, he'd do ten minutes on Karl Marx and "false consciousness," the tendency of Americans to vote against their own best interests.

He loved to talk about what he was reading. I loved to listen. Between the two of us—not to mention Uncle Bill—I guess we bored Mom into infuriation.

I'm sure we did. Dad had this oddly distracted quality, like the absented-minded professor. With his crooked little smile, he always looked like he'd lost something, but if he just thought about it hard enough, it would come back. The car keys, for instance, would just fly from some forgotten pocket directly into his hand. "Aha, now we can go someplace!" He seemed just on the verge of a remarkable discovery. It was a very appealing aspect of his whole manner. His appeal contributed to our trouble, no question.

Even though he was selling Buicks and GMC trucks, Dad often sounded like an enthusiastic anti-capitalist socialist. Not exactly a dreamer of revolution, but an idealistic admirer of the Scandinavian countries. No matter how you approach it, disquisitions on working class rights and economic imbalance are not exciting, certainly not to Mom. Though some women found such subjects fascinating, I later learned.

If my dad had a major flaw—and as I said, it's not my place to judge them, but doing so anyway—Dad would not confront any issue head on. We should have done something for and about my Mom, but he just did his best to avoid trouble.

Looking back on that time, I think both of my parents, in their own ways, were like Madame Bovary. They both seemed to be searching for something just over the horizon. Unrealized possibilities.

"Can you imagine what it's like to live with you two? It's like watching paint dry. Nothing happens! NOTHING! You know what I'm looking forward to? MY SUICIDE!"

"Now, now, Honey."

Again, the mistake of taking that drippy placatingsome tone. *Dad! Never, never, never call her "honey."* I don't know why, smart as he was, he didn't know that. But he just couldn't help himself, I guess.

"SUICIDE JEFFREY! Wouldn't that be messy to clean up? How would you explain that to Martha? She knew it was a mistake to marry you. Would I listen? How could I have been such a goddamn fool? Answer that? How could I? You don't know, do you?"

"I do as a matter of fact."

"Oh, go back to old Martha."

"She hasn't talked to me in fourteen years."

"You think she talks to me, Jeffrey?"

"You said you never wanted to talk to her again."

"That's one of the terrible things about you, Jeffrey. You think everything people say is what they mean. I haven't seen Martha since— since way before she moved into that fancy apartment on the Park. I've never been in it. And whose fault is that, Jeffrey? You evil FUCK!"

It's getting to be pretty deep when she uses that word. He was smart this time and didn't say anything.

I was surprised, though, by what came next.

"Jezebel, Jeffrey? That's what we used to call her."

Was she talking about Aunt Martha? I don't think so. What an odd reference. It sounded like some Egyptian queen Miss O'Malley might mention. I'd heard the name. Something Biblical, but I couldn't place it, and I certainly wasn't going to pipe up, "Who?" at this time.

"Come on, Chris. You have to get up for school." Dad guided me out of the room.

"Don't you sleep too comfortably, boys. I may get a steak knife and stab you BOTH in your sleep!"

Off to bed. Dad slept with me sometimes after these apocalypses and he put his arm around me.

"What's she talking about? 'Jezebel?'" I asked.

"I have no idea, Chris." I knew he did, but I didn't want to pursue the issue. Later it turned out I should not have been so totally trusting, but my Dad was my greatest comfort—"the warmth and security of a loving home" as Doctor H. so eloquently put it.

On more than one occasion, when my dad and I had retreated from a blistering tirade, Mom would walk in on us in her nightgown and just stare at us.

If I felt that stare, and I did, I would sit straight up and bite my hand to keep from screaming. She would turn and leave. Without a word. She wasn't sleepwalking like Lady Macbeth. She knew what she was doing. I just wasn't sure what it was. Dad told me she was just, as Maria had put it, "high strung." That did not comfort me one bit. The fact that the wedding picture had disappeared also made me nervous.

We never really knew where she went on her rides except to look at the houses on Summit and Pearson. Once she mentioned the Falls, but nothing more.

She quit her job at Talbot's.

It gave her headaches.

I was sorry she did that. Maria had helped her get the job. Mom once said she had run her father's optical shop for him while he saw patients, but that was a long time ago. I really thought some nice work, like Talbot's, might be very good for her. So did Dad. "Get her outside herself," as Mrs. Whitestone might say.

I told her I was proud that she worked at Talbot's. She dressed up to go there. Looked very nice, I thought.

"Yes, it's wonderful taking orders from some nobody like that Sandy Rothbart person. When I ran the optical shop, I was in charge. I gave the orders. Nobody looked down on me then."

Whatever the situation at Talbot's, she quit. And took her strange rides.

Then, much to my relief, she stopped going for rides. I'd come home from school and find her curled up on her bed in a fetal position. She'd lift her hand and indicate I should go away. Or sometimes I'd find her lying on the couch with a cloth on her forehead. Sometimes she would acknowledge me with a wan little smile. Sometimes she would surprise me and be quite pleasant for a bit.

"Is school all right, Chris?"

"Fine."

"You're smart, you know."

"I guess."

"Do you have any friends?"

"Amy."

"Besides Amy."

"Not too many."

"You really ought to have more friends. When I was your age I had twenty-two people to my sixteenth birthday party."

"Maybe I will, too, when I'm sixteen. I've got three years to build an enormous following, Mom."

"If your father had any sense he'd take some of your friends to some nice place for pizza or something. Celebrate your next birthday."

"We can think about that, Mom."

"You should be invited to some parties. There must be parties going on. They're probably not inviting you because of where we live. People know your father isn't anybody worth knowing. And you're always with Amy. She keeps you from meeting the popular kids."

I don't know what to say when she talks like that. She sounds a little like Mrs. Whitestone urging me to get outside of myself, but at least Mrs. Whitestone leaves my dad out of it.

There's no point in defending Dad. She will never get over the ordinariness of his selling cars and the fact that they are really such ordinary cars. Buicks. Rolls Royce might be better for Mom but I don't think he'd ever sell one of those around here. Come to think of it, I've never even seen a Rolls Royce except in pictures of Princess Diana.

"Remember how much fun we used to have playing hide and seek, Chris?"

"I do."

"You were very little then."

"Yes."

"You'd crawl into that cabinet with the pots and pans, making all kinds of noise. I'd call, 'Where is my precious baby? Where are you?' I'd look everywhere but there. Finally, you couldn't stand it any more. You'd jump out, big as life, pointing at yourself. 'Here I am, Mommy!' Oh, how you had fooled me. Remember, I'd be so surprised and then we'd laugh and laugh. You were so cute. I really adored you. I still do. I do."

"I know."

"Life changes. It can't be helped. Be a dear and run some more cold water over this cloth, Chris."

I thought this might be an opportune time to mention the possibility of medical help again. Not smart.

"You ought to see Doctor Shore, Mom. Really. Please."

"He's a jerk-water quack."

"He went to the University of Pennsylvania, did his residency at Brigham and Women's—

"That doesn't mean he knows anything."

"He could run some tests. Maybe refer you to a psychiatrist or a therapist—"

Another mistake.

"A PSYCHIATRIST!? Have you ever known a psychiatrist who wasn't half nuts himself?"

I didn't know any psychiatrists.

"Don't you ever tell me that I have some kind of mental illness! No one in MY FAMILY has ever had a mental illness!"

I'm in a bad situation here. I have to cool things down if I can. But she goes right on.

"You and your father are the ones who are crazy! Oh, hell, you're just like your father. You create a problem and then you insist it has a solution."

Mom in sing-song: "'It'll work out. It'll work out.' Well, this one won't! You want to know what's wrong? Ask HIM what's wrong!"

"All I mean is it might help just to see somebody."

"IT WON'T HELP ME!"

"Okay."

"You did this! How can a woman be attractive to anyone when she's a goddamn diaper-changing MOTHER? Things were not too bad, until you came along!"

"I'm sorry. I didn't mean to come along."

She slapped me.

She had hit my dad. Pulled my hair. Slapped me. I guess I loved her, but I became frightened of my own Mom.

Last Monday, the debate squad was in a tournament at our school. Even though I wouldn't be actually debating, Mr. Olson wanted "the whole team" to appear at the tournament in a "white or blue shirt" and a "conservative" tie.

The night before, Dad had taken one of his ties, showed me how to tie a simple overhand knot, and I did it fairly well, except, it being my dad's tie, the back hanging part was much too long.

"Easy to fix, my boy." He got a scissors and snipped it off. Just like in the cartoons. It broke me up. "Very cleversome, sir," I said.

He left the tie tied, so the next morning I'm in my blue shirt, just slipping the tie over my head, when Mom walks in.

"Did your father give you that?"

"Yes."

"He just cut it off?"

"Yes."

"What a jerk."

And she jerked the tie off me. Went to the closet, got another of his ties, and put it under my collar, around my neck. She began to tie it, and was having some trouble. She was handling me pretty roughly.

"I can do it," I said.

"You can't. I'll do it."

"Dad showed me."

"Shut up."

"Mom, I don't need you to do this for me."

"Oh, you don't need me?" She tightened the tie. "You don't need me? Maybe you need Jezebel? Maybe you need Brenda McCauley? I'll tell you when you don't need me!" She kept tightening the tie, and tightening it. I was coughing and choking, when Dad walked in.

"What the hell, Mary?"

She stopped. He picked me up like I was three years old. I was sobbing on his shoulder.

"Let's go," he said. He took me to school that day, and he went on to Bigley Buick.

"ONE OF THE MOST IMPORTANT LESSONS WE CAN TEACH OUR CHILDREN, ESPECIALLY AS THEY GROW INTO THEIR TEENS, IS THAT OUR ACTIONS HAVE CONSEQUENCES." -DOCTOR H.

I was concerned that the incident with the tie would not be the end of it, but that Mom would be provoked further.

That afternoon, I came home. Once again the old BMW wasn't there. My mother wasn't there. At first I was actually relieved. But gradually it got dark.

And this time she didn't come back at all that night.

We talked to Maria to see if she saw anything, knew anything. Nothing.

Dad called the town police and the county Sheriff's office to see if there'd been an accident involving the BMW. Nothing.

Dad and I looked at the three suitcases stored on the top shelf in Mom and Dad's bedroom closet. All there, as far as we could tell. I thought there used to be a pink one under my bed but Dad thought Mom threw that out because it was so old. He looked in her dresser drawers, checked her clothes hanging in the closet. There didn't appear to be anything missing, but he really couldn't tell.

We got into the Bigley Buick and drove around town, going up and down Summit and Pearson, passing where Mom's old house had been. We went down to the Talbot's parking lot.

Then Dad said, "We'll go up to the Falls."

"Why? Does Mom even mention the Falls? We never go there."

"That's where we met."

"I thought you met at the fire."

"That's right. But we went on a picnic up at the Falls."

"It's dark you know. We won't be able to see the Falls."

"We'll be able to see if her car is in the lot."

Oh, God, I hoped it wouldn't be. If we found the BMW and she wasn't in it—the implication was something I didn't want to think about. I was getting more anxious by the minute, that awful feeling that she might have done what I knew she could do.

When we got to the Falls we couldn't drive into the parking lot. The park people had put up chains, closing the park for the night. But we got out of the car, took the flashlight, and walked around the lot looking for the old BMW. I was afraid we'd be arrested for trespassing on government property. Or we'd meet a bear. But nothing happened. And we didn't find the BMW. The only vehicle was a yellow park maintenance truck.

When we got home, Dad looked through her purses, the photo scrapbook, her address book, and *The Joy of Cooking*.

"Why are you looking in that cook book?"

"Her father told her a woman needed to have "mad money." I thought she might have hidden some cash there."

"If she hid it and took it, Dad, it wouldn't be there."

"Right. Right."

He continued to prowl all over the house, the carpot, every closet. He looked in the washing machine.

"What're you looking for, Dad?"

"A note. Something. Where did she go?"

He looked and looked until finally I fell asleep on the couch. I felt him putting the old afghan over me.

I went to school the next morning. When I got home, she still wasn't there.

When Dad came home that evening, we ate some eggs. The Sheriff called to see if Mom had come home. He had no information for us. He'd let us know if they heard anything.

I found Aunt Martha's phone number in Mom's old address book. "Maybe Aunt Martha would know something, Dad."

"Your mother doesn't talk to her."

"But she sends us a card every Christmas."

"Well, your mother doesn't send a card to her. Your mother would kill me if she knew I called Martha."

I don't understand anything. I certainly don't understand my mom. And I can't figure out my dad. He is my only solid ground. I love him so. And yet—and yet—here is my mother, God knows where or in what shape, and *he's worried she'll be mad at him!* If she's dead, he's still concerned that she'll somehow kill him if he breaks the silence with Martha!

If you can figure people out, please let me know.

"Call anyway. She might know something, Dad." He called. No longer in service. According to information her number is unlisted. In Mom's book I found the number where Aunt Martha worked fourteen years ago. I asked Dad to please try that tomorrow.

Next day, I went to school as usual and this is where I messed up big time. In this stupid school, of all places. "Speech is silver." Uncle Bill said once. "Silence is golden." Would that we followed this little proverb. Would that I did. Me and my big mouth, my out-of-control, unformed-brain, adolescent mouth. If I'm so smart, how come I say such stupendouslysome stupid things. I think like a sausage.

"Never think like a sausage."
                    -Uncle Bill

It was a very cold November day, a rehearsal for real winter, the sky mottled like an old piece of aluminum. The kind of moody day I normally like. Miss Austin stood there in front of the window, the light fading outside, and she read.

> *"If I should die,*
> *And you should live,*
> *And time should gurgle on,*
> *And morn should beam,*
> *And noon should burn,*
> *As it has usual done;*
> *If birds should build as early,*
> *And bees as bustling go,-*
> *One might depart at option*
> *From enterprise below!*
> *'Tis sweet to know that stocks will stand*
> *When we with daisies lie,*
> *That commerce will continue,*
> *And trades as briskly fly.*
> *It makes the parting tranquil*
> *And keeps the soul serene,*
> *That gentlemen so sprightly*
> *Conduct the pleasing scene!"*
> —Emily Dickinson

I felt the tears. I may cry at home when I just can't help it. But I don't cry in public. Not even when they hit me in the head with the dodge ball. But I was crying. Not sniffling. Not making a sound. Just feeling tears form and run down my cheeks.

The bell rang. The day was over. Everyone left. I still sat there. Crying. Amy was at the door, then came back to me. Put her hand on my shoulder.

"Go away. Please."

"Chris—"

"Please."

"What did the Sheriff say?"

"Nothing. I don't want to talk now."

She backed away.

"He'll be okay," Miss Austin said. And Amy was gone. Miss Austin, the beautiful Miss Theresa Austin walked over and knelt down beside me. She smelled like vanilla. She patted my arm. Handed me a Kleenex.

"I know it's sad to think of life that way —"

"It's not that."

"What then?"

"My Mom left."

I heard a loud, wrenching wail. It must have come from me. I threw my glasses on the floor and sobbed, rubbing my eyes, blubbering like a three year old. Miss Austin put her arm around my shoulder and patted my hair.

"It's my fault."

"I'm sure it's not, Christopher."

"She's been very upset with me."

"It'll pass. It's a misunderstanding. She'll be back."

"No she won't. You don't know her."

A girl in a short red skirt appeared in the doorway. She had a little stack of papers in her arms and was wearing a white sweater with a red "JW" on it.

"What's wrong with him?"

"He'll be okay."

"I hope it's not like serious."

"No. He'll be fine."

"Can I put up a homecoming poster on your bulletin board?"

"We don't have a bulletin board."

"Yes, you do. Over there."

"Oh, I never noticed."

Kimberly went over and put up her homecoming poster, eyeing me with a mixture of concern and suspicion.

"You're sure he's all right?"

"I'M FINE!" I shouted.

"Okay, okay. See ya around, Chris."

"Sure." Kimberly left. Miss Austin picked up my glasses, handed them to me, and walked to her desk. She came back with another Kleenex. I blew my nose and gradually got myself under control. I was proud of the fact that I was usually under control in most situations, and now here, with my best teacher, this lovely, fragrant creature, I had completely lost it. I was ashamed. I got up to go.

"I'm sorry, Miss Austin."

"For goodness sake, Christopher. You don't have to apologize for something like this. Just sit there until you get hold of yourself."

"I'm missing my bus."

"Where do you live?"

"Frog Pond Lane. It's back of the Home Depot."

"I think I know where that is. Just wait 'til I finish up a few things, then I'll take you home if that's all right."

We walked out to the Avanti, passing Stephanie, Kimberly, and Nicole in their Peppy Pep Girl outfits.

"Hello, Chris," they simpered. "Hello, Miss Austin." Gigglesome twits.

"Hello, girls."

I could feel their idiot eyes burning into my back as we continued on to the car. Miss Austin handed me the books and papers she was carrying and she unlocked the car. I held the door for her while she slid into the driver's seat, then I went around to get in the other side. I didn't want to look back. I knew my face was bright red. Crying and blushing are not good for the complexion.

The Witches of Watson were still sniggering on the sidewalk. Why didn't they just go practice their peppishsome routines? You know how incredibly, totallysome stupid Kimberly, Nicole and Stephanie are? At a football game Amy and I went to once because Josephus wanted to go, our team, the Watson Warriors, had the ball at the opponent's two. We're trying to score and these girls were yelling "Hold that line! Hold that line!" They would have flunked the Penis Breath gym test.

The Avanti came to life, and we escaped.

Miss Austin found Frog Pond Lane like she'd been born there.

"What a charming little lane, Christopher. Have you always lived here?"

"Since we came from Texas."

"Would you like me to wait while you see if anyone is home?"

"No, no. I'm going to call my father to see if there's any news. Please don't mention this to anyone. I'm sure Mom'll come right back."

"I'm sure. I know you're worried, but I'm sure things will be fine," she said (not at all sure things would be fine at all).

She drove off, putting her arm out the window to wave. I waved back.

Dad wasn't in his office at Bigley. Anita, the receptionist, said that he'd been over at the Sheriff's office since about one-o'clock. I called the Sheriff's office. They said Hennessy, the Sheriff, and Deputy Clover were still talking.

"This is Chris Mullins. Could I possibly talk to my dad?"

After about what seemed like a lifetime, Dad was on the phone. He sounded very tired.

"There's no news, Chris. Her car hasn't turned up anywhere."

"Did you call Aunt Martha?"

"Yes. That bank has been taken over and merged and what all. Nobody knows Martha Harvin."

"We got a Christmas card from her."

"I know, but we haven't talked with her since we got married. Your mother doesn't want anything to do with her. Sit tight, Chris."

"What if she did kill herself?"

"I don't think so. That bottle of those old sleeping pills is still in the cabinet. I'll be home soon."

"Maybe we should just drive up to Aunt Martha's apartment in New York."

"If we did that, and your mother comes right back, do you have any idea how really upset your mother will be?"

I realize I've been slow to recognize the truth. Somehow, Dad, my tall, strong dad, has become very much afraid of Mom.

"We'll find her."

"Who? Aunt Martha or Mom?"

"Both. I don't know. I'll be home soon."

Next day, Mrs. Leitner, Doctor Waltzman's secretary, was standing at the top of the stairs when I arrived at school.

"Oh, Chris, hold up a second. Doctor Waltzman had to go to a Curriculum Conference at Rolling Hills today, but he asked me to ask you if you've been having any trouble in Miss Austin's class?"

No, no, oh for God's sake no!

"No. Why?"

"Kimberly Wellborn stopped by the office and said she thought you were crying in Miss Austin's class. She said she was concerned."

"I have this terrible allergy."

"That's what Miss Austin said when I asked her about whatever it was that was wrong. She said the fall pollen was very heavy yesterday."

"Yes."

"I just wanted to check. You know what might be helpful? Nasonex. It works wonders for me. Try it."

"I certainly will."

"Miss Austin is our youngest teacher you know, Chris, so anything you can do to make her job easier, would be good."

"I'll try, Mrs. Leitner."

Well, off we go. Have a nice day, Chris."

"You, too, Mrs. Leitner."

They actually went to ask Miss Austin about me. Kick myself, kick yourself, Chrissy boy. The news is all over the school, by now. Alert the media Chris Mullins had a breakdown in Miss Austin's room. I had to blubber, blabber, bawl like a baby. Well, I did it. I couldn't take it back now. "What's done is done," as Will said. His mother screams in Talbot's. He cries in class. It runs in the family.

Again, Dad was held up by Sheriff Hennessy. When he got home he was slumped down like his head was too heavy for his body.

"They asked me to come down. I went. You know what Hennessy did? He kept asking me where she was, Chris. Again, and again. And I kept saying I don't know. I asked them, 'What have you guys found out? A banged up old red 1978 BMW

99

shouldn't be hard to spot.' 'We're on it day and night, Jeff. We're in touch with all the surrounding states. It's a big country. "'

"Dad, is there anything I should know about anything? Something that caused this. I mean, I know she wasn't happy, but was there anything—?"

He looked at me like a hurt puppy. I shouldn't have asked because, in truth, if there was something I should know and it wasn't good, I really didn't want to know. He took both my hands in his.

"I'm sorry, Chris." He was crying. "I never made her happy, Chris. I wanted to make her happy, but I never did. I'm not a good person."

I don't know what I'll do if something happens to Dad.

"AS CHILDREN AGE, THEIR TYPICAL FEARS CHANGE. TYPICAL CHILDHOOD FEARS INCLUDE FEAR OF DARKNESS, FEAR OF STRANGERS, FEAR OF INSECTS, FEAR OF ANIMALS, FEAR OF BEING LEFT ALONE, FEAR OF ABANDONMENT. SEPARATION ANXIETY IS NOT UNCOMMON, SOMETIMES EXTENDING INTO EARLY ADOLESCENCE." -DOCTOR H.

This time Mrs. Leitner, came and got me out of Beverly Beatrice Spurling's class. It was with mixed emotions that I followed her down to Doctor Waltzman's office. I didn't want to talk to the principal. On the other hand, Spurling was in the midst of obfuscating polynomials, so leaving wasn't a total loss. He had so many of those poor juniors in this class so completely confused they would be wandering in a wilderness of polynomials for the rest of their lives.

Doctor Waltzman came bounding out of his office to greet me like I was a long lost relative.

"Christopher Mullins, our resident prodigy! Good to see you. How are your classes going? You know what? We tell everyone, someday that Chris Mullins is going to be on Jeopardy!"

"That'd be tough."

"Not for you, Chris. No, sir. Some day, when you're a successful lawyer or author…or educator or…the potential is limitless, Chris…and someday we're going to point with pride and say 'That young man is the product of a Waltzman education!' Come in, come in. Sit there. Have a jelly bean. President Reagan, bless him, kept a supply of jelly beans in the oval office you know."

"I didn't know that."

"There isn't too much you don't know, Chris, so I'm delighted to be able to impart some new knowledge. Ha ha. Even if it is rather, ah, trivial."

This man is not only an *Educationist*. He is an Educationist with pompsitysomeness of the highest order. Did I mention he also wears cologne? You've probably seen the ads—Eau de Testiclés. I made that up.

"Chris, we want you to know (arm around me) how sorry we are. Sheriff Hennessy, has been in touch with me regarding the disappearance, or I should say alleged disappearance of your mother."

Waltzman talked to the Sheriff? Why?

101

Big smile. "They tell me you're quite the teacher's pet of that pretty English teacher."

"Miss Austin?"

"Yes, that's right. She certainly is attractive, isn't she son?"

No, she's as ugly as that green witch in the Wizard of Oz. What does he want me to say?

"I spoke to her about you."

And?

"She didn't seem to know anything about your mother."

I'm so glad she didn't say anything. She said she wouldn't and she didn't. What is this Waltzman trying to do?

"You were crying in her class."

"Allergies, sir."

"Yes, apparently. You know that according to Sheriff Hennessy we don't have all the facts on your mother's disappearance."

He looked at me very intently as if I did, in fact, have some facts that I was hiding. The Waltzman stare. He took another jelly bean from the jar and popped it into his mouth.

"We wonder, Chris, has everything been all right at home?"

You're kidding, right Doctor Waltzman?? My mom left us. Poof. Not there. Does that sound like things are *ALL RIGHT?*

"I mean up until now, has everything been all right? Normal?"

Normal, yes, absolutely a model of sweet domestic normalcyness.

I said, "Yes, sir."

His mustache was twitching. I think he may have some sort of chronic motor tic disorder. "Well, let me ask this—in the strictest confidence, mind you—do—did your mother and father get along?"

"Most of the time," I lied.

"When they don't get along does your father threaten your mother?"

"No."

I can't believe this. Waltzman has talked with Sheriff Hennessy and they're trying to get me to implicate my dad. In cases like this, as they say on television, the prime suspect is the husband. Furthermore in a Waltzman school we do things a certain way, and one of those ways in a case where the father is the prime suspect is to subject the only son to the unctuous concern of a Nazi-like interrogation.

I tried to smile. Too much of a smile, probably. How should I behave in this absurd situation? Don't think about it. Sit there.

"We want to help."

"I'm sure."

"We are your friends, as you know, Chris. If there's anything we can do for you, anything you want to tell me or discuss, just make an appointment with Mrs. Leitner. Meanwhile, I don't think you should bother Miss Austin with your, ah, personal life. That's what your counselor Mrs. Whatshername is there for. In fact, I think it would be a good idea if you went down to see your counselor, Mrs. Whatshername as soon as possible."

"Whitestone.

"Right." Calling into the next room with authority. "Mrs. Leitner, call down and see if Mrs. Whitestone is in? Chris, I strongly suggest you see her today if possible, to help work things out. One of the reasons we have Mrs. Whitestone is her extensive knowledge of grief. So, confide in her."

"Yes, sir."

He looks at the battery-powered, fake Regulator on the wall.

"Oh, we're almost in the next period. Better run along. Good to see you, Chris, and, I repeat, if there is anything, anything your principal Doctor Waltzman can do to make things a bit easier, Mrs. Leitner always knows where I am. 'Principal' ends with the word 'pal,' you know." Big smile.

I feel sorry for Mrs. Leitner. I really do.

When I saw Mrs. Whitestone that's when she suggested the pen pal in Denmark or Poland or the Baltic.

Amy and I got off the bus and they were there waiting in the Sheriff's car, Sheriff Hennessy and Deputy Clover. Deputy Clover is a short, chubby black lady with a big smile and this enormous gun on her hip that made her look even shorter. The barrel reached halfway down her thigh. If it went off it would probably leave a five-foot crater. She took my hand in both of hers.

"Chris, I'm Deputy Sheila Clover. It is so nice to meet you."

The Sheriff chuckles, "You probably know who I am."

Not at all, sir. Despite the fact that your super-serious chubby pink face was plastered on every visible surface in the county prior to the election, and you're wearing a big shiny badge and a name tag and that silly Smoky-the-Bear hat, not to mention the really cool brown costume, I have no idea who you might be—Dudley Do-Right? Inspector Gill?

"I'm Sheriff Dan Hennessy. Can we come in a minute?"

What am I going to say? Do you have a warrant? No, sir, the Fourth Amendment to the Constitution guarantees that my home is my castle.

"Sure. Come in."

They take up a fair amount of space in the living room, these two, but there they are. Looking in all directions.

"Would you like to sit down?"

"No, no. We just want to make sure you're doing okay."

"I'm fine."

"Your dad's at work, right?"

"I hope so."

"What do you mean you 'hope so?'"

"I meant I hope he's okay."

Big smile from Sheila, "Would you mind if I used your bathroom?"

Yes, I mind. Go at the office.

"Not at all. Over there."

Bathroom, my earlobe. Looking for blood, aren't you? Looking for whatever you people look for.

"Chris, let's sit down." Hennessy sits on our couch, right in the center, spreading his legs in a wide-flung masculine manner so that there's no room anywhere on that couch for anyone except him and his bulging pants and leather jacket and belt and about twelve pounds of keys, and, of course, the giant flashlight, black holster and big gun. Heavy-duty manly costuming. He gestures to the little ottoman. I sit.

"Can we talk turkey?"

Gobble, gobble.

"Man to man?"

"Sure."

"Do you have any idea what your father did with your mother?"

"WHAT'RE YOU SAYING? MY FATHER DIDN'T DO ANYTHING WITH MY MOTHER! SHE LEFT!"

"Calm down. I didn't mean to imply anything. I meant do you have any idea where your mom might have gone."

"No."

Sheila comes back. She says, "You have just two bedrooms, right? The one that's yours and your parents?"

She's been all over the damn, fucking house.

"Right."

"You're an only child?"

No. We buried the others in the backyard.

"Yes."

106

"I want you to relax, Chris. Don't worry, we'll find your mom. We've got everyone everywhere looking for that little red Beamer. It'll show up. Well, nice talking to you."

They're gone. But before they drive away, they walk around Dad's garden, looking at the three trees he planted in the corner. Winter is the time to plant trees I read, I think.

He looked gray and bedraggled, my dad. He slumped in the chair in front of the TV, but didn't turn it on.

"Come here." I went over to him. He hugged me as if he might never have another chance to hug me. "I'm not perfect, Chris. But you know how much I love you. More than anything. And your mother does, too. In her own way. She was just born with a silver spoon in her mouth and I came along with a stainless steel fork, I guess. However this all comes out, you have a brilliant, brilliant future."

"Did the Sheriff talk to you again?"

"The son-of-a-bitch. He stopped by Bigley and told me not to leave town."

"What would happen if you did?"

"Who knows? I'm not going to leave town. What does he think I am?"

A *murderer!?*

Miss Austin leaned against the corner of her desk, twisting a small strand of her hair, smiling at us.

"Hamlet? Important actors have played the part, right? But I think they've all been wrong. Why? They've all been what?"

"Too short?"

"No."

"Too weird?"

"Maybe, but in my opinion they've all been too old. Hamlet is a teenager—a pouting teenager at that. Think about it. Your father is the king. You adore him. And what does your mother do? She marries your uncle, whom you can't stand. Not only does she marry him, she marries him when his father is 'But two months dead: nay, not so much, not two.' He is furious that his mother has married his uncle so soon after his father has died. He is developing a contempt for his mother. He's on stage, alone talking to himself, as he often does, and he feels the way many teenage boys or girls might feel:

> *"Let me not think on it — Frailty, thy name is woman!*
> *A little month, or ere those shoes were old*
> *With which she follow'd my poor father's body,*
> *All tears: — why she, even she —*
> *O God! a beast that wants discourse of reason,*
> *Would have mourn'd longer — married with my uncle,*
> *My father's brother, but more like my father*
> *Than I to Hercules; within a month:*
> *Ere yet the salt of most unrighteous tears*
> *Had left the flushing in her galled eyes,*
> *She married. O, most wicked speed, to post*

108

With such dexterity to incestuous sheets!
It is not nor it cannot come to good!"

"Now, we all know what's going to happen, but it unfolds in such a fascinating and complex way. An important part of the genius of Shakespeare is that he knows how human emotions ebb and flow, how they can confuse a person even as he or she is feeling those emotions. Life is not simple."

Boy, Miss Austin, you can say that again. The bell rings.

"Read to the end of Act Three, scene four. And remind your parents again about Parents' Night."

Miss Austin closes the book.

"Christopher?"

"Yes?"

"Are you okay?"

"Yes." Something about her brings tears to my eyes. I have to go. "I can't miss my bus."

Beverly Spurling is slinking around outside Miss Austin's classroom door again looking like he has something ulterior on his mind. Creep.

Time wore on for three more days and my mother did not come back. Winter was settling in with chillingsome authority. It snowed.

Every day I walked by the Fowlers, got Amy, and we went to school like always. Every day Amy asked if there was any news. Every day there wasn't. After school Maria and Josephus asked if there was any news. There wasn't.

On the fourth day there was news—a small item in the Courier, our local daily paper.

> Slide County Sheriff, Dan Hennessy, reports that officials are looking for Mary Mullins, wife of Jeffrey Mullins (pictured above) who, according to Mr. Mullins, went missing some time Monday, November 8. Mr. Mullins said she was probably driving a red 1978 BMW 325, license number KL 7144. If anyone has knowledge of the whereabouts of Mary Mullins or has seen her car, please contact the Slide County Sheriff's office at 679.252.6000.

It was a three-or-four-year-old picture of Mom. Smiling. She looked very nice, young, beautiful. Who knows, maybe she could have been in movies.

The snow continued to fall. After school, at night, Dad and I hunkered down in the house like we were on a camping trip—not that we'd ever been on a camping trip. "I can't imagine sleeping on the ground with all those crawly things," Mom said. So, we didn't camp.

But if we had I think it would have been like these last few winter nights with Dad. We made chili and meatloaf and roasted a chicken. We had Hungry Jack mashed potatoes out of a box and Heinz gravy out of a jar. I'm sorry to say this, but in those few days, when Dad and I were together, I don't think either of us missed Mom very much. Whenever I thought about her during the day, riding the bus, coming home to the empty house, I did miss her, and I would feel tears coming on. But once Dad came home, we were pretty much okay.

I didn't question him any more about what I should or shouldn't know. I really didn't want to take a chance on upsetting things with Dad. Of course, I was bothered by Mom's references to Brenda McCauley and, particularly, "Jezebel." Clearly Mom was suspicious of Dad's relationship with Brenda McCauley, but whatever that was about was long ago. However, Jezebel came on the scene about the time of Mom's Talbot's tantrum, so Jezebel was a more immediate concern. I looked her up in a guide to the Bible, which I was pretty sure was the context. I must say I wasn't terribly enlightened except to learn that Jezebel worshipped Baal and she'd been thrown out of a window and eaten by dogs. If there is someone by that name in our town, I doubt that she worships Baal. She's apparently also associated with prostitutes but I'm not exactly sure why. As far as I could read in the Bible guide (Dad says I should read the whole Bible some time cover to cover to broaden my education) where I found Jezebel mentioned I found nothing about prostitution. I could ask Miss Austin, but that doesn't seem wise. Josephus, Amy's dad, knows the Bible backwards and sideways, but I don't want to bring it up with him either. Maybe I should talk about these women with Uncle Bill.

Maybe I should just let all this go. Attribute the references to Mom's unbalanced condition—whatever that condition is.

The fourth night. Parents' Night.

It was parents' night at the school. Both parents are supposed to come, if possible, but, in my case, of course, it wasn't possible.

Dad came, however. He knew that the teachers and, probably by now, quite a few of the other parents were aware that Mary Mullins, my Mom, was missing. After all, it had been in the paper. I told him he didn't have to go, but he came to school anyway. I loved him for that courage.

"I think I have to do this, Chris. We can't hide."

I think we could hide, we should hide, but we didn't.

We went right up to the heavy swinging gates of the underworld, through them, past the plaque identifying Jason Willard Watson, and on into whisper land.

In the auditorium heads are turning and a low buzzing begins when he and I walk in, then an unnatural quiet. We spot a couple of seats in the center of row "N". Perfect. About fifteen pairs of feet to step over. Excuse me, excuse me. Now, more buzzsome buzzyness, hornets looking to sting. I can't get my jacket unzipped and have to stand up to get the stupid thing undone. Stephanie and Stephanie's parents, the Schallers, are just a couple of rows in front of us. Stephanie turns and waves. Then the three of them, the Mr., the Mrs. and the darling child turn and smile. Dad nods. I am red.

Not red as a beet. Red as a tomato. Red as a speeding fire engine. My acne is acneying up. I never had any of that hideous affliction until the last few days. I'm sure it's what leprosy or the bubonic plague probably looks like, or necrotizing fasciitis, that flesh-eating disease for which there is no known cure.

"UNDERSTANDING YOUR TEEN CHILD'S ACNE: ANDROGENS ARE HORMONES THAT INCREASE IN BOYS AND GIRLS DURING PUBERTY CAUSING THE SEBACEOUS GLANDS TO SECRETE MORE SEBUM AND CLOG THE PORES. EXCESS SEBUM BREAKS DOWN THE CELLULAR WALL IN THE PORES, ALLOWING BACTERIA TO GROW, CAUSING ERUPTIONS OF VARYING SIZE. ACNE MAY BE EXACERBATED BY CERTAIN MEDICATIONS, DIET, AND STRESS." -DOCTOR H.

Stress. *STRESS, PEOPLE. YOU'RE LOOKING AT PIMPLESOME STRESS DISORDER!!* That's all it is, for God's sake. Look that way, look at the stage. There's Waltzman. Listen up!

The routine for Parents' Night is the epitome of *Educationist* dumbsomeness.

First, you assemble in the auditorium and Doctor Waltzman himself welcomes and thanks you and blah, blah, "our philosophy of EDUCATING the whole student at Watson—high academic and ethical standards in a Waltzman school" blahblathersome and you're off, zipping around at a trot, meeting each teacher, your counselor, and finally back for concluding remarks from the good and great Doctor

Waltzman, in whose school we do things "the Waltzman way."

You have about eight minutes with each of these people. Just enough time to hear, "Chris is such a joy to have in class," but not enough time to ask a meaningful question or even find out what's going on in the class. This arrangement is a ploy by the *Educationists* to keep parents in the dark. They say they want parents involved in our Education, but they really don't want some smart-ass parent spouting off and interfering with what they're doing, no matter how vacuous it might be.

Beverly Beatrice Spurling is especially sensitive about his advanced algebra class because so many of the kids in the class are completely clueless and the parents know it, but they can't figure out a way to unclueless their offspring without setting off Spurling into a spate of retributionsomeness on the kids. Thereby affecting their grades. Thereby ruining their chances of getting into Princeton or Stanford or even the state university. Thereby completely ruining their lives. Finished even before they start because some parent thoughtlessly pointed out that no one, NO ONE, Mr. Spurling, knows what's going on in your unadvancing advanced algebra class.

However, the exception that proves the rule is guess who?

"Chris is such a joy to have in class. He doesn't want shortcuts, like, sad-to-say, so many of the students do. He goes beyond the superficial and grasps the larger concepts that I'm trying to impart."

114

"It must be frustrating," says my dad.

"Oh, Mr. Mullins, you have no idea. I try to get them to look at problems from various angles, and all they want to know is will this be on the test, what's the answer and what's the easiest way to get it?? Frustrating."

"I sympathize," says my dad.

"By the way, I heard about Mrs. Mullins. Any word on—on her?"

"Not yet. Thank you for asking."

Penis Breath Himoski was one teacher who didn't find me a joy. Not unlike Beverly Beatrice Spurling, Himoski, the soul of personal sensitivity, finds it frustrating to have some highly unmotivated students in his gym class, which, as he points out, is just as important as every other class. Maybe more so in terms of health and longevity.

"I tell them school should not be just your academic classes. To have a healthy mind, you have to have a healthy body, too, don't you agree, Mr. Mullins?"

"I do. I was an athlete myself. And I keep telling Chris that what good coaches are looking for is not ability, but effort."

Dad! For God's sake!

"Right on, Mr. Mullins. The old Big E!"

Vomitsome nauseousness, PB.

Dad goes on. "But sometimes, when you are working so terribly hard in all your other classes, sometimes, it's good to have one class that is a haven from all the pressure. It's good to have one teacher who understands."

"Well, I certainly try to be understanding, Mr. Mullins."

"I can see that, Mr. Himoski."

"Paul. Paul Bruce. Everyone calls me PB."

"I'm Jeff."

"Jeff, your Chris here is a good little boy." Pats me on the head. "I know things aren't easy right now, but as Pappy Martin used to say, 'It's always darkest before the storm.'"

"That's true."

Jesus.

Off to our next stop.

"Who is Pappy Martin?"

"Must be some famous coach I never heard of, Chris. We'll certainly want to look him up, won't we?"

"Absolutely."

Mrs. Whitestone. Mrs. Whitestone is sitting in her office, with a kind of lavender poncho woolen thing draped around her and that hideous jewelry on her chest. She's on the phone with her daughter discussing some sort of party that her daughter is going to or giving or something. Big smile to Dad and me standing in the doorway as she motions us in, while holding up a brightly manicured finger to indicate that she'll be with us in a teeny weeny moment.

"Honey, I don't think gifts are necessary, but we can talk about it when I get home Sweetheart. Try not to worry, okay? Bye, bye."

Now to us.

"Chris, at last. I thought maybe you didn't come. And this must be your father. Mr. Mullins, I'm Trisha Whitestone, Chris's guidance counselor."

They dance around a bit, agreeing that I am exceptional, and I should just cover my ears because she and virtually everyone on the faculty have such high praise for me, and then we get to it.

"I take it your wife is still missing."

"Yes."

"We've all been concerned, of course, but I've been especially concerned because, well, I'm the one responsible, in the long run, for Chris's mental health and his psychological well-being."

"We certainly appreciate your concern."

"Chris and I have had some long talks about this—this situation. Haven't we, Chris? And I've suggested he find ways to get outside himself, reach beyond the immediate. You know what I'm saying?"

"Yes."

What, Dad? You and I know she's just blowing smoke up her own ass.

"Do you mind if I ask—have Chris and you and your wife been churched?"

"Uh—"

Aha! Dad is speechless.

"Churched?"

"Do you go to church with any regularity? Prayer, you know, is a powerful thing."

"It is, yes."

"I think the three of us should pray."

She takes my hand and my dad's hand and bows her head.

"Father, in heaven, we ask in the holy name of your only son that this (Pope-ish hand waves over my head) only son's mother and this man's wife be returned to us safe and sound. We pray that no harm has come to her and that she will take her place in this family to once again nurture and care for—"

The phone rings.

"—them. Amen. Hello. Yes, Sweetie, can I call you back in a sec—I know the other girls have decided—"

Dad stands up, points to his watch, pantomimes that we have to be on our way, and we are.

"What the hell? What's happened to the separation of church and state?" That's my dad when we are clear of the doorway. "This might be the ideal time for me to file a complaint with the Sheriff."

I laugh. He laughs. We are like a couple of little kids. How can we possibly be laughing when you and I know this whole evening compares unfavorably with an hour on the medieval rack?

Onward, right? We zip into the penultimate class, Mr. Stetlik's physics. He seems to be in a very mellow mood, praising me extravagantly, especially my outstanding ability to work with others in *Group*

118

Projects. "Even though Chris is younger, his classmates have a very collegial view toward Chris. They even ask to work with him."

Then he says, confidentially, "Mr. Mullins, this can be a mean place. Your son is tough."

"I'm proud of him," Dad says. "Thanks for being so kind."

Miss Austin is our last stop before returning for the Waltzman benediction.

She's sitting on the edge of her desk, talking quite seriously with Mr. and Mrs. Quinn and their daughter Keri. Keri is a junior, or a senior maybe, and very, very serious—earnest really. Anything remotely connected with love or sex seems to make her nervous. She asks a million questions in class and is always frowning because she tends to take everything quite literally, which can be a disadvantage when you're dealing with poetry and literature. Searching for exactitudeness in absolutely everything can really slow you down.

The Quinns, her parents, have that same intense look, like the people you see at health food stores. People obsessed with regularity. They seem concerned and Miss Austin seems to be explaining why they shouldn't be concerned. They look doubtful, but somewhat mollified. Eventually, the three of them exit and Miss Austin hurries over to greet us.

"I'm sorry to keep you waiting. I was trying to explain to them that 'frailty thy name is woman' is not my sexist view of womankind but Hamlet's view—oh, sorry—hello. You must be Mr. Mullins. I'm Theresa Austin. Nice to meet you."

"And it's nice to meet you. My son thinks very highly of you."

"And I think highly of him. Turn your back, Christopher, we are saying nice things about you."

"I won't listen."

This polite small talk has got to improve. Whitestone wants me to cover my ears. Miss Austin wants me to turn my back. I'm becoming a circus act. We only have about thirty seconds of interaction with my favorite teacher left before we have to run back to hear Waltzman.

"I'd like to talk about Christopher's work, but do you mind my asking—"

"No. We still haven't heard from my wife—Chris's mother."

"I'm so sorry. You should know that Christopher has held up very well here at school during these few days. This place is a hotbed of rumor and gossip and he's been very strong."

That's not true. I'm a mess. But I try to smile at her. At least I hope my smile comes out like a smile and not like that Munch painting, *The Scream.*

However, there is the promise of relief just around the corner, in the auditorium, where this ordeal will soon conclude right after we are privileged to hear the Waltzman closing, which is pretty much what he said in his opening educationist salvo, but with an additional appeal for the Principal's Discretionary Fund for needy students. As far as I can tell, Amy and I are two of the neediest students in the school so I think we should apply, don't you? Me especially. I'm really needy in so many ways.

On the way out of the auditorium Mrs. Quinn stops my father with her severely intense gaze. "You know, Mr. Mullins, as far as I'm concerned we still have the rule of law in this country. No matter what people may think or say, a man is not guilty until proven guilty in a court of law. Hearsay is just hearsay."

Oh, God. Why did I let my dad come to this place? I should have saved him from these people.

"I appreciate that."

We can't get out fast enough. Run! He doesn't. He walks very deliberately, very tall, Clint Eastwoody. He's even wearing his old Tony Lama boots from Sheplers.

He smiles and speaks to them all—the Schallers and the Wellborns and their daughters, Stephanie and Kimberly. And there's Mrs. Findley and Nicole. They are just behind us going into the parking lot. Mrs. Findley is on the School Board and appears, wearing her Ronald McDonald smile, at every school event. Stephanie and Kimberly say, "Good night, Chris. Take care, teddy bear."

Need I say it? They giggle. It's all *SO-O-O* funny—bunny—honey—sonny—*shit!*

At the end of the week of Mom's disappearance, Miss Austin is talking about the Greek

121

story of Oedipus. Keri Quinn is saying he's committed this terrible sin by marrying his mother and Miss Austin is saying not really because he didn't know that Jocasta was his mother. Keri is insisting when the bell rings. Miss Austin says "We'll continue this tomorrow." Then, as I'm on my way out, "Just a minute, Christopher."

I stop. Amy turns. "I'll be right there," I say.

"Don't miss the bus," Amy says, leaving.

"SOCIALLY AND EMOTIONALLY COMPETENT TEACHERS DEVELOP SUPPORTIVE AND ENCOURAGING RELATIONSHIPS WITH THEIR STUDENTS, IMPLEMENTING BEHAVIORAL GUIDELINES IN WAYS THAT PROMOTE INTRINSIC MOTIVATION, COACHING STUDENTS THROUGH TROUBLING SITUATIONS, AND IN CASES WHERE HOME LIFE MAY BE DESTABILIZED OR IMPOVERISHED, PROVIDING APPROPRIATE EXPRESSIONS OF EMOTION AND SUPPORTIVENESS AND RESPONSIVENESS TO INDIVIDUAL DIFFERENCES AND STUDENT NEEDS.
-COLDMAN & DUVOS,
PSYCHOLOGY OF EDUCATION JOURNAL

Miss Austin looks at me like she's assessing my health. "Your father seems like a very nice man, Christopher. If I may ask—since your mother has been absent, who's been fixing your dinners?"

What? Miss Austin, come on. You don't care about that, do you?

"Dad and I both cook. We're pretty good at it."

"I'm sure." She hesitates a second then says, "Would you and your father like a little break from that chore?'

"Oh, sure, but we're doing fine."

She hesitates another second, then says, "I wonder if you and your father would care to come to dinner Sunday evening? I live with my aunt and my cousin. They're very proper, I assure you."

Oh my God! Can you believe it? Dinner. With Miss Austin. My two favorite people in the world—my father and Miss Austin. Well, Amy is too, but I didn't see that there was anything to be gained by trying to expand the dinner party.

Now, I wish I'd had Amy with me. It might have changed something. I'm not sure what, though.

Sunday. Mom has been gone six days. We're going out to a dinner that turned out to be a somewhat pivotal point in the year, in my life.

"PSYCHIATRISTS GENERALLY AGREE THAT MOST AFFAIRS STEM FROM SOME DEEP HURT AND A WISH TO REINVENT THE SELF."
-DOCTOR H.

"You're sure this is the address she gave you, Chris? The corner of Summit and Pearson? That's the old Auttenberg house. I don't think this is right."

"200 Summit, Dad. That must be the house."

The house is an old pale-yellow brick Georgian style. Dad said it was probably built around 1920. I'm sure Mom had driven by on one of her peculiar house-seeing rides. It has a center entrance and two chimneys. I note all this because if something in the entertainment world doesn't work out (who am I kidding, right?) being an architect really appeals to me.

Dad still hesitates. "Her name is Austin, Chris. Not Auttenberg,"

"Dad, let's just see, okay?"

We pull into the side driveway precisely at 7:32 by the car clock, and Dad drives on to park around back, near the alley.

"Why are we parking back here?"

"We'll leave room for others out front."

Others? What others? Maybe Miss Austin has invited the entire class and when we walk in they're all going to shout "Surprise!" My birthday maybe. It's coming up in barely a month.

We crunch along the gravel to the front of the house. Dad has picked up a little box of candy. We talked about wine, but he thought for a teacher candy would be more appropriate. We leave our winter coats in the car. Too much trouble. He looks great in his blazer and tan sweater. I'm wearing my "good" dorky shoes, my nicest V-neck sweater with what Dad calls, "An old school tie." It's also dorky I know, but I like the tie. I tend to identify with old British styles, as does Ralph Lauren. (Born: Ralph Lifshitz. Don't you love that name? Say it real fast.)

The door bell chimes, a dog barks, the door opens, and there she is. Miss Austin. Jumping around at her feet, eager to be petted, is a West Highland Terrier.

Miss Austin is wearing a tight gray wool dress with a very high turtleneck collar and long sleeves. That beautiful dark hair that she has at an angle across her forehead seems to shimmer under the overhead hall light. I know I tend to be, as Dad says, "grandiose" in my descriptions, but she deserves lots of grandiosityness, in my opinion. I feel suffused with warmth. My "heart leaps," as they say.

"Hello, hello, thank you for coming. This is MacDuff—Duffy. Duffy, this is Christopher Mullins, and his father, Mr. Mullins. Come in. We're having Coq Au Vin. I hope you like Coq Au Vin."

"My favorite," says Dad as we follow Miss Austin into the living room, or in this case I suppose I should call it the "parlor." There's a flowered oriental rug with an antique white curvy sofa, and several other curvy chairs, lots of pillows and paintings. It's cluttered, but bright. I could live here. Mom would kill to live here. Although I'm sure she'd rearrange it after a few weeks.

Dad is looking back to the hall, all around. He is exceptionally alert, to say the least.

Seated on the couch, doing needlepoint or knitting or something, is a woman in a dark brown dress. She's, what? Maybe ninety. I can't judge.

She's very old. But very perkysome looking. Like a wobbly but bright-eyed sparrow.

"This is my aunt, Aunt Elissa Auttenberg."

Introductions. Aunt Elissa invites me to sit by her. Miss Austin points to a little portable bar, invites us to have something to drink. Aunt Elissa wants her usual—a dry Beefeater martini, straight up. Two olives. Miss Austin proceeds to make it for her while pouring white wine for herself. My father indicates he'll have the same. White wine, that is. Aunt Elissa says that I should have some sherry which, she says, aids the digestion. Some discussion about my age. When Aunt Elissa was my age she drank beer and wine. A tiny glass of it is put in my hand. Aunt Elissa requires another martini. She asks me if I've read much of Philip Larkin? None at all. She gestures toward one of the floor-to-ceiling bookcases. She snaps her fingers.

"Theresa, the boy should know the foibles of humanity. Lend him that green copy of Larkin."

Miss Austin says she's not too sure about that, but hands me the book anyway.

A tall woman sweeps into the room. She looks to me like someone who was once on the stage. She smiles at the whole room.

"Am I too late for cocktails?" she purrs.

She's about Dad's age. She's draped in scarfeylike things and lots of what look to me like sleeves, but there seem to be more than two sleeves. Maybe four sleeves. She has long hair, speckled gray. She's beautiful.

"This is my cousin, Adalicia Auttenberg. My star pupil, Christopher Mullins, and his father."

"Jeff," he says, softly. I can hardly hear him.

She shakes his hand. I look at her. I look at him. It's clear—

They know each other!

Miss Austin doesn't know that they know each other. Aunt Elissa doesn't know that they know each other. But Dad knows and I know and Adalicia knows that *they know each other*.

She quickly but nonchalantly explains.

"Actually we know each other. I directed a little TV spot for Bigley Buick and your father was the star."

You didn't tell me that, Dad.

Miss Austin explains further.

"Since Adalicia got back she's been teaching film at the college and doing some directing on the side."

"Just a few little TV spots. Mostly local."

"She did a great job for us. For Bigley."

"Jeff was very good."

I'm looking forward to seeing this, Dad.

Dinner is, as Miss Austin said, Coq au Vin. I guess it was delicious. I'm just trying to figure out what's going on. There is, I feel, some tension in the air between Dad and Adalicia, but I could be wrong.

127

Miss Austin explains how she ended up teaching here in this county and how her aunt and cousin have graciously provided a room for her while she gets settled in her first year of teaching.

They talk about the Peace Corps, which only Miss Austin has been in but they all heartily agree it is a wonderful experience and good for America. Miss Austin says that some people like Doctor Waltzman and some of the parents think it's filled with a bunch of communists, but fortunately Superintendent Prevell thought otherwise so they hired her anyway, even though Acting Vice Principal Himoski told her he hoped her foreign experience hadn't given her too many foreign ideas and Miss O'Malley hoped she wasn't as "green behind the ears as she looked." Everybody laughs.

Adalicia pours wine, red, for everyone, including me.

Dad talks about how actual communism has never been properly practiced as a form of government. Adalicia agrees. Though, she says, "political ideology doesn't matter that much in the long run—wars are constantly caused by religion and ethnicity." Dad agrees. Adalicia has spent years in Europe, mainly France, but is "more spiritually connected" with Italy. She and Dad think the world of the "neorealist" Italian movies. Dad is at his most appealing, absent-minded, idea-wandering best as he leads the conversation in ever more arcane circles. Médecins Sans Frontières comes up. Aunt Elissa falls asleep at the table. No one seems to notice.

I never have seen Dad drink anything other than beer with Uncle Bill, but Dad has another glass of wine. Adalicia has another glass of wine. I have another glass. Miss Austin thinks this is not a good idea. "Nonsense," says Adalicia. "You live longer if you start drinking early in life." Dad laughs. I think maybe I imagined the tension. It seems to have abated. I notice the candles are dripping on the table. No one seems to notice that either. Mom would have put them out before real damage was done to this nice furniture. Adalicia pours more wine. I ask to look at the bottle, intending to indicate that I've done a good deal of reading on wine and how the French owe us Americans because it's our vines that make their vines possible because of that disease that—"Dad, what was that disease?"

"What disease?"

"That the wine vines got."

"Wine vines?"

"They grow right next to the spaghetti trees in Tuscany," Adalicia says wittysomely. She and Dad laugh. She touches his hand. No, I was right the first time, but it's not tension. It's attraction.

"It's snowing," says Miss Austin bringing creme brûlées in from the kitchen on a tray. As she passes me she says in what I would call a breathy sotto voce, "No more wine, Christopher."

Everyone, except Aunt Elissa, goes to the windows to see the snow. It's really coming down now. Perfect dendrite flakes. It's a blizzardsome blizzard of Russian cinematic proportions.

The "great, wise snowflakes cover the earth" as I read. It's beautiful. Adalicia is beautiful. The windows and drapes are beautiful. The candles are beautiful. And, of course, Miss Austin is beautiful.

I wake up the next morning in a foggy state of complete disorientationsomeness. I'm in a single bed with tall posts. The high ceiling is grayish white with spidery cracks. The walls are faded cabbage roses. There's a dark dresser with an oval mirror and a white pitcher and basin next to a blue towel. Covering me is an old Hudson Bay blanket smelling of moth balls. I know it's a Hudson Bay blanket because my mom has one handed down from somebody in the Harvin family back in the Pleistocene Epoch. Ours has moth holes.

I feel like I'm in a hotel room in a Western movie set in the 1880s.

What is this place? Well, Stupid, it's pretty clear someone has put you to bed in some sort of small bedroom in the Auttenberg castle. I'm over the kitchen where I can smell coffee and hear activity below. Dishes and silverware rattle. A TV set or radio is going somewhere. Women are talking.

I climb out of bed and stand there looking out the frosted window at the snow-covered trees. This room is cold. I'm wearing a voluminous white man's shirt. Except for my underwear, which I have on under the shirt, the rest of my clothes are neatly folded on a spindly black wooden chair. I have a minor headache—something between acute concussive necrosis and a tympanic mine explosion.

I tiptoe to the open doorway and look down the long hall. No one. The hall ends in a big black-and-white-tiled bathroom. I gather my clothes, dorky shoes, and the towel, and walk down to the bathroom. I splash water on my face, smooth my hair as best I can, and put on my clothes, folding the "old school" tie into my pocket, hanging the borrowed white shirt on the doorknob.

Next to the bedroom where I spent the night is a narrow, curving back stairs for the servants. I go down. At the bottom is a small hall next to the kitchen where Miss Austin and Adalicia are in a heated conversation. The little TV in the corner of the kitchen counter is broadcasting weather reports. The weatherman is saying, "One snowflake melts. A whole bunch of snowflakes stops traffic. And we've got us a bunch!"

I sit on the stairs.

"How many times do I have to say this? I admitted he was a married man!" That's Adalicia.

"I cannot *believe* this." That's Miss Austin.

"How was I to know he was THIS married man?"

Miss Austin says, "The name Mullins didn't ring a bell?"

"No. All that registered with me was 'Christopher,' this poor, brilliant, really young student of yours whose mother has disappeared and he needs

131

a little comfort. A little 'home cooking' as that idiot neighbor of ours, Franny whosits might say. I told you it was a bad idea. I didn't like any part of it."

"Well, like it or not, that's what I had in mind. I didn't know your latest conquest was going to trot in."

"He's not a conquest. We worked together. He's got troubles."

"Don't they all?"

"Don't get so shirty with me, Theresa. He's one of the nicest men I've ever known. I only hope I haven't done irreparable damage to him."

"You probably have."

"Yes, I probably have. I've been careless. I'd forgotten what this tight- assed, hyper-Christian small town was like. It's like Russia. Everybody spies on everybody."

"Now what?"

"Now, nothing, you'd better hope."

"To top it off you kept pouring wine."

"Two glasses. Three. Besides, it was a very light Pinot Noir."

"Oh, for God's sake. What am I going to say?"

"Nothing. Grow up, Theresa. The less said the better. I'll break off with him eventually but right now he needs someone."

"God, I wish I could be like you. Utterly blasé."

"Cousin, I am not utterly blasé or you wouldn't be here. Now, put this in perspective and eat your Cheerios."

I was sitting there. I didn't know what I felt. I didn't know if I could keep from crying—or screaming. Worlds on worlds—spinning out of spinning–this stairs smelling of wax and long-dead servants. My *DAD*. My goddamned head!

There ought to be a pill or a drug that will erase all this, turn the time disc back to the beginning and let the year start all over, someplace else.

Miss Austin steps into the little hall headed for the closet and she sees me sitting there.

"Christopher?!"

I turn away. I'm close to crying. Lately I seem to cry at the drop of anything.

"Christopher." She reaches out to me.

"Don't touch me."

"I'm so sorry."

Adalicia appears. She, too, is sorry. Everybody's sorry. I'm sorry. God, I wish against wishing I'd been nicer to Mom. Dad? What? What? Nothing is going to be right ever again.

Adalicia says, "Come. Have something to eat."

Eat? Eat? I feel like my mom, "Is that all you people think of?"

Adalicia goes back into the kitchen. I push past Miss Austin and run to the front of the house. I look out the window. My dad's car isn't there. I forgot. We parked in the back. I run back through the kitchen to the back door. No car. Adalicia is scrambling eggs. A time like this and *she's scrambling fucking eggs!*

133

"Where's my dad?'

"He slept on the couch. He went to work. Here." Adalicia hands me a glass of tomato juice and two aspirin. I take the aspirin, drink the tomato juice. I don't even like tomato juice.

"School is delayed two hours for the plows," says Miss Austin. Adalicia hands me a warm plate of scrambled eggs. I'm going to turn into a scrambled egg. I eat them. They're good. They have smoked salmon in them.

Aunt Elissa walks in wearing an oriental-looking kimono and green rubber boots. She pours herself a glass of tomato juice, takes a bottle of vodka out of a cabinet, pours a dollop into the juice, and says, "How are you?"

"Fine," I say. She tousles my hair.

"I'll get the paper."

"We got the paper, Elissa. Have some breakfast."

Aunt Elissa sits next to me. She smells of lavender and alcohol. Adalicia gives her a plate of eggs. Adalicia tousles my hair, then sits across from me, smiles, and looks at the paper. "I wish he hadn't put Hillary in charge of their health plan. Stupid, stupid. They hate her."

Miss Austin is at the end of the table pretending to work the crossword. She eyes me like she expects me to cry or throw up. "Have some toast, Christopher. It's raisin bread."

I do. In spite of myself, I like it here. Even the table itself seems perfumed to me. It smells like rye bread with caraway seeds, which I love.

Aunt Elissa says, "I hate raisins. They stick in my teeth. Why aren't you at school, Theresa?"

"Delayed for the plows."

"You know how they are," Adalicia is saying. "An inch of snow, and everything shuts down. Our street has been cleared for hours, though." She gets up. I like the way she smiles.

"Coffee?"

"Yes, please."

She continues to chatter, "Of course, it doesn't hurt that the esteemed Big Normie Schaller lives across the street. So-called public servants always get the first plows."

"Who?" I ask.

"Schaller. Our sleaze-ball councilman. The developers have been paying him off for years, you know."

No. I didn't know. Wait. Schaller? Could that be Stephanie Schaller's parents. Could Stephanie Schaller be lurking right there in the house across the street?

"The whole family is crooked, always has been," says Aunt Elissa.

As it turned out Stephanie and her mother were both lurking. And back of the Auttenberg house is the Wellborn house, home of the tattler snake,

Kimberly. Nicole's house is probably next door. Nice neighborhood? I don't think so. It's like living in an alley full of human rats.

I ride with Miss Austin to school, slipping and sliding in spots as the temperature was rising and the sparkling white snow was turning to gray slush. We ride in silence. She's gripping the wheel.

"I haven't done a lot of driving in these kinds of conditions, Christopher. Bear with me."

"We have rough winters," I say.

What are we doing? We're talking now and what are we talking about? The weather! The cosmos has been tilting out of control and we're talking about the weather!

I don't say anything else for some minutes. Neither does Miss Austin, until—"I'm awfully sorry about last night, Christopher."

"Who put me to bed?"

"Your father and Adalicia."

Jesus.

"I don't hold my liquor very well," I say.

"That was my cousin's doing. My fault actually. I should have put a stop to it. I'm sorry. I am very sorry."

"We have to take responsibility for our own behavior."

She looks at me as if to say, "I can't really believe you said that." Then, she smiles. "Yes, we all have to do that, don't we—Doctor Waltzman?"

She understands. Damn it—topsy-turvy as things have evolved, these Auttenberg ladies understand.

Miss Austin grips the steering wheel with determination. She's biting her lip. We're going about eleven miles an hour.

A yellow school bus passes us in a wake of slush. A school bus? That's a good sign. We're in the vicinity.

And at last—"Well, here we are. We made it, Christopher. Just in time for lunch."

The buses have rolled in just ahead of us and there are kids everywhere. And who is standing, talking with who and who on the steps? Stephanie, Kimberly, Nicole and Todd. They see this incredibly conspicuous car and me—and Miss Austin—getting out.

Moving as clumsily as possible, I see both of my feet zipping out ahead of the rest of my body which is now seated on its behind. I'm sitting down in wet slush.

"Oh, you poor boy. Are you hurt?" says Miss Austin.

"No, no. I just slipped."

"I'm so sorry. You're all wet."

The Man Todd yells, "Way to go, stud."

"I'm fine. Really."

"You're sure?"

"YES!"

"Don't shout, Christopher. Everything will be fine. I'll see you in class."

She's off.

Amy runs up to me. "Where the hell have you been?"

I don't know how to explain, even where to start. I don't have to. Amy goes on.

"They came to your place this morning just before I left."

"Who?"

"The Sheriff, that lady cop, and a city worker."

"What're they doing?"

"I don't know. When I left they were just walking around, sticking this big stick or bar or something here and there in the garden."

"It's all slush."

"Some places are melted completely. I think they're looking for your mom's body."

"Oh, God, oh God."

"Josephus called your dad."

"Where is my dad?"

"At work. At Bigley. Where were you?"

"I'm not sure."

> "If you're not where you want
> to be, go someplace else."
>
> -Uncle Bill

If I ran away from school right that minute, where would I go? It was about a twenty-minute ride on the school bus, so if I started walking now, assuming I could cover maybe three-and-a-half miles an hour, I'd probably get home by dark. Not a good plan.

My usual sparkling clearheadedsomeness is failing. Let's face it, I'm not clearheaded at all. Who blubbered that Mom was gone? I did. In a way, I have further compounded this compounded calamity at every turn.

I could take a taxi home. I had two quarters. Here, Mr. Taxi Driver, keep the change. I could call Dad, but how do I begin that conversation after last night? Call anyway. I went to the pay phone outside the lunchroom and called Dad. Anita said he had left.

"Where was he going?"

"An emergency at home, he said."

I called home. Dad answered. He said he was sorry about how everything had gone last night.

Don't even get into it. "Okay, but what's going on there now?"

"The Sheriff and Deputy Clover are walking all over the place, poking around. They have no right to do this. Uncle Bill is on his way."

"What can he do?"

"He's an old friend of Hennessy's."

"Dad, do we need a lawyer?"

"Possibly. We'll see. Go to class, Chris. There's nothing you can do."

Why does everyone say, "There's nothing you can do" or "It'll be fine" or "Take it easy?" That's probably what they told those people who were working at that Chernobyl place.

What did Himoski's friend, Pappy Martin say? "It's always darkest before the storm?"

A wonderfully reassuring thought.

*"Families are like cockroaches.
They can sneak in on you, even
through a fake keyhole."*
                                    -Uncle Bill

MARY

It's getting dark. There's a strong wind coming from between these buildings, I can feel it rock the car. I left without my address book. I left in a hurry so I'd get away while my thoughts were clear, before *they* got home and messed me up again.

I confess I didn't have an absolutely, one-hundred-percent worked-out plan in mind. I've always been a spontaneous person. I just took it one step at a time.

First, my suitcase. There it was, still under Chris's bed, the pink Samsonite case Daddy got for me to take to college. How many times I wished I had gone. I could have taken classes in acting. I really believe Mr. Lubinoff was right, I would have been in lots of plays. Producers and agents, so I'd heard, often went to colleges looking for new talent. I wish I had been there to impress them.

Just one more disappointment caused by Jeff.

But that's over. I should have done this years ago.

I took the three hundred dollars in mad money I had tucked into *The Joy of Cooking* (irritating title!). I threw a sweatshirt, jeans, underwear, two pairs of my highest heels, and all my good make-up into the case. And that was it. I put on my cute powder-blue down coat with the monkey-fur-trimmed hood and shot out of there.

Once I'm determined, I'm not a dawdler. I move fast.

But now, here I am and I'm wondering, what if, God-forbid, this isn't the right place? I can't spend another night in the car.

Stop worrying. I'm almost positive this is the right place. Number 37. There it is.

But it's not on the Park! The Park is down there, almost a block away. Typical. She made me think it's on the Park. What's she going to say? "It was on the Park at one time, but they put buildings in front of it?"

Really now. Where else could I go? Daddy's dead.
Don't say that!
Well, he is. His own fault, I must say.

Uncle David and Aunt Cheri? They must be in their eighties. Jeff stayed in touch with them, but they never did like me. This was the only place. So here I am.

Eat some Fritos. Go around the block again. How do people live here? There's no place to park at all. I just won't keep the car. I'll sell it. But what if I need to get away from here? Maybe there would be a place to park it further away from here. I'll decide that later.

Park in front of that fire hydrant. The police will see that it's clearly an out-of-state car that is just visiting.

What if—what if she isn't even in town? But her cards were always sent from New York—she used to say she always wanted to see China—oh,oh, *oh*—a woman is coming down the street. Sneakers. Briefcase. Trench coat. That's the beat-up old Aquascutum! Yes. Yes! That's her! Oh, thank heavens! Lean on the horn. She's looking. Get out of the car. *Wave!*

Martha froze, her face a mask of utter disbelief. Horror.

I went toward her. "I had the right address, didn't I?"

"Mary?"

"You recognized me. I'm so glad."

"Mary—Mary—what—?"

"I'm so glad to see you."

"For God's sake, Mary, what're you doing here?"

"I came to see you."

Martha just stood there, looking at me. She must've thought I was a ghost. I shouted, "YES, IT'S ME!"

I spread my arms wide and stepped forward to embrace my sister. I hugged her. She just had to understand. This was the only place where everything could be made right again. Martha was the only person who really knew me. The only one. I held Martha tightly. She patted my back. She said nothing. But I knew everything would be all right, just like when we were small. People walked by, faces pinched in the wind, indifferent to our reunion, but I felt like I could cry right there on the street.

Martha stepped back, put her hands on my shoulders and looked me up and down. "You haven't changed much," she said.

"Oh, yes, I have. I've become an ugly old housewife. You look wonderful."

"Let's get out of the middle of the sidewalk and go inside."

"I probably shouldn't leave my car there."

"God, no. We'll give the keys to Albert, the doorman."

Martha and I and my pink suitcase rode the elevator up to Martha's surprisingly small three-room apartment on the 8th floor. We were greeted by the saddest-looking basset hound since that one on that stupid Dukes-of-something show. Drooling dogs are the worst! But I couldn't just ignore him–her–it.

"What's its name?"

"Officially, it's Woebegone, but I just call him Woebee." She petted it and looked at me.

Say something.

"This is a beautiful apartment, Martha."

"Thank you. The building is pre-war, built in 1929. See the molding?"

"Why did I have the impression it was on the Park?"

"It's just down the street. Mary–really–what are you doing here?"

"I told you. I came to see you."

I explained to Martha that I'd thought about calling her, oh so many times, but I wasn't sure of the number. She said her number was unlisted because she didn't want the people at work pestering her at all hours. That's what she had Norton for. Norton was her assistant.

Martha said she was sorry, but she had to walk Woebee. What a bother that dog was already turning out to be, but I smiled and said I'd go along with her.

> *"New York can be cold enough to freeze the brass off a bald monkey."*
> *— Uncle Bill*

The wind was really howling by the time we got back to Martha's, and I was chilled to the bone. The old-fashioned radiators in the apartment made noises which reminded me of our old house. I imagined perhaps that was why Martha had chosen this apartment. It had a familiar feeling.

I couldn't tell if Martha was upset with me or not. She just kept considering me like she'd never seen me before in her life. Well, it had been fourteen years, but blood is thicker than time. No. That's not the saying. Blood is thicker...than something. Surely, she must sense my need, my desperate need. I went up to her and threw my arms around her neck. Again, she patted me.

"Oh, my God, Martha, I've missed you so much. You were right about everything. But it'll be all right, won't it? Just like it was before the trouble, before everything. I'm here now."

When I was young and beside myself with frustration, I would sort of—I wouldn't say whine–I've never been a whiner—but I'd make a soft, unconscious whimper—just to myself. I was hardly aware I was doing it.

I hated schoolwork. I hated doing geometry problems. I hated writing those awful research papers. I found that a tiny whimper distressed

Martha, and she'd help me with that hateful homework just to get me to stop.

It got to be a habit when I wanted her help. I'm not proud of it, but I guess I was doing that now. Martha handed me some tissues and guided me to the couch. We sat down.

She soothed, "It's okay."

I straightened up. I didn't mean to do what I had just done. But then again, I had to do something to get her full attention.

Martha said, "Well, now..." and pointed to my suitcase. "You've had this awhile, haven't you?"

"I still have the whole matching set that Daddy got me for college...."

"Well...."

I didn't really have her attention. Martha was looking at the ceiling now.

How stupid of me! I should have known. She did not want me here. She didn't want me at all. All the trouble I'd gone to, and this was the welcome I got! I stood up.

"I should leave."

"Mary, no, no."

"I'm going."

"Mary, be sensible!"

Isn't that just like her? How many times had I heard that, in just that tone? I could close my eyes, and it's years ago. Martha was going on now, making me sensible.

"Mary, it's freezing out there. You'll stay here. The couch makes into a bed. It's pretty comfortable, I'm told. Please sit down."

Maybe I'm wrong. Maybe she is glad to see me. I can't read her most of the time. Martha was never like me. I always wore my heart on my sleeve, according to our mother. I can't help it. Martha is cold, secretive.

She pulled the couch open. The mattress was about two-inches thick, but I said that it looked fine.
"You have just the one bedroom?"
"Yes. I like having the larger living space and open kitchen."

Martha walked into the kitchen area. "We should have a drink, don't you think? Yes, we should have a drink. What would you like? I'm having a vodka on the rocks."
"I'll have that, too."

She made the drinks. I sat on a hard wooden stool at the kitchen counter. We clinked glasses, and toasted, "To the Harvin girls," and I suppose we would have laughed if we could have. We drank and discussed—of all the ridiculous things—the ingenious storage that had been built into this small apartment by clever architects who had experience in boat building. I said our Cape Cod cottage had many similar features, also quite ingeniously designed. She nodded.

All was calm now. I relaxed. I had done the right thing.

We had another drink. Martha asked was I hungry? Did we want to go out?

"Or we could just send out," she said.

"Let's do that," I said.

"You used to love egg rolls as I recall."

"Oh, I still do. Jeffrey brings them home sometimes to surprise me."

The subject. The elephant in the room. And I brought it up! *Him!*

"How is he?"

"Fine. Just fine. He wanted to come along, but couldn't get away from his work. You know how that is."

"I do. I do. I wish I'd known you were coming..."

"It was a spur of the moment thing. I just had to see you. Touch you."

I truly meant that.

The only sound for a long moment was the clink of ice as Martha topped off the drinks. Flipping through a compact Rolodex on the counter, she found Grand Szechuan, and ordered Kung Pao Chicken, Shrimp with Broccoli, and Egg Rolls.

I walked to each window and looked out at the city lights. The view wasn't as spectacular as I had anticipated, but I felt Martha would expect me to say something nice, so I did—with a good deal of feeling.

"Oh God, Martha, you live wonderfully!"

"I like it."

"Oh, God, Martha—" The feelings I had managed to enact caught up with me, and I finally did cry. Real tears.

I went to her, reached out to her.

"There, there."

"I've missed you so," I said. I was weeping now.

I thought she would probably be crying, too. It seemed only natural. But I realized she was not. I pulled away from her and looked her right in the face.

"Please don't patronize me with your false comfort, Martha."

She stiffened and I feared she was about to say something awful, but she didn't. Instead she went to the kitchen and repaired her drink, asking me, "Ten more drops, as Father used to say on his eleventh drink?"

The cloud had passed. I said, "Why not?" I had been needlessly concerned. Martha was just Martha.

The buzzer from downstairs. The food arrived. I commented that you still couldn't get decent

Chinese at home, though there was a good new Thai place.

"We've never been there, of course."
"Oh, well...."

The battery clock on the kitchen wall softly pulsed second after second while Martha studied a floret of broccoli while I studied Martha. Now was as good a time as any.

"I'm LEAVING HIM, Martha! I can't STAND IT any more!"

Okay. There it was. Out in the open.

I watched her. Was she shocked? She didn't react at all as far as I could tell. She just said, "Does he know you're here?"
"I left a note," I lied. "I had to get away. I didn't know where to go."
"So you came here?"

I thought I had already explained why I was here, but I guess not. So, I'd better just tell her the whole shameful story about my miserable life with Jeffrey. "We live in a trailer, Martha! A fucking trailer on muddy Frog Pond Lane back of Home Depot. He doesn't care. His nose is in a book and his head is in the clouds. And Chris is turning out the same way."
"You want to leave Chris, too?"

"Yes."

I took another bite of my egg roll. It tasted flat.

"Do you use this restaurant often?"
"Sometimes. Why?"
"I just thought it would be...I don't know...better. Not that there's anything wrong with it—it's just that this being New York, you'd think they'd have more zip in their egg rolls."
"Put more mustard on it."
"This mustard is too hot."

The evening continued in its uncomfortable pace. I reminisced about how wonderful everything used to be in our old house on Pearson while Martha got sheets and blankets and struggled to make up the damn fold-out bed. I talked about how much I used to enjoy running the optical shop for Daddy, and how much I hated working at Talbot's, and that I'd finally had to quit because of the way customers treated me. Then Martha asked me where I intended to go and what I would do, now that I was leaving my husband and son.

"I don't know. I haven't thought that far ahead. You know how I am."
"Yes."
"I have to get on my feet. I was thinking of taking a business course of some kind."

"Where?"

"Well—probably some of the best business schools in the country are right here in New York, wouldn't you say? I could go to school here."

"Mary, you can't live with me."

There! I knew it, felt it from the start. I told her, "I'll go right now!"

"I just meant you can't live with me permanently—on a protracted basis. I'm sure you understand—"

"I've never understood why you're so jealous of me. You weren't even there for my wedding."

"You told me to leave!"

"You're twisting things around."

"Mary, you yelled at me, *'Get out—I never want to see you again!'*"

"It was my special day, and you couldn't stand that I was going to have a big, beautiful wedding. You said it was inappropriate."

"I said that just once, when you started making the grand plans."

"You and your words. 'Inappropriate!' In-fucking-appropriate!"

"And a poor use of father's life insurance moncy, yes."

"What? I should have gone into a convent?"

"Don't be crazy."

"Is that what you think? I'm crazy?"

"Unpredictable, maybe."

"Have you talked to the other girls behind my back?"

"What girls?"

"My so-called bridesmaids. Louise and the others."

"Why would I?"

"If they want to see me socially, let them call me. I've always tried my best to be a good friend to them."

Martha regarded me with a sad expression on her face. I thought maybe now she might cry. Instead, she said, "Don't you recall? You yelled at them, too. At the rehearsal. Over the shoes."

"They wouldn't dye them to match the dresses."

"You were vicious to them."

"I was not."

"You called them vile names. Told them you'd never speak to them again."

"Bridesmaids are supposed to do whatever the bride wants."

"Oh, Mary. It was such a small thing."

"Not to me! You've always thought better of them than you do of me!"

"I never had anything in common with your silly friends, but I do think you should be fair in your recollection of what happened."

"If Jeff had only done better, they wouldn't matter, would they? Did you ever see the ring he finally gave me?"

I got my purse, fumbled through it, and found the pathetic ring. I still couldn't believe the thing. It had this bitty diamond on top of a Tiffany setting. It was insulting, grotesque. "What do you think that is?"

"A diamond," said Martha.

"A quarter of a carat? An eighth? It could fall out and you wouldn't notice it was gone. Would you be seen wearing such a thing?"

I don't know....It's hard to know what anybody else really feels, but looking at the goddamn ring, now–*now*–her eyes water up. Some people.

We argued into the night. Round and round about who did what and said what when. Why didn't Martha know that I didn't mean she should *actually* leave when I told her to get out? Martha had the same blind failing as Jeff. She took me literally without taking the time or having the compassion to understand what I really mean. I really wanted Martha to be maid-of-honor. Martha should have known that. As it was, no one was willing to be maid-of-honor.

"Sure, lots of the girls were jealous because so many boys took me out."

"That's true. Lots of boys did take you out."

"I was Homecoming Queen."

"No, you weren't."

"Louise cheated. I was runner-up."

"No."

"Goddamn it, Martha. You are making me MAD AT YOU!"

"Shh! You'll set off the smoke alarm."

That struck me funny and I actually laughed. Martha smiled at me.

The level of tension between us fell. Then it rose again. Martha just couldn't let things alone. She kept asking me endless questions. Was there going to be a divorce? How did I intend to handle it? Did I have an attorney? Had I told Jeffrey and Chris exactly what the hell I was doing? Did they really know where I was?

"They know where I am. I TOLD YOU! I LEFT A NOTE!"

As for the divorce and all those details, I finally had to scream at Martha that it wasn't all worked out. That I'm not a machine like the chilly Martha Harvin. I have REAL FEELINGS! "I don't know how things turned out the way they did. All I know is that I deserve more out of life!"

Martha said I had known that Jeffrey didn't drink much, and I got him drunk and took him up to the Falls. What an outrageous accusation! I didn't remember anything of the sort and I told her so. All I knew for certain was that Jeffrey had gotten duller and duller, and he had not a shred of ambition.

I ticked off some of his shortcomings: the goddamn garden, Uncle Bill, Uncle Bill's chickens, boring conversations with Chris about God-knows-what! The list of his shortcomings was limitless.

"He knows what a wonderful life I came from and he doesn't give a shit."

"Everything was not sweetness and light on Pearson, Mary. Father drank like a fish. Probably a whole lot of people in town were half-blind because he fitted them with the wrong glasses."

"He did not."

"He hit mother. Often."

"Why are you saying these things? Lying about Daddy. He was the dearest man in the world!"

"Is that why you had all those tantrums? You screamed at him when he wouldn't get you a horse to prance around on. You were screaming the night of the fire. 'I want to go to Florida with the rest of the girls!' You kicked him."

"LIAR!"

"I have to get some sleep. Good night." Martha whirled and went to the bedroom.

"He's having an affair!"

"I don't blame him. Good night." The bedroom door shut.

That's it! I went after her and wrenched open the door.

"Don't walk away from me when I'm talking to you! I'm telling you he's fucking some other woman—Jezebel, as a matter of fact. You remember her. And I'm sure there've been others."

"You should talk, Mary."

"What??"

157

"Was Jeff your one and only, the true love of your life, the prince riding up to the castle? Those castle gates were wide open for years."

Three in the morning, fire trucks going by over on Broadway. Terrible bed. I got up, picked my way around the clothes that I had unpacked and went to the kitchen and selected a large chef's knife from the wooden knife holder. I examined it, traced my finger over the German maker's marque, "Wusthof." I held the knife so it was silhouetted against the window. Then I put it back in the holder.

I went to the window. I could see lights in other apartments—small warm spots in the cold city.

I went to Martha's bedroom and opened the door. I stood and looked at her sleeping. She woke. I held my hand out to her. She came to me and brought me back to bed with her. We slept entwined as in some of those nights long ago, when indeed Daddy had been drunk and Mother had bruises on her face, and Martha was my comforter.

A cold sunny November morning. I found myself alone with the dog. It had wriggled up onto the bed when Martha left and had drooled all over the pillow.

I got up and went to the kitchen. There was a note: "Strawberry Pop-Tarts in cabinet over fridge. Love, Martha."

We always liked Pop-Tarts. We still shared so much.

The New York Times was on the counter. Vladimir somebody was forming a government in someplace called Slovakia.

I found the Pop-Tarts, toasted one, walked around looking at various tchotchkes and photos of people I didn't know. I was wondering if Martha had anyone in her life besides the dog, when I heard a key in the door. I froze. Looked at the clock. Martha wouldn't be coming home at this hour.

I realized when Martha had gone out the chain lock and the swing lock on the door were left unfastened. I grabbed the chef's knife and faced the door.

Albert, the doorman, stepped in and the dog came running to him with the leash in its mouth.

"Hi there, Woebee!"

I coughed to indicate my presence. Albert jumped.

"Yee—oh, wow—sorry, Miss. Sorry. I forgot you were here."

"Sorry. I didn't know who it was."

"Woebee's walker is here. I'll call up before I bring Woebee back. Will you be wanting your car?"

"No, I don't think so."

"Very good."

He and the dog left and I put the knife back. If I'd stabbed the doorman, that would have been a fine mess. Martha should have warned me that Albert just comes and goes as he pleases. I turned the bolt lock on the door and put the chain and swing lock in place.

What to do now?

I certainly didn't want to go back. Taking me for granted all these years—enough of that. I wanted them to worry.

What would they think? That something must have happened to me. Some harm. The police would probably be suspicious of Jeffrey. Serves him right.

He wouldn't hurt a flea, of course. That's part of his problem.

I meant to leave a note. I almost did leave a note explaining that I was only going away to try to get a break, to breathe some different air, to try to get my head straight so I could maybe be a better mother.

And wife?

Yes, maybe, if I could just make Jeff understand what I had hoped for in life.

Of course, I knew that many men had affairs, but successful, sophisticated men—because they were successful and sophisticated—knew how to carry out their affairs in a refined and discreet manner. They had a sense of style. They went to Las Vegas and brought home beautiful jewelry to their wives. They knew how to maintain respect in society. It wasn't the affair with the damn woman! Boys will be boys. It was the tacky way he had done it in full view of half the population of the town, and, to make it even more tasteless, in the old neighborhood. It made me mad all over again just to think about it.

Don't think about it.

Chris? Well, I find myself confused about him. I love him, of course, but I want him to be so much more than Jeffrey.

I don't want him to settle—to be content to live like the Fowlers. Nice people, certainly—kind even—but look at them. Would they even be allowed to step into Adrian's restaurant? And that girl, Amy. Chris says she plays a terrific game of chess. Who in the world would ever care about that? What goddamn good is chess?

I'll eventually have to go back, I guess. Someone has to save Chris from embracing low standards. He's never been in a really nice store in his life. I could weep for what he doesn't know about looking—what? Elegant? Yes. Albert the doorman has a better sense of style than Chris is likely to develop, the way he's going. Such tacky influences on his life.

Jeffrey looks good, I'll give him that. Women notice him. Idiots.

Jezebel. That Auttenberg woman. The one who spent most of her life someplace else. I haven't seen her in years, but those...what's that phrase Mother liked?...*"nouveau riche."* Those nouveau-riche Wellborns with their high nasal voices—they seem to think she's fucking around with Jeffrey. What would Jezebel see in him? Fuck him. I won't go back. Even for Chris.

We should have stayed in Texas. Jeffrey should have known I didn't-want to come back home to those jealous people. Even if his mother was in that wheelchair. She died anyway, didn't she?

Enough! I can't think about all these things. I should do something today. Something fun—daring.

Martha could have taken the day off, but obviously she didn't want to. She's just like she always was. She knows I'm disturbed. No. Not disturbed. Never say that. Unsettled.

I stopped in front of the hall mirror and addressed my messy-haired, unmade-up reflection out loud. "Mary Harvin—Mrs. Jeffrey Mullins—God, how sick I am of being Mrs. Jeffrey Mullins. You are an unsettled woman. I can see that. *But, listen—it's not your fault.* You simply misjudged how Daddy would react to a simple request. Enough, enough, *enough!* Tidy up! Put on make-up! Smile! Compose and pose yourself like a queen!

I marched off to the bathroom, took a shower, and assessed my body in front of the full-length hall mirror. I might meet someone interesting yet in this life. I put on my panties and bra and went to Martha's closet. Martha was somewhat taller, but we

162

had been close enough in size that I could always borrow.

Yes, I'll borrow that nice, heavy brown knit with the long vest, and I know exactly what I'm going to do. I haven't been in Bergdorf Goodman since I was fifteen and went there with Mother. And Saks. I'll get my hair done with that new layered look. I'll just tell them that I'm recently divorced and my accounts are a bit muddled but just send the bill to me, Martha Harvin, at 37 West 72nd Street. They'll believe me because when I tell them, it will be very close to true. If something you say is so close to true that deep inside you convince yourself that it is true, people will believe you, and what you say becomes true. Especially if you are attractive and have an engaging smile.

I did my make-up very carefully and practiced smiling into the elevator mirror all the way down. Albert took me by the arm and helped me into the taxi. He has such a commanding way of hailing a taxi.

It was late by the time I got back to the apartment. Martha was just coming home after walking the dog. Good—I didn't have to do that with her. I was eager for her to see my new haircut and my new toast-colored dress with a plunging neckline, like the beautiful one Daddy bought me so many years ago.

She plopped down and I modeled for her. She applauded.

"How daring," she said, smiling.

I giggled. I felt sixteen again. I felt like I did when I was the Golden Girl and everybody—*everybody*—loved me. Louise and Franny and Polly—all of them were so jealous of me.

That evening, after eating Greek take-out, after I suggested we have some more of that chilled vodka, Martha sat down directly in front of me. We were knees to knees. She took my hands.

"Mary, dear, you have to go back to get everything properly settled. You know that, don't you?"

I looked down at Martha's left hand, turned it to expose the scar, ran my finger along the scar.

I whispered, "I'm sorry."

I don't know if she heard me because she went on, "You know you have to make things right with Chris—and Jeffrey. You can't just leave them. It doesn't work that way."

"I HATE THE FUCKING WAY THINGS FUCKING WORK!"

I slapped Martha. The stupid dog growled.

Now I'd done it. Why do people do these things to me anyway? It's not what they do so much as the way they do it. Provoking. I certainly did not mean to slap her. It's just a natural reaction—automatic. Like when someone shines a bright light into your eyes, you close your eyes and hold your hands up simply to stop the light. Totally normal.

Martha's cheek was red. Not really *red*-red. Just a little pink. I wasn't sure what to say. Then I said, "I'm sorry. I'm sorry for everything."

She sat there a second, then got up and folded my new dress back into the Saks' box. I went on, trying to explain.

"But seriously, I think if I could just take some time and get enrolled in a business class, I would be in a stronger position. You see what I mean? I used to have a pretty good head for business. Daddy said I was the best manager the optical shop ever had."

"Mary, I think you—we—can start to make everything better if we are honest with each other. You know you never did anything in that optical shop."

"Who ran the shop when Daddy was...not feeling well? Answer that."

"Mother did. Sometimes I helped."

"What was I doing there, then?"

"You came by when you felt like it. Showed off your cheerleading outfit. Smiled at the customers. You were an ornament."

Once again, Martha and I had trouble finding common ground because we remembered everything so differently. She admitted that I was not totally wrong. Daddy didn't mind having me, "his pretty, bouncy daughter," dropping in on the shop. After all, he could brag that I ran for Homecoming Queen at the high school and got my picture in the Courier. I was probably good for business. Especially good for some of the older men who, while they didn't see so well, appreciated the charms of youth.

But Martha insisted that I did not, in fact, do any of the technical tasks or paperwork.

I wasn't going to argue. It was pointless. I knew what I knew. Martha knew what she knew. Besides, I had a wonderful idea.

"I'll go back, but I don't want to drive alone. Drive back with me."
No response. Not a move.

"Please, Martha." I couldn't help myself. A small whimper. I don't think she even heard. So, I piped up. "FOR GOD'S SAKE, MARTHA, HELP ME! I NEED YOU!"

Martha just continued to look at me steadily.

I calmed myself down and tried a different tactic. I reminded her of how she had always helped me when I really needed it. I almost made light of it, hoping she, too, might remember with some affection, even amusement.

"Do you remember when I was in seventh grade and I had a paper on the Civil War due the next day, and Mother was so mad that I had waited until the last minute and Daddy was threatening to belt me, and you wrote the whole thing for me—remember?"

"I remember," she said.

"You always helped me."

"Yes," she said.

"Remember that night Daddy had been drinking and he shoved me into the corner, and you picked up the poker and told him to go to bed?"

She started to fuss with the damn bed, moving the couch pillows, pulling on the fold-out handle. Was she even hearing me?

"Yes, I remember all of it. I remember all of the high drama. The dishes thrown against the wall. I don't want to go back there, Mary. I'm sorry, but I just don't want to be needed by anyone anymore.

Selfish! Uncaring! OLD BITCH!

I threw myself down on that hard, awful mattress and began to cry. I knew now that no one would help me—no one! I was sobbing. My nose was running. My hair was getting into my mouth. I didn't care!

The bed squeaked as Martha sat down next to me. She smoothed my hair and stroked my cheek. She said, "Shh, baby, shh."

> "There's no such thing
> as a free lunch."
> —Uncle Bill
> As Quoted by
> Milton Friedman

CHRISTOPHER

The day after the famous Auttenberg dinner, and my slipping on the ice getting out of the Avanti with the whole world watching, I finally got to my last class with Miss Austin.

It was not the old comfort zone. I wanted to ask her about her cousin, my dad's chummysome friend, Adalicia. For no rational reason I felt like telling Miss Austin that Adalicia reminded me a little of Susan Sarandon's character in *Bull Durham*—and I actually liked her. Even though the situation was what one might call one of extreme duress, surprisingly the dinner and breakfast with my dad's girlfriend were two of the least stomach-churning meals I'd had in years of eating with Mom.

But I couldn't do that. If someone said to you, "I don't mind that my father is disloyal to my mother because my mother is difficult," what would you think of that person? I'd have contempt for that person.

And I do. I have contempt for me. I'm an accomplice and I don't want to be my father's accomplice. I want out. I want out of this whole fucking morass. And go where, you little, little shit?

I really would like to talk to Miss Austin. But I shouldn't say anything. How could I bring anything up? No matter what I do, I'll make it worse. Let the whole thing go. Get home. But then what? What will I say to Dad?

For the first time, I wanted Miss Austin's class to be over. We were covering early nineteenth-century novels, specifically Jane Eyre. Miss Austin was talking about the attitude toward madness at that time and how we were much more enlightened today. It made me very uneasy. I visualized Dad locking Mom in an attic somewhere off in the hills. A ramshackle old house up beyond Uncle Bill's place. With bats. If there was an Olympic event in creating horrors in the head, I'd win the gold medal.

At that moment, I couldn't trust either of my parents or Miss Austin or anyone, and least of all myself. At the bell, Miss Austin said, "Christopher?!" But I dashed out.

When I finally got home there was the Sheriff's car and Uncle Bill's old truck and Dad's Buick parked in our yard. The Sheriff had been poking around. Had he been poking around all day? At the door I heard Uncle Bill.

"Dan, for Christ's sake."

"I know Bill, but like I told you, I can't ignore the talk ..."

As I let myself in, a 'sudden silence descended' as I'm sure someone must have written someplace in one of those nineteenth-century novels. They all looked at me like they'd never seen me before, like I'm ET.

Uncle Bill came to and acknowledged me, "Hey, Chris. How was school?"

Like ho-humness, it's just another day, right? Sheriff Hennessey here just popped by to borrow some fingerprint ink.

"What's going on?"

Sheriff Hennessy: "Just more routine paperwork, son."

Dad? He's scowling at Hennessey, a cold black look that is frightening. Dad? Don't do anything more stupid than what you've already done, please. Please don't hit the nice policeman.

Deputy Clover gave me her warm, reassuring deputy smile. All's well as far as she's concerned. We've just been digging in your garden as part of our agricultural duties.

Then, all of a sudden, the Sheriff and Deputy Clover excused themselves. They're not going to keep talking in front of me. They suddenly realized they had to be someplace else. She picks up a large envelope conspicuously lettered "Slide County Sheriff's Office, EVIDENCE." They nod to Dad as if to say, "To be continued."

As they drive off, the Sheriff turns on his siren.

Uncle Bill: "Fat-assed stupid son-of-a-bitch. He couldn't pour piss out of a boot if the instructions were on the heel."

Me: "What's in the 'EVIDENCE' envelope?"

Dad: "That old wedding picture. They found it buried in the garden. Bastards."

"Mom actually went into the garden and buried the wedding picture?"

"Apparently."

"Mom buried it before she left?"

"I guess."

"You're sure we don't need a lawyer?"

Uncle Bill says no one is charged with anything. Let's save our money until we really need one. Implying that we will. Need one.

I look at Dad, at Bill, back at Dad. What should I know about what? I'm getting tired of being perpetually clueless. The Sheriff mentioned "talk." What talk? I'll bet I have some idea. Okay? Okay. Maybe this is the time to just blurt out the words ADALICIA AUTTENBERG! What kind of a name is that anyway, Dad? Explain this Adalicia Auttenberg! And don't tell me she's pretty and exotic. I know that! I had eggs and raisin toast with her this morning!

But maybe Uncle Bill doesn't know about her and Dad wouldn't want him to know. Maybe there's really nothing to know. Who're we kidding, Chrissy, boy? Of course there's something to know. This woman? Was this woman there long before Mom left or disappeared? Or? How should I bring this up?

Dad saves me the trouble.

Dad gets up and starts to walk around the room. He picks up an empty glass, puts it down. He picks it up again and gets a glass of water. He comes over to us and puts his hand on my shoulder. "There's something I've got to talk to both of you about."

I don't know what he's going to say. I'm afraid of what he might say. It could be the worst possible thing he could say.

Dad clears his throat and says, "I've been seeing—not seeing but I've seen this woman."

Whewwhew! Uncle Bill and I both exhale. Relief. Thank God. He just wants to tell us about—about what?

"I've seen this woman a couple of times."
Okay. I think I've seen this woman, too, Dad. Well?

"I had lunch with her. We worked together on this commercial for Bigley, and she—"
Lunch? Lunch? Dad, watch TV. People having affairs meet in smoky hotel bars. Besides, you also had dinner with her. Remember? I was there. You slept on the couch. Right? Right?

"Lunch? Who cares about lunch?" said Bill.

"At her house."

"Ah," said Bill.

Well, now—I look at Uncle Bill.

Bill shrugs, says, "Nothing like home cooking."

Dad continues his feeblesome explanation.

"A couple—two—three times. At her house up on Summit. I don't know what kind of talk is going around."

"Whose house on Summit?" Uncle Bill asks.

"Auttenberg."

So! All the fuss over "this must be the wrong address!" And we parked in the back to avoid what? Prying eyes?

"Jesus H. Christ. That was really, really stupid, Jeff," said Bill. "There are eyes everywhere in this town. Especially regarding those women. I've been there, worked on the young one's Avanti. Those women are drop-dead gorgeous and you're messing around in broad daylight having lunch? Half the women in town would like to stick an ice pick in the older one. Both of them, probably."

"She had nothing but nice things to say to me—"

Well, la-dee-da, Dad. 'Nice things to say?' What're you doing? Attending a class in self-esteem? Your wife is missing!

Dad says, hangdogsomely, "It was just such a refreshing change—"

Bill, latching on to this bright thought: "Well, I'd be the first to say that anyone would be a refreshing change from Mary. You understand, don't you, Chris?"

Sure.

No. NO!

"No, I don't understand! I know how Mom was. Is. But you shouldn't have done something like this! You shouldn't have!"

"I'm sorry."

"Mom's right. You're always sorry."

"I won't see her again. I know this is all my fault."

"All what? You're pitiful, Dad. You're pathetic. NO WONDER SHE LEFT!"

Bill puts his arm around me. I shake him off. I've never had a big fight with Dad. I need him more than anything, but I hate him for doing this. How can your own father, the one person you depend on, count on—how can this man have a GIRLFRIEND like some pimpled idiot kid at school?

"YOU MADE HER CRAZY!"

I ran out the door and went down to Amy's. She and Maria were gone, but the door was unlocked as usual. Josephus was studying his chessboard, seeing moves in his head, I guess. He looked up. "Hey, Chris. Got those sneakers tied, I see."

I stood there, trying not to cry.

"Come over here, boy."

I went to the side of his wheelchair. He put one arm across my skinny shoulders. His arm is so muscular it envelops me in warmth. Tears came to me so easily these days. I am such a dippysome twelve-almost-thirteen crying diphead. I am an embarrassment to young American manhood.

Josephus doesn't ask what's wrong. He just says, "You're goin' through some heavy times, Chris. But they say the Lord doesn't give you a heavier load than you can carry."

"Do you really believe that?"

"I don't know. But it comforts me to think it might be true."

Me, too.

"IT IS NOT UNUSUAL FOR ADOLESCENT CHILDREN TO CRAVE THE CERTAINTY THAT SOME RELIGIOUS EXPERIENCES CAN PROVIDE." -DOCTOR H.

I went home. Bill was bundled up in his ratty sheepskin coat, standing on the porch, smoking a joint. He motioned me toward him, put his arms around me.

"What can I say, Chris? Women like him. He likes women. He talks. They talk. Troubles drift away. You know him, if he finds smooth water, he doesn't like to make a ripple. He loves you more than anything in this world, son."

In the house, Dad was sitting just where I left him. There were tears in his eyes. God, he's a baby. I'm a baby. It's genetic. I went and got his old cowboy hat, put it on him, and put Stevie Ray Vaughn on the old Sony.

He put his arm around me and we just sat there listening to the music. Everybody is putting an arm around me these days. I need them to.

JEFF

No question, I had betrayed Chris. I certainly didn't mean to.

Oh, ho, Jeff, my friend, you know that is the universal excuse for all crimes from adultery to murder to stealing candy in the supermarket checkout line. The Mullins family on the male side found it particularly convenient. My great grandfather, it was said, ran a still. My own father was no saint.

But—well—most saints weren't saints, were they? Witness Augustine's famous prayer, "Lord, make me chaste and celibate. But not yet."

I don't imagine Mary would be much impressed with Augustine.

I had my arm around poor Chris and we sat there in semi-darkness listening to the music, saying nothing.

We both became aware of the lights outside at the same time and stepped out onto the porch to see who had come calling at this hour. I hoped our intrepid sheriff had not decided to come back to dig around in the dark and ask some more questions. It wouldn't surprise me.

Four familiar headlights were bouncing their beams along the ruts of Frog Pond Lane, coming toward us.

I'll be damned! I'll be goddamned!

"Dad, that's Mom's car!"

Yes, sir. There it was. The old BMW pulled up and Mary got out of the passenger side. "Hello!" she yelled.

A sad-eyed basset hound wiggled out from the back seat and flopped to the ground. The driver got out.

Martha? Jesus Christ! Is that Martha?

It was.

Chris ran to Mary, "Mom! Mom!"

I didn't move. I couldn't move. I stood there looking at the women, the improbable dog, Chris hugging Mary, Martha wrestling with some things in the back seat. I was watching a movie.

Then I found myself in it, arms around Mary.

"Mary, my God! Thank God. Thank God."

Mary hugged me, "I'm so sorry, Jeffrey. I explained it all in the note."

178

"What note?"

"I'm so sorry, Jeffrey. Oh, I'm so sorry."

"No, I'm sorry." I pushed my hat to the back of my head, kissed Mary, then turned, not saying her name out loud, but mouthing it, "Martha."

"Hello, Jeff."

Back of me, through the open door, I could hear:

> *"Well hello baby, Tell me,*
> *How have you been?*
> *We all have missed you,*
> *And the way you grin*
> *The day is necessary,*
> *Every now and then*
> *For souls to move on,*
> *Given life back again."*
>
> *--Stevie Ray Vaughan*

Neither Chris nor I asked a real question, like "What the hell?" and "Why didn't you let us know where you were?" and "How come you're here, Martha?"

Instead, the four of us just waltzed around the car, retrieving Mary's pink suitcase and Martha's black roller, an open bag of Fritos, empty Coke cups, the dog's treats, an old trench coat, Mary's familiar blue coat, a computer that had to be Martha's, a couple of Saks boxes, and what was left of a box of Pop Tarts. We dragged all this stuff into the living room of our double wide—what Chris calls our "ersatz Cape Cod Cottage."

179

We were saying things like: "Who would have thought all this would fit in this small car?" "The dog's name is Woebegone but I call him Woebee." "I wanted to surprise you, Jeff." "Well, I'm so happy to be surprised." "We've really missed you." "Well, we've missed you, haven't we?"

Things like that. Meaningless things.

People go away. They come back. It happens all the time. People die. A few words are said. At the funeral the talk is about how tasty the country-ham sandwiches are. Reality, hard-hitting, life-changing reality is never real at all. You can't feel what's happening when it happens. "It"—whatever it is—like the wise bumper sticker says, just happens. The tree falling in the forest is not the question. For me, the question always has been, "What is the question?"

So, "it" was with us. It was unreal, as it probably is in all moments that really matter to the people involved. It was as if these two women had suddenly noticed that they hadn't spoken to each other in fourteen years, and they thought it would be a fun idea if they dropped in on me, this nice but not totally trustworthy man, and his son for a little visit. Meanwhile, the man and his son seem not at all surprised.

Chris and I acted as if such events were practically a daily occurrence. Who knows? Tomorrow President and Mrs. Clinton might drop in! Mary hadn't been missing at all. She'd just been out visiting!

180

Martha said, "Between Mary's need for Fritos and Woebee's needs for rest stops I thought we'd never get here."

I said, sagely, "Traffic is terrible."

Everyone agreed to that. And how confusing construction signs were. The women mentioned some detours. I said there was a new detour on the road leading up to our road. They said they almost missed the correct turn because of that.

I asked if they'd eaten, and in the midst of my question, Maria appeared at the door with a lasagna, which she handed to Chris as she threw her arms around Mary. "I saw the car. Oh, thank God. Thank you, Jesus. I knew it. I knew you were all right."

Amy appeared. Mary hugged Amy tightly. "Martha, this is Maria's dear daughter Amy. And this is my dear sister, Martha."

Maria said, "Pleased to meet you." To me, "Leave this covered and put it in at three-fifty for, oh, thirty minutes." I said we'd do that.

Martha smiled. Chris smiled. I smiled. Mary actually laughed. She was in a wonderful mood. It was all just marvelous.

I never mentioned that I had been suspected of murder.

That night, when Chris headed for bed, Mary went with him to "tuck in my little boy."

I watched Martha cover the leftover lasagna with Saran Wrap. She didn't look directly at me for a moment, then she did, studying me, not necessarily approving or disapproving. Just looking.

I picked up a little dust kitty and twisted it into a thread.

I said, "We had big plans, didn't we?"

"Yes, we did."

"You did anyway. Plans for us at the University."

"The world is full of plans that don't come true, Jeff. I'm here because I want to see that Mary gets help."

"She won't do it."

"I think she will. On the trip back—which was hell by the way—she finally agreed to see this psychiatrist acquaintance of mine. Barry Kandleman. About forty-five minutes down the road."

"She's been acting erratically for years," I said. "Worse and worse, lately, but I never could persuade her to do anything."

"I told Mary that Kandleman is known as a Diplomat in the medical community. He delivers lectures in Paris. In French."

"I'm sure that impressed her."

"That was the clincher."

When Mary returned from Chris's room, she said she was worried about Chris. He'd changed. Something was different. He seemed, oh, she didn't know, she said—"devious." She said Chris wasn't the way she had remembered him when he was younger.

Martha said that might be because he wasn't younger any more.

"He's only twelve."

"Almost thirteen, Honey," I said.

Why do I do that? It's some kind of reflexive action that I can't help. I know it's a mistake. I know that Chris knows it's a mistake. No sooner was the word "honey" out of my mouth than I wished I could take it back.

Mary's eyes narrowed and she gave me that suspicious, kill-me-if-she-could look as she assessed her "honey"-tongued husband.

"What kind of conspiracy have you Mullins boys cooked up while I was gone? Uncle Bill's been here. Smell the pot, Martha?"

Martha said that all she smelled was lasagna.

"What have you told Chris about Jezebel, Jeffrey? I told you, Martha, didn't I, that he not only cheated on you but he cheated on me?"

I couldn't help but shrug, gave out a little half laugh and stepped into the kitchen. "Beer anyone? Something harder?"

"Beer? You hear that, Martha? We drink chilled Russian vodka, don't we? Beer? What is this? A ball game? God! I apologize, Martha."

"A cold beer might be good, Mary. Why don't we have one?"

We did.

MARY

Jeff had gone off to sell cars or do whatever he did during the day. Chris was at school. Martha and I were home eating Pop Tarts, looking at the Courier. They ran this item:

> Slide County Sheriff Hennesy announced Tuesday that Mary Mullins, wife of Jeffrey Mullins, thought to be missing since November 8, has returned home after visiting her sister, Martha Harvin, in New York City. Faulty answering machines and telephone lines downed by the recent storms caused a communication breakdown within the family. Sheriff Hennessy said, "They simply couldn't get in touch with each other." He went on to say that both Mr. and Mrs. Mullins are very sorry for any inconvenience or concern the misunderstanding might have caused.

That afternoon the phone rang. Martha answered.

It turned out to be this eighty-four-year old reporter named Talia Tyler. Everybody knew Old Miss Tyler. Her job was to be nosy. She not only followed up on the "personal angle" of some newsy stories but also wrote a gossip column called "Talia's Tales" in the Style section. I could tell that Martha was trying to get rid of her and was reluctantly answering questions about what she did, where she lived and so on. Martha finally promised to call back, and hung up with a sigh of relief.

What a pesky old woman. Martha certainly had better things to do than talk to her. As a matter of fact, she had agreed to accompany me on my first appointment with Doctor Kandelman.

And I have to say that appointment seemed to go quite well, though at first it didn't look like it would because I had to talk with a "counselor," a rather dumpy woman named Sharon who asked all kinds of very personal questions, took my blood pressure, listened to my heart—I thought she would never finish. I have always hated the name Sharon ever since Sharon Bixler called me a slut in seventh grade. But then having cleared the Sharon hurdle, I was ushered in to see the diplomat Doctor himself and that was an immediate success as far as I was concerned.

So many of these medical people act like you are a pre-school child, or probably don't speak English. They talk down to you. Doctor Kandleman didn't. He didn't even act like there was any reason I should be there. It was like a pleasant social call, and I was the most important woman in the room.

He listened to me. He seemed to have all the time in the world, unlike that old fool of a doctor Jeff likes, Doctor Shore, who was always rushing around.

I wasn't too sure it was a good idea, but Doctor Kandelman talked to Martha and Jeff as well as me. He must have been satisfied with whatever they said because he was optimistic, cheerful even. My blood pressure and heart rate were those of someone ten-years younger. Imagine! I was very impressed with his manner, his wavy gray hair, his suit. Clearly a bespoke suit. Very tasteful.

Doctor Kandelman said that as far as he was concerned there was hardly anything amiss with me. He took my hands and told me I was a smart, sensitive, very attractive woman who simply had been through a good deal. That's all. But professional integrity dictated that he do some further evaluation. Meanwhile he prescribed a low dose of lithium just to tide me over until they could determine what would be the optimal cocktail of effective medications for what he described to me as "your very mild, very understandable nervous condition, which is so very treatable." He scheduled the first follow-up appointment for two weeks from Tuesday. He handed me orders for a CT scan and an MRI just to "rule out" anything that might be causing the headaches, though I assured him I hadn't had one in quite some time.

"I am ninety-nine percent sure these tests will reveal nothing, but they'd drum me out of the Doctor Club if we weren't absolutely safe rather than sorry, Mrs. Mullins. And remember, Sharon is usually available as well as my associate, Doctor Schwartz. We're all here for you." He took my hands again, and I felt, definitely felt, that he held my hands longer than he needed to for an ordinary medical visit.

I thanked Martha for introducing me to Doctor Barry Kandelman. "He's just what the doctor ordered," I joked.

I couldn't tell. Maybe it was the lithium. Maybe there was just something about Martha and me being back together again. Whatever it was, our situation seemed a little better. Jeff was more considerate. Chris was more loving. His skin looked better, too. Very few of those hideous little pimples that he sometimes had on his forehead.

I said that we all ought to go someplace exciting to celebrate how nicely things seemed to be going. Like an amusement park. Unfortunately, they're closed here in the winter.

But not in Las Vegas. Or Florida.

Wouldn't it be fun if we could all go to Florida now? Right this minute—just get on a plane and go—*someplace!*

JEFF

In these days together I think Mary had come to rely on Martha, and, while I'm sure she wouldn't admit it, on Martha's judgment. No question, Martha had a calming influence on our household.

She reassured both Mary and me that our problems could be overcome. And, amazingly, I believed her.

Chris instinctively trusted her. Despite an occasional lashing out by Mary over some irritation, while Martha was on hand she brought a sense of stability and predictability to daily life that neither Chris nor I had known for a long time. No food was thrown. No threats were made.

Sadly, Martha could not stay long. Mary pleaded with her to stay just a little longer, but Martha said Norton was getting antsy. Clients needed attention. She had to go.

Soon it was time.

Mary said she had a terrific idea and ran out to get a "going-away surprise." Chris had gone next door and I had been out in the garden fixing the little gate that Hennessey and his people had jimmied up. I walked in and found Martha packing.

"You have to go?" I said.
" 'Fraid so."
"Will you be back?"
"Probably not."
"Chris has really taken to you."
"I've taken to him. Let him come visit me."
"I will."

I didn't know what to say to her or what she expected me to do. I was standing like a sack of potatoes. I could feel my shoulders sagging. Martha seemed to be standing the same way. The years that we had missed together, the lost dreams—they seemed palpable at that moment. They seemed like a weight on each of us and we leaned toward each other for support.

We held each other so tightly, the kiss was so intense, that we staggered back against the door. I stroked her hair, kissed her neck. Her back arched and her lips found my lips again, again.
I whispered her name.

She stiffened. She came to attention—the good soldier once again.

I backed away. "I'm sorry. I didn't mean for that to happen."

"Me, too. But I'll admit it—I think I'll always miss you, Jeff. I'm afraid there is a hole in my heart that will never quite heal. I pray God takes care of you and your beautiful boy."

Mary came back announcing that she had the surprise—a cake mix. She was going to make a birthday cake and they would celebrate Chris's thirteenth birthday a couple of weeks early. Martha could help by making the seven-minute frosting their mother used to make years and years ago.

When the three of us took Martha and Woebee to the airport, I knew that each of us was missing Martha even before she was gone.

Before leaving, she gave Chris her unlisted number and made arrangements for him to be able to get immediate access to her through Norton, any time. She told Chris that if he desperately needed a lifeline, to call. She hugged him so hard that I saw him take a deep breath to recover. He was holding back tears, standing with his head up and shoulders back.

Martha hugged Mary the same way. And me. I stood like Chris—head up, shoulders back, holding in tears as Martha waved and disappeared into the boarding ramp.

It was lonely in the little double-wide without her. Mary and I, each of us in our own way, had found in Martha some remembrance of the joys of better days. She was a link to whatever might have been good in the past.

A family is lucky to find someone who smoothes the waters, even if only temporarily. Many a relative will dance into a family situation and think they can alleviate tensions by joking, making light of matters with encouraging slaps on the back. Uncle Bill had tried that briefly with Mary. It didn't work. The life-of-the-party is seldom the party to a better life. Martha, on the other hand, was the embodiment of a quiet hope that somehow whatever was wrong could be, if not resolved, at least eased.

Chris told me that he wished Aunt Martha had been there for Parents' Night along with me. He said he wished she could be there to protect him and Miss Austin from the Witches. And, he said "from Mom."

I wasn't sure exactly what he meant about the Witches. But I knew he would miss Martha.

So would I.

MARY

The day after Martha left I read in "Talia's Tales" in the Courier:

> Martha Harvin is visiting her sister and brother-in-law, Mary and Jeff Mullins, 210 Frog Pond Lane. Martha has been living in Manhattan for the past fourteen years where she works as an executive with the financial firm of Cordemon Stein. In talking with this writer, she remarked on the amazing growth in our beautiful county and the cultural vibrancy of our fair town. Martha said she would definitely be back to visit as often as possible.

That very afternoon one of my bridesmaids, Polly Findley, called. I've been back here all this time and not heard a word from any of them. I know, I know—like Martha said, I told them I didn't ever want to see them again. But lots of people say things like that when they are disappointed, and I was.

However, wouldn't you know that as soon as Martha's name pops up in the Courier, one of them—in this case Polly—would decide to call?

At first I had no idea who it was. Polly had acquired some sort of British accent. She invited Martha and me for "luncheon Wednesday week." Polly rattled on, telling me she thought it was absolutely ridiculous that we didn't see more of each other. *"You don't appreciate your oldest and dearest friends until you suddenly realize something bad might have actually happened to one of them!"* She said that they all were so concerned when I seemed to be missing. Thank goodness it was just a big mix up. Every one of the girls would love to see me and my sister again. Plus there was something they wanted to talk with both of us about.

When I informed Polly that Martha had already gone back to New York, Polly was disappointed—I could hear that in her voice. But, the luncheon would go on as planned she said. Polly would pick me up and we would all go to Adrian's. They have the most mouth-watering potato-wrapped black bass that you've ever tasted.

I could hardly answer her. I guess I mumbled something about how nice it would be, but *I was not ready for this!*

I immediately called Doctor Kandelman and told his nurse or appointment person or whoever the hell answered the phone that I had to see Doctor Kandleman right away. Sooner than two weeks from Tuesday, certainly.

No, I did not want to talk to Sharon!

He would call back. When? The totally uninformed person I was talking to didn't know.

I can't believe this!

I just saw him. And now this.

What am I supposed to do? Sit by the phone all day just waiting for his call?

I realize I am not an ordinary patient. I know that. Sometimes things in general can be a little too much for my system. But Doctor Kandleman himself has said that whatever is wrong with me is so easily treated. But that means *IT HAS TO BE TREATED WHEN IT HAS TO BE TREATED!*

Now what? Dare I just go out for a little drive? No. He might call.

Watch television. I don't want to watch television.

Take a shower. I did that this morning.

Do *something!*

I read about people with hobbies. Collecting jars or old toothbrushes or glass slippers, or Jesus knows what. In *Parade* there was one man who collects train schedules. I don't know what I could collect. I don't want to collect anything. Some old lady in Mother's family tatted. I can't recall what that was, but she did it.

194

Doctor Kandelman called. Thank God. I had to see him. There was no one I could talk with to sort this mess out. Martha had, as usual, left me. Jeff understood nothing. Maria was practically illiterate. Josephus was home, of course, but he was black, and crippled to boot. Plus, come to think of it, I'd never spoken to him.

Doctor Kandelman listened to me. He understood perfectly. He would see me just as soon as he got back from his short ski vacation. Meanwhile, he felt an additional medication would help the situation. Something new called quetiapine. I would have to be fair and give it some time, but he was sure I would find that I could cope by adding this to my treatment.

I was particularly reassured when Doctor Kandelman said that Janine Turner and several other stars, as well as some prominent women supporters of the Metropolitan Museum of Art, were using quetiapine with excellent results. Plus, he joked, if the Nazi maître d' happened to still be working at Adrian's, I should simply smile at him, and if I felt like it, wink.

I loved Doctor Kandelman. What flair.

I wore my new toast-colored Saks dress with the daring neckline. Thank you God for making me buy it. Perhaps a little too much for lunch, but I was entitled. It made me feel...special again.

The color was so good on me. You wouldn't think, after all I've been through, that I would age well, but Doctor Kandelman said that I had. And I had. The mirror didn't lie. Daddy had been right. I was the Sweetheart of Slide County.

Polly Findley picked me up in her new Lexus. Louise Schaller was already in the car, and Franny Wellborn would meet us at the restaurant. Louise pressed my hand. Polly, the driver, blew me a kiss from her glittering fingers.

Polly said this was going to be so exciting! And so long overdue!

No one knew why they hadn't done this many months ago. They knew I was back from Texas. They'd seen me at Talbots—well Louise and Franny had—but life had been just spinning. Busy schedules, raising children, Normie Schaller's political career, Polly trying to get the new house in Florida decorated—so many factors that intervened and made it almost crazy just trying to find time to get your hair done!

They went on like that for what seemed like miles, but finally we got to the restaurant.

The Nazi was not on duty at Adrian's. I was disappointed. I'd been looking forward to giving him a big flirty wink. Well, you can't have everything.

Franny was already at the table in the quiet section looking out on the bird bath and winter-bare garden. What would Franny say? They must all know that Kimberly had seen Jeff sniffing around Jezebel's house. Well, screw it. I looked terrific. A million times better than fat Franny. I turned on my best Homecoming Queen smile.

Franny hugged me and said that it was a shame we hadn't seen each other since she and Kimberly were in Talbot's. Was I still working there? Oh? What a shame I wasn't because it was always so helpful to have someone you knew in a fairly nice clothing store.

Polly Findley had never been in that store. She did most of her shopping in New York or—whenever she could "hop across the pond"—London, she said in her British accent.

Louise Schaller had been in Talbot's with Stephanie "but you weren't there, Mary." She and Stephanie agreed it was a good place to find jeans that fit well and didn't cost an arm and a leg.

Speaking of clothing, they all reminisced— "Remember how beautiful Mary's wedding gown was?" oh, yes, and "How handsome Jeff had been!" The man wore a tuxedo like he'd been born in it. How was he? Still selling cars? Fat Franny asked if he still drove that lovely green Buick? All the women had seen him at Parents' Night, looking dashing as ever.

My, we all had "so much to catch up on," it was a shame we had to stop talking to look over the menu and order! White wine? Why not? It was a shame we didn't do this every week! Maybe we should!

197

Form the Old Girls' Lunch Club just like the men's Rotary, which Normie Schaller was president of!

Years and years to talk about. A shame not to just make time. A shame.

So much was a shame. "A shame, Mary, that you hadn't been able to be with us in the Theta house at the University."

I kept smiling. I was doing fine.

The conversation turned to the children. That is, Louise and Franny turned the conversation to the children. Stephanie and Kimberly just loved J.W. Watson High School. "Nicole, as well," Polly echoed the endorsement. Was Chris enjoying it? The girls say he's brilliant. But what would you expect from Jeff's son. And so cute.

"Chris?" I said somewhat doubtfully, thinking of his occasional flare-ups of acne."

"Stephanie says he's adorable, and has an adorable little girlfriend. Annie somebody."

"Amy," corrected Franny, who seemed to be in close touch with what was going on at the school. As was Louise, though not too sharp on names.

"Stephanie says that little Annie has a rather unconventional look. What is she?"

"Italian," I said.

"That English teacher, Theresa Auttenberg...er, Austin...certainly has a look, doesn't she?" said Louise, knowingly.

"Who??" I startled, suddenly alert.

198

"She's some Auttenberg relative," said Franny. "And she's almost black."

Louise and Franny looked as if they were about to barge into the planned pièce de résistance of the luncheon, but Polly held up her hand as if to say "Not until I explain!" Then she explained:

"It's true, this young woman claims to be an Auttenberg cousin, and it's true she is rather dark. However, she had an excellent curriculum vitae, and we on the School Board had hoped that she would expose the children to a higher quality of diversity. Superintendent Privell was the deciding factor. Jolly keen on her."

"I don't think she's actually BLACK black." said Franny. "Her nose is very, whatdoyoucallit? Aquiline."

"Many of those African tribes, particularly in the desert parts, have very fine, light features, and thin lips," averred Polly. "But Cal and I believe she is Arab."

"Well whatever she is, she's clearly another odd Auttenberg in my mind," said Louise. Those Auttenberg women have always had a sort of foreign look, dramatic in an off-center way."

"We used to call Adalicia 'Jezebel,' remember?" blurted Franny, then instantly clapped her hand to her mouth. She looked furtively to Louise, who looked quickly at Polly, who smoothly asked, "Where did that name come from anyway?"

"Didn't Father James refer to her in some sermon?"

"Adalicia?"

"Jezebel. I think she was one of the heathen prostitutes that Jesus saved."

I could tell, now that Franny had mentioned Jezebel, that the three women were watching to see my reaction. For once in my life I said and did nothing. Nothing. Not a tremor. I sensed that they had more important matters in mind, so I just kept smiling. My face was frozen into that smile for so long that my cheeks were beginning to ache.

Polly smoothly transitioned away from Jezebel, "You ought to come hear our new priest now, Mary. He did graduate work in England."

Louise added that the new priest's wife told them her husband was fluent in Greek and Hebrew. No one knew quite what to say about that impressive fact, except to nod.

Thank goodness the arrival of the food interrupted this line of the conversation. Everyone knows that religion is a touchy subject. Jeff loves to talk about it. I just shut my ears.

Which is what I did now. I sipped the wine and ate a bit, and listened while they got into a discussion about what seasonings Adrian used in his hummus. Polly said there were many different kinds, including a scrumptious seafood hummus they served at the Ritz-Carleton in Naples. Naples, Florida, Polly informed us, was not as easy a place to live as you might think. Why, the new house she was trying to make livable as quickly as possible was practically

200

cursed with the incompetence of Mexican-speaking workmen and the unavailability of some materials.

"They don't have any really interesting tile," she said.

"You would think they would," said Louise.

"No. I finally found something suitable in this little place in Tampa. They had to ship it in from Italy. And when the cartons arrived, what do you think?"

"What?"

"Broken, cracked, smashed!"

"No!"

"It all had to go back. Another month's delay. Cal says we should just go over with a bunch of empty suitcases and bring it back ourselves!"

The women agreed that Cal had always been something of a wit. But then, so was Normie Schaller. Have you seen his golf cart that he uses to walk the dog? He's put a Rolls-Royce radiator on the front of the golf cart! What a hoot!

God! They laughed like this was the funniest thing anybody ever did. I was beginning to think about climbing the drapes and swinging across the table.

But then they all got quiet. I saw Louise sit up straighter and taller in her chair. She cleared her throat and said, "One of the main reasons we're here–outside of the wonderful chance to all get together

201

again—is that something has been bothering Franny and me." Louise looked at me like I should know what's been bothering her.

"Mary, has Chris said anything to you about this Theresa Auttenberg?"

"Austin," corrected Franny.

"I think he and Amy have mentioned her. They seem to think she's a good teacher. Why?"

"As you know, I supervise the cheerleaders. The girls, Stephanie and Kimberly—Nicole, too—"

"Yes," Polly jumped in. "Nicole is especially concerned."

"What about?" I asked. This was becoming stranger and stranger.

"This is very awkward."

"And there may be nothing to it."

"But you should look into it."

"If you need any help, I'm on the School Board, as you know," offered Polly.

"And we're all very active mothers. It's good to volunteer at the school just to know what's going on," Franny chimed in.

"Stephanie says some of the teachers are decidedly weird," added Louise.

"If you met the Jewish physics teacher he'd scare you to death," said Polly, "but the Board was very impressed with his curriculum vitae."

"What were you saying about this Auttenberg teacher?" I asked. Now I could hear a little quaver in my voice. I hoped they couldn't.

"Austin," corrected Franny, seemingly irritated with Louise. Then she put her hand on Louise's arm supposedly to show that she wasn't really miffed— but I think she put her hand there right in front of me so that I couldn't miss all those diamonds! Why don't they get to whatever it is they want to say? What is going on?

"I don't think you should say anything to Chris," said Polly. "I think we should nose around a little more. Talk to Doctor Waltzman."

I finally couldn't stop myself. I shouted, "ABOUT WHAT?"

"My goodness, Mary," said Louise. "We don't really know anything for sure, but Stephanie and Kimberly and Nicole think she may be bothering your son."

I suppose my expression and reaction was all any of them could have hoped for. My mouth was open, but nothing came out.

Franny chimed in like maybe everything they'd just said, they hadn't meant to say. "They're possibly imagining things," she said. "Although, you can't be too careful these days."

"You could never trust any of the Auttenbergs. Right up until he died, old man Auttenberg tried to get Normie off the council. Had the nerve to call him a crook at an open meeting!"

I couldn't wait to get out of this restaurant and get home to call Doctor Kandleman, but the rest of the women lingered over another glass of wine. They chatted about a shoe sale and this show in New York that some business friends of Cal's had seen and said it was just awful—all about these gay people with AIDS and one woman discovers that her husband is also a homosexual. Polly couldn't remember the title. Something about angels. You don't know why some plays are ever produced. And books! Louise said she has practically stopped reading because everything is about sex, sex, sex! Television, too! Polly said, "Well, you can't get away from it. There does seem to be a lot of sex in the world."

I thought I would scream. Or sweep the glasses off the table. You would have thought they had never said what they said before about the teacher and Chris. Bothering him? What? How?

I held tight to the edge of the table. I said nothing. The drugs were working. How smart of me to have doubled the dose.

At last, at last, the waiter brought the check. Another eternity. They had forgotten to ask for separate checks. Polly said she would just take all of them. Her treat. I was relieved by this sensible decision. Let her pay. Let's go.

Oh, no. Louise and Franny wouldn't hear of it. If they were going to do this again—and they were going to do it again and often—they had to go Dutch. Mary's share, computed by Louise on a little calculator she carried in her Marc Jacobs (so practical!) purse, was seventeen dollars and thirty-seven cents.

For lunch! As if I didn't already feel sick about what I'd been told, (though I wasn't sure what I'd been told), and now this expense, which made this one of the worst luncheons of my life!

Still...it *was* nice to be accepted again. And even though I had so strongly felt like it, I didn't actually scream or throw anything.

I was proud of myself. I was doing this. I was looking right at all of them and smiling. Bless Doctor Kandelman.

I planned to call him as soon as I got home to tell him how well I had coped with the lunch. And I'd ask him what I should do about this teacher matter at the school. It was disturbing, no question.

Should I actually let Franny and Louise help? Fat Franny and Louise suggested they would pave the way for a meeting with Doctor Waltzman, to see if this could be quietly looked into without upsetting

Chris. They said the girls, Stephanie and Kimberly and Nicole, might be helpful in getting to the bottom of this, whatever it was, since they were right there in the school every day, and they were *so very fond* of little Chris.

Somehow I doubted that. But, then again, if these were popular girls, it wouldn't hurt Chris to know them better.

As we left the restaurant, Louise squeezed my hand. "Isn't this fun being together again?"

After Polly dropped me off at our crappy house on our muddy road, I went right to the phone.

The phone person said Doctor Kandelman was on a vacation until the end of the week. Why hadn't he told me? The stupid phone person had no idea. She thought he had.

"Well, dammit, I have to talk to him!"

He was way off at a place called Whistler Blackcomb in the Arctic or some place but they would get a message to him if it was urgent. *OF COURSE IT WAS URGENT!* Sharon, or Doctor Schwartz, Doctor Kandelman's associate, would be happy to talk to me. They both had my records.

No. That would not do!

All right. There's no point in wasting time with these people. Just tell the good doctor that I am waiting cheerfully *IN DISTRESS* for him to call me from wherever the hell he is!

It was all so, so irritating! Maybe I should call Martha? No. I knew what she would say. She would tell me to calm down and just have a talk with Chris. Well, who's the crazy one there? Just talk to Chris? Even if that made some sense, Martha should know that I wouldn't be able to just talk to Chris. I couldn't really believe him about anything now that he was older and more devious, and that would make me angry. Martha should know that.

Martha had gotten awfully close to Chris while she was here. Too close. And Jeffrey. That was to be expected, wasn't it?

I was too nervous right then to talk to Chris or Jeffrey under any circumstances. And God knows, Jeffrey wouldn't have the vaguest idea what to do. I had to think this through on my own. Thank goodness, I had time to think before Chris got home from school.

CHRISTOPHER

I was in front of the odoriferoussomely locker just about to change into my stinky gym clothes when PB came to tell me Mrs. Leitner wanted me to come to Waltzman's office as soon as possible. As you know, I'll take any excuse to get out of gym, but this did not sound like an excuse I was going to welcome.

Mrs. Leitner was right outside the gym, waiting. Now what?

"THERAPIES FOR ADOLESCENT ANXIETY DISORDERS ARE WELL DEVELOPED WITH MANY NEW TREATMENTS THAT CAN HELP MOST TEENS WITH ANXIETY DISORDERS GO ON TO LEAD PRODUCTIVE, FULFILLING ADULT LIVES." -DOCTOR H.

As we walked up to Waltzman's office Mrs. Leitner asked, "Has there ever been a problem between you and Stephanie Schaller?"

Warning, warning, dive for cover, dive, dive!

"No." Pause. "Why?"

"She and her mother just left the office and then Doctor Waltzman asked me to get you. Do you know Mrs. Schaller? She supervises the cheerleaders. She's something of a busy-body, I should warn you."

"Thank you."

"We were so pleased to hear that the whole concern about your mother was just a misunderstanding."

"Yes, ma'm. Answering machines didn't work."

"I hate them. I wish we still had the old phone company."

Doctor Waltzman is all eager, smilingness, directing me to the witness stand in front of the jelly beans, offering me one, popping one into his mouth, looking down at some notes on a yellow pad, looking up.

"How're you doing, Chris? It's wonderful that your mother is back. We were all relieved. You and your father must be so happy."

"We are."

"Is there anything we can do for you, Chris?"

"Not that I can think of."

"Anything you'd like to talk about?"

What's going on here, Doctor? Why am I here?

"Classes going well?'

"Yes, sir."

"Good. Good. Ah, you're in that advanced English Class, aren't you?"

"Yes, sir."

"Pretty teacher, don't you think?" He winks.

"Yes, sir."

"Miss, uh...?"

We've been through this before, Doctor, and you know her name as well as I do. But, just answer respectfully.

"Austin."

"Yes, Miss Austin. What're you studying in that class now, by the way?"

"Waiting for Godot."

"Thought-provoking novel, as I recall."

Don't say 'it's a play.' Don't say it. Agree with him.

"Very."

"Ah, Chris, while we're talking about Miss Austin's class, I just wanted to ask you — how do you feel about Miss Austin?"

Again, the Waltzman stare. Where is this going? He looks at me with those beady little eyes, like an alert terrier. Waiting. What should I say?

"She's a very good teacher."

"She is, yes. That's what we've heard. Now that you've brought her up, is there anything we should know?"

"I'm not sure I understand, Doctor Waltzman." And I didn't bring her up. You brought her up, old chum, old fart. What is this about?

"Has Miss Austin ever made you feel—well—(he makes little air quotes) uncomfortable?"

Oh, God. My crying. My blubbering crying in her class. Kimberly saw, everybody knew.

"Is this about some people thinking I cried in her class one day? When people think I cried in Miss Austin's class that day, it was allergies—and, then, too, we thought maybe something had happened to my Mom and I was—"

"No, no. We understand that. I was just talking 'uncomfortable' in general. What she has you reading, etcetera."

"No—?"

"Oh, well, one of our girls' mothers here at Watson happened by and said she, they, the girl and her mother, that is, were worried that Miss Austin might be (more air quotes) 'bothering' you. Taking you for rides in that car, for instance. Etcetera. She apparently brought you to school the day of the big snow—big slush, really. Ha."

> "Never pour cold water
> on a hot moose."
> -Uncle Bill

Whoa! The day after the damn dinner. Dad and I. Stephanie and her mother lurking across the street. What should I say? No stopping the good Doctor now. He's rolling. Does he relish the idea that Miss Austin is, in fact, actually, as he put it, "bothering" me? Or is he looking for an excuse to in some way "bother" Miss Austin. I'm not the most perceptive person on earth, but I don't think he likes her.

I mumbled something about everything was just fine, and the only reason I ended up in Miss Austin's car was that I was late, and she did me a favor.

His face was a question mark of raised eyebrows and twitching mustache parts. I was hiding something. He knew in the depth of his *Educationist* Ph.D. soul that at some point he would manage to worm an acceptable version of the truth out of this little smart-ass bastard.

Suddenly he shifts gears.

"By the way, while we're on the subject, one of the mothers said she didn't want her daughter in that advanced English class because of the reading list. Not that that girl would have qualified, but would you mind dropping off a copy of the reading list for Miss Austin's class when you have a chance, Chris? We can't seem to find our copy."

"Yes, sir."

Sure. Certainly. I wasn't aware there was a reading list, but if there is, I'll be very happy to drop it off. Or make one up and drop it off. "We" are very happy to do anything "we" can to lubricate the gears of *Education.*

"So—your mother is doing well, is she?"

"Yes. That was all a mix-up."

"Yes, so we understand. You wouldn't mind if we called her sometime, would you? We respect your privacy, of course, but we are always looking for parent volunteers to interact with faculty committees, chaperone activities, etcetera."

Please, no. Please don't call Mom. You don't know Mom.

"That's fine."

"Good. Well—good talking with you, Chris. Back to class with you. And don't forget that list."

On the bus home Amy said she heard I was called to Waltzman's office. What was up?

"Have you ever seen a reading list for Miss Austin's class?"

"No. Why?"

"Waltzman wants to see a copy of it."

"Anything else?"

"No. Why?"

"You seem like something more is going on than a stupid reading list."

MARY

After I got off the phone with the useless doctor's office person, I went into the bedroom to change out of my new "luncheon" dress. I looked in the mirror. My make-up was still intact. I had definitely aged better than the others. Surely they had noticed.

It didn't matter what they noticed. I was feeling very uneasy. I needed to talk to Doctor Kandelman about what I should do about the black teacher and Chris.

What should I do? Where there's smoke there's fire. "Bothering?"

I wished now that I hadn't thrown out all my CDs. Some music would be comforting. Maybe I'll go see Maria. No, Maria would still be at the store. What time is it? I wish I had a watch. Not a Timex or whatever imitation junk Jeffrey tried to pawn off on me, but a real diamond watch. God, those stupid women had diamonds!

I picked up a book that Chris had left lying there. *Madame Bovary.* I'd heard of it. What was it about? What a pity I never went to college. If only I hadn't married so young. Well, that wasn't my fault.

I think I'll take another lithium. I've already taken—what—four? 1800 milligrams. But surely another little 450 milligram pill wouldn't hurt. Or would it? How dangerous are these drugs? The phone rang. At last, Doctor Kandelman.

"Hello."
"Hello, Mrs. Mullins. This is Doctor Waltzman. The principal at the high school."
I felt my heart jump. My tongue seemed stuck to the roof of my mouth.
"Mrs. Mullins?"
"Yes."
I have to respond like a real person and not the zombie I feel like.
"This is Doctor Waltzman," he repeated more slowly. "I'm the principal at Watson High School, Mrs. Mullins."
"Oh, my."

There, I'm talking. Keep it up. Show interest, concern. Say something.
"Has something happened to Chris?"
"No, no. We were just wondering if you and your husband could find time to come in and talk with us—some time at your convenience?"

Okay, okay. This is going along now. Ask why.

"Why? Has Chris done something wrong?"

"Not at all."

He's being evasive. I'm starting to feel angry. I'm not going to be pushed around by this principal. I'm not afraid of a school principal.

"Well, WHY do we need to come in?"

No, no. Slow down. Don't—don't yell at this man. He could make trouble for Chris. Think of a quiet pool of water. Be still now. Let him explain.

"We are talking to a few parents about some faculty issues, and we'd like your help. But it would be best if we discussed this in person."

Something is very wrong. Something is seriously wrong. My brain is moving a million miles a minute now. I have to say something, do something. Think clearly. Get up and do something— *SOMETHING!*

"Would it help if I came over to the school right now?"

"Well, the school day is over, but we'll be here for another hour or so." He emitted the great sigh of those straining under enormous administrative burdens. "Our work never seems to be done, unfortunately."

Why did I say that? I don't want to go to the school. People knew I'd been missing. Why don't they just leave me alone?

No, I don't care. This man wants to see me. I'll go. Hurry up. He's waiting. Wear what? The gray tweed suit from Talbot's. That would be fine, wouldn't it? Yes. Put it on. Get into the car. Hurry over there. Where is J.W. Watson High School? I passed it on one of my drives. There. NO PARKING? Park anyway.

I ran up the steps and almost knocked over a girl in a cheerleader's outfit.

"Hi, Mrs. Mullins. Remember me? Kimberly? Wellborn?"

"Yes, how are you, Kimberly?"

"I'm good. Can I help you find something?"

"Doctor Waltzman's office?"

"I'll take you there. I'm on my way to the gym anyway."

Kimberly was on her best society hostess behavior, introducing me to Mrs. Leitner, and then before skipping off, inquiring if there was "anything else I can do for you, Mrs. Mullins?" She sounded like a TV puppet, just as high and nasal as her mother. I thanked her, and Mrs. Leitner ushered me into Doctor Walzman's impressive office with its big desk and a shiny conference table.

"Ah, Mrs. Mullins. Sit down, please. Will Mr. Mullins be joining us? Of course not, he must still be at work."

I noticed the framed Ph.D. certificate on the wall. I was certainly glad Jeff wasn't here. Doctor Waltzman would immediately sense that he was dealing with a Buick salesman.

"Do you like jelly beans, Mrs. Mullins? I'm afraid I'm addicted to them."

He offered me the jar. I declined. He popped one into his mouth.

"Can Mrs. Leitner get you something to drink? Coffee? Water?"

"No thank you."

He got up and closed the door. I now wished I had taken another lithium. I smiled at him. He noticed that I'm pretty, didn't he? I wish I'd worn something else. Say something.

"You   have   a   very   nice   office,   Doctor Waltzman."

"It's not mine, you know. It belongs to the taxpayers. We never forget the fact that in a Waltzman school, everything belongs to the people. And the most important people are the students and their parents."

I didn't know what I was supposed to say to this, so I just nodded. He continued.

"Paramount is the quality of our faculty—and the quality of their relationships with our students."

"Of course," I said.

"Your son seems to be thriving. All his teachers say that he is exceptional."

"That's good to hear."

"Has he ever mentioned an English teacher? A Miss Austin?"

The black Arab teacher Louise and Franny and Polly say is "bothering" Chris! That's the teacher! Should I just blurt that out?

"Not that I recall."

"Has he been disturbed by some of the things he's been reading in that class?"

I wondered what that "Madame" book was. I should take a closer look. I don't know if Chris has been disturbed or not.

"Not that I know of. Why?"

"I don't mean to alarm you," reassured Doctor Waltzman, "and there may be nothing to this. In all probability, there is nothing to it. But some of the mothers say their daughters think that Miss Austin may be, in some way, bothering your son."

There's that word. "Bothering!" Bothering, bothering, bothering!

"Bothering? How do you mean?"

"I'm not at all sure. These could be nothing more than rumors. That's why we'd like your help. There is probably nothing to this, but..."

"WHAT IF THERE IS SOMETHING TO IT?"

"Please. Mrs. Mullins. We will investigate thoroughly, and furthermore, we are putting together a faculty committee to probe this further."

I felt myself getting upset now. "For God's sake, what good will that do? Whatever this teacher did, just GET RID of her."

"We don't know for a fact that she did anything. That's one of the reasons we wanted to talk with you."

This is worse than the luncheon. I'd like to throw the jar of jelly beans at Doctor Waltzman. *This black Arab teacher should be fired! Now!* But Doctor Waltzman keeps talking.

"Mrs. Mullins, we're very sensitive to the fact that Chris is only twelve, and exceedingly smart, and he's been troubled by your, ah—disappearance—but rest assured, we have experience and trained expertise in matters such as these."

"My son is *not* troubled. And I did *not* disappear."

"I understand."

"If my son is hurt in any way—who is more important, Doctor? My son or this black Auttenberg woman?"

I swallowed my shouting impulse and straightened my jacket. I felt slightly dizzy. Perhaps I had taken too many pills. What if I fainted in this man's office? Don't faint. Don't say anything. Listen to Doctor Waltzman.

"Please. We don't know if she did anything, Mrs. Mullins. If she did nothing that violates our strict code of ethics—and our code of ethics is stricter than the state education department standard, let me assure you—but if she did nothing to violate our exceptionally strict code of ethics, and we tried to, as you say, 'get rid' of her, we, meaning the school, that is the School Board and thus the taxpayers, could be sued. Which is why I'd like your help—"

"My help—??"

"It is my contention, based on many years of experience, that often a boy's best friend is, in fact, his mother."

Well, now. This may be going better than I originally thought.

"Or in some cases, his father."

If Doctor Waltzman knew Jeffrey, he'd just leave him out of this matter. Jeffrey would think this Arab teacher was just fine. In fact, Jeffrey had gone to that Parents' Night thing while I was away, and he seemed perfectly happy with the school.

Doctor Waltzman went on, "Perhaps he might tell you things that he wouldn't tell us."

"Chris?"

"Yes."

"Yes, perhaps."

"Don't put him on the defensive about—about whatever he might feel defensive about. Which is probably nothing. But if there is anything amiss, we all need to know about it as soon as possible so that the proper remedial action can be taken—or not taken—as appropriate. We have to work together. You and I. Don't you agree, Mrs. Mullins?"

"Very much so. Yes."

"We are after all, a small, close-knit community, that depends on intelligent, interested people like you."

"Well, I'm happy to do whatever I can."

"It has been a great pleasure. You can reach us any time."

He took me by the arm as he moved to open the door. It may have been my imagination, but I'm sure he squeezed my arm. A small man, but very nice hands.

"Mrs. Leitner, would you give Mrs. Mullins our card so that she can call us directly any time she might need to?"

I said how nice it was to meet him, and told him how much I appreciated what he was doing. He assured me this was all possibly a tempest in a tea cup. I, in turn agreed, collected my card, and waved good-by to Mrs. Leitner, who was on the phone. As I went out, I heard her say,

"Doctor Waltzman, Mrs. Schaller is on the line."

When I got to the car, I had a parking ticket. I dropped it on the passenger seat and drove home.

"High school doesn't end
until you die. If then."
—Uncle Bill

CHRISTOPHER

I got home from school and the BMW was gone. Not again?

I went over to Amy's. Maria was home from the store. She said the BMW was there that morning.

It was the early dark of December. Cold. Should we start to worry again?

No. Headlights. Here it comes. I ran home, fearful but curious.

Mom looked okay. She looked nice. She hugged me.

"How was school, Chrissy?"
"Just fine."
"How's that English class?"
"Good."

Everyone is interested in "that" English class. Physics? Ancient History? Not a word. "That" English class! What have I said about that English class?
Nothing.

Waltzman and his "One-of-the-girls-and-*her-mother*-think-Miss-Austin-might-be-'bothering'-you" garbage. I haven't said anything to Mom or anyone about the class or Miss Austin. Have I? Do I talk in my sleep? No. If I did Mom or Dad would have noticed and said something like, "Chris, you talk in your sleep."

Mom says, "Is that black teacher easy to get along with?"
"What black teacher?"
"In that English class."
"She's not black."
"Oh?"
"She's part Persian."
"Is that what she says?"
"Yes."

Don't go on, Chris. Don't say "what if she were black?" So much stuff is bubbling up from the lagoon of my little mind that I am very close to drowning. It wouldn't surprise me a bit if someone knocked on the door right then and there and said, "Hi, we're from '60 Minutes' and we'd like to talk to you about Chris Mullins and his father and their dinner with Jezebel, a known communist strumpet and Aunt Elissa who drinks like Hooch the Hound."

Why is Mom interested in that class? What does she know that I don't know she knows? Or that she imagines. Mom put her hand on my head and played with my hair. She was considering what to say next. I was considering what she might do next, alert to any possibility.

"Chris, why don't you go see Amy?
"Why?"
Oh, Chris, why would you ask her 'why'? Dumb. Hold your breath. Here it comes.
"I WANT TO MAKE A PRIVATE PHONE CALL TO MY PRIVATE DOCTOR. IS THAT OKAY?"
"Yes, yes. Absolutely."

I scooted out. Going past the BMW I saw a parking ticket on the seat. Ever the Junior Detective, I looked at the ticket. Oh, Jesus. Mom had been at my school! Do you hear me, God? *MOM HAS BEEN AT MY SCHOOL!*

I saw Dad coming home. I flagged him down.

"Mom has been at school. She's asking questions about Miss Austin and that English class. Waltzman asked me questions about Miss Austin. He knows she brought me to school the morning after THE dinner."
"How would he know that?"
"The Witches of Watson saw me get out of her car and fall on my ass!"
"So?"
"So Mrs. Schaller and Stephanie talked to him."
"Mrs. Schaller and Stephanie? What do they have to do with anything?"

"They live across the street from the Auttenburg house."

"Ah."

"They wonder if Miss Austin is quote 'bothering' me."

"What the hell? What's your mother doing now?"

"She's talking to Doctor Kandelman."

We went into the house with trepidationsome jitteriness. The lithium and quetiapine seemed to be working, but you could never be sure with Mom.

And sure enough. She was crying and pulling at her hair. She picked up my copy of *Madame Bovary* and threw it in my general direction. She was breathing very hard when she turned to Dad. "YOU!" she shouted. Then she just sort of slid into herself like a Slinky coming together after a trip down the stairs. She continued to slide down to the floor. She looked up at us like a hurt animal. Against my better judgement, I went to her and hugged her. She sobbed and said, "I'm sorry. I didn't mean to do it."

"Do what?"

"You know."

Dad helped Mom to her feet and brought her over to the couch. She seemed to have made contact with another voice deep inside her, a harsh, raspy sound as if something bad was stuck in her throat.

"That patronizing son-of-a-bitch. That quack. He didn't care what I had to say. All he cares about is did I get the CT thing and the other thing? He makes money on those, you know. Did you see his suit? I'm his goddamn meal ticket to go skiing. He pretends to like me, to care about me. He flirted with me. You saw him. You can see what he has in mind."

She was gasping, spittle on her lips as she talked, stamping her feet.

"Jeffrey, you fool, you should have known. Martha should have known. That conceited Jewish fuck. I told him to go rot in hell and never, EVER TALK TO ME AGAIN!"

On wobbly legs she went to the kitchen counter where she kept her medications. She took— we couldn't tell—how many of each, and then straightened up.

"I'm in no mood to discuss this. Good night."

As she went into the bedroom, she was unsteady but managing to navigate. Dad was right with her, helping her into bed. She was mumbling something about Florida. In bed, she turned to us both.

"See what you've done to me?"

Then her head hit the pillow and she started to snore.

Had she tried to kill herself? I went and checked the pill bottles. Not empty. Dad thought if she was trying to kill herself she would have taken all the pills.

The next morning Mom was still deeply asleep, breathing regularly. She looked fine. Dad had sat by her all night. He looked terrible. He said we would have to do something about finding a new doctor, although maybe, possibly with a bit of luck, she might be persuaded to go through the tests and return to Doctor Kandleman.

Ever the wishful thinker, my dad.

He decided to stay home from work to keep an eye on her, but sent me off to school. Which I wish he hadn't done.

Between Spurling's class and O'Malley's, as Amy and I walked through the hall, the three Witches and The Man Todd were grouped into a smirking quartet in front of us.

> *"Double, double toil and trouble;*
> *Fire burn, and caldron bubble."*
> *--Shakespeare, Macbeth*
> *--Also the Olsen Twins*
> *--Also the Witches of Watson*

"Hey, super cool guys," says Stephanie.

"How's your Mom?" says Kimberly.

"Is it true you're fucking Miss Austin?" says The Man Todd.

Without my usual caution and hesitation, I charge toward him, leading with my head, attempting to slam him against the lockers. Instead, he trips me. I struggle to get up and he's grabbing my shirt when suddenly he falls backward, holding his bleeding nose. Amy has clobbered him in the face

228

with an unabridged hardcover edition of *Moby Dick*.
She really is quick. It's amazing.

"You little bitch," says Stephanie. "You broke
his nose!"
"Back off or I'll break yours!" says Amy.

At that point Miss Austin appears. The deep
voice again: "You, you, you, you—all of you—stop
this nonsense now!"
"She broke Todd's nose," says Kimberly.
"It doesn't matter, everyone here is guilty. You
(Todd)— go down to see the nurse about that nose.
The rest of you move on and if this ever happens
again outside my classroom..."
Miss O'Malley barges into the scene. "Just a
moment, Dear, let me handle this. Now, children tell
me exactly what happened."

The end result of this bloody episode is that
Amy and I find ourselves in Doctor Waltzman's office.
We are both to see Mrs. Whitestone and attend a
class in Anger Management on Saturdays, which she
will arrange. I can go now. He'd like to talk to Amy
for just a moment.

On the bus going home Amy and I are holding
hands. We need to.

"He asked me about Miss Austin," says Amy.
"He goes 'What is Chris's relationship with Miss
Austin?' I told him you are one of her best students.

Waltzman says, 'Anything else you think I should know?' He gives me the stare. I'm supposed to say something. I just say, 'No.' He pats me on the head. If you ask me, that's close to assault. You heard Todd, though. This is serious stuff, Chris. What'll we do?"

Whatever the implied issues are in this whole situationness regarding Miss Austin and me, they are fraught with too much dreadfullosity to contemplate. I mean whatever this all is, the consequences could be really, really horrible. I know this. Amy knows this. I don't want to talk to Dad any more about this because he's already mixed up with Miss Austin's cousin. I don't know when he last saw Adalicia, or if he's seen her, but I don't think that between an exotic girlfriend and a crazy wife he needs more worries at the moment. I've already said too much. In fact, behaving just like my sometimes-feckless father, I just hope the whole situationness I'm in will turn into a big misunderstanding, the way Mom's disappearance was made out to be.

The next day Miss Austin comes into class several minutes late. I think she had been crying. Did she hear what Todd said? Did the Witches say something to Miss O'Malley? Are the Witches' mothers, the older Witches, wandering around the school generally doubling the trouble? I feel so sorry for Miss Austin.

"Of a Ministry pitiful, angry, mean,
A gallant commander the victim is seen.
For promptitude, vigour, success, does he stand
Condemn'd to receive a severe reprimand!
To his foes I could wish a resemblance in fate:
That they, too, may suffer themselves, soon or late,
The injustice they warrent. But vain is my spite
They cannot so suffer who never do right."
                                              --Jane Austen

MISS THERESA AUSTIN

Something is wrong. I'm not sure what, but I fear my days here may be numbered. I have made too many mistakes, been too young, too enchanted by the music of the words and the dazzling precocity of some of my students.

I was stopped by Doctor Waltzman today on the way to my wonderful AP English class. He smiled and said this is just a "heads-up." For what? Well, there may have been some complaints about some aspects of my teaching, the readings, my "behavior, etcetera!" He refused to be specific, but instead rattled on, promising that "in a Waltzman school we think the best judges of peers are other peers." So he would reserve judgment. On what? I begged him to tell me what was wrong, but he continued smiling, saying we mustn't be premature until the facts are "established" and "We're looking into it." He concluded our brief and highly disturbing encounter by saying, "By the way, we can't find the lesson plan for your AP class."

Being told something is wrong but not being told what is wrong is frustrating enough to make even someone who has eaten Giant Rat meat with the Peace Corps in Cameroon come to tears, so I came to tears. I'm pretty sure I must have filed a "lesson plan" of some sort for the AP English class, but among my other shortcomings, I don't pay much attention to such things. I know this much. It's not the lesson plan. It's me. I have been cocky—arrogantly holding myself above the boring requirements of pedantry, teaching my classes, living as though I were free. Almost openly irreligious. I have been foolish beyond belief.

Worse, I have been naive.

Before I came to Watson I had finished my commitment to the Peace Corps and was headed toward graduate school at Columbia to get a Master's degree and, at the same time, to get back together with Vikram, the young man I'd met in Cameroon. Vikram is Indian, and an aspiring and gifted poet. Our romance, such as it was, was suddenly cut short when he was called back to India by his father. In a short while, he wrote me a long and beautifully-written letter explaining how highly he thought of me and how much he regretted having to fulfill his obligation to enter into an arranged marriage to Nipa, the daughter of a prominent politician and owner of a large drug manufacturer in Patna.

I can't say I was distraught. Just disgusted that I'd let myself become so unguarded. However, more schooling didn't seem like quite the thing I ought to be doing at that juncture in my life. I ought to be moving on. I ought to be doing what I always wanted to do—teach. Happily, a friend at Columbia put me in touch with Dalton Prevell.

Superintendent Dalton Prevell, a very dashing young Princeton-schooled idealist with a law degree to boot, recruited me to Watson High School with descriptions of an educational Elysian Fields. They wanted young teachers exactly like me, who would infuse the very fine, highly rated J.W. Watson High School with "new blood, new ideas that would make learning even more exciting." He wanted to "shake things up a bit."

Dalton Prevell was a very persuasive man. He's tall, rumpled, preppy-looking, with unruly reddish hair and a boyishly enthusiastic manner. I was quite smitten with him. As my cousin Adalicia might say, "It's a shame he's married." Although that never did stand in her way.

Dalton convinced me that my Peace Corps experience was just the kind of background they were looking for. I could create my own lesson plans within broad and flexible guidelines. I would only have three classes, plus a study hall, and ample class preparation time, which all sounded just great. It would be, in short, what every girl who saw herself as a teacher since she was six-years-old dreamed about: my classes pretty much on my terms in which I could help young people appreciate the literature I loved, and, I have to be honest, have the fun of performing without actually having to be an actor. It would be a dream world.

The school district itself was quite small but very prosperous, a relatively autonomous community set in an exurban, semi-rural county, offering a higher than average starting salary. And, as a great bonus, my excitingly strange and unconventional cousin, Adalicia Auttenberg, had moved back to her roots in the town after many years of having adventures on the production side of making movies and, apparently, making love to men all over Europe. I'm not sure why she came back. Nostalgia, perhaps? No, I doubt that, because she has very little good to say about the people in the town. More likely she came to protect the family finances. Adalicia and her brother Andrew, who lives in Arizona, I think, still owned a good deal of farmland north of town that was being encroached on by politically-connected developers.

Whatever her reasons, I was delighted she was there. She lived with her very aged charmingly alcoholic Aunt Elissa in their big old family home on a beautiful street. They had plenty of room for me, rent-free. They also had a 1963 Avanti that old Mr. Auttenberg had restored and kept in the garage. He had died a couple of years ago, and Adalicia told me that if I could find a mechanic who could get it running, I could use it. Ivan Stetlik, the physics teacher, referred me to this charming country eccentric and fellow cannabis aficionado, Bill Davlin. He got the Avanti going in nothing flat.

He told me to call him Uncle Bill, and that if the car or I needed "a little helpful handy hand," to just give him a ring. He is what you might call a really "nice" dirty old man.

The car is a gorgeous work of art.

Adalicia did warn me that driving a work of art every day to school was perhaps not the most prudent way for a new young teacher to modestly present herself in a mostly ultra-ultra-conservative community, but I gaily went ahead. I thought, well, why not? What I drive is my business.

I may be fairly smart, but I'm not wise.

My first couple of months at the school were pretty good. Not all of the teachers were as warm and welcoming as I might have hoped, of course, but I'd dealt with social coolness before. However, I should have paid more heed to Ivan. He told me to be watchful. "This can be a mean place," he said.

I thought he was merely referring to the tendency of many children in their teens to be cruelly cliquey and downright mean, which can affect their behavior in a classroom. I understood the potentially negative effects of that kind of distraction from my own days in high school. However, I should have been even more alert to slings and arrows slung by the school's adult faction, including some of the teachers, administrators and, surprisingly, intermeddling parents.

Doctor Waltzman, the principal, is somewhere in his late fifties. Before they brought him to this school when it was built in 1982, he spent some years as headmaster at Saint John's, an old private school to which he makes frequent reference. In fact, he proudly and often describes himself as "old-school." Whether it is an intentional allusion or not, I think my youth and inexperience offend him. He apologized that we do not have a "mentoring" system here for first-year teachers, but he suggests that I should not hesitate to consult with veteran teacher Miss O'Malley on any questions I might have regarding school protocol, classroom management, and as he put it, "appropriate workplace attire and grooming." At times he makes me feel like I am about four years old.

To be fair, in my first few weeks, (while he was always quite full of himself), he did seem to be trying to be helpful, at least from his perspective. However, I must say, he caught me completely off-guard when he suggested, at one of our little "what-can-Doctor-Waltzman-do-to-make-your-job-easier?" meetings, that I ought to consider finding a church and teaching Sunday school. I said that I wasn't very knowledgeable nor very religious. He said it didn't matter. It would be good for my image. It would polish my "Christian bona fides." I told him I would think about it, and he surprised me by saying, "If I were you, I'd think about it quite seriously."

As the fall wore on I came to realize that I was not destined to be Doctor Waltzman's favorite subordinate. He likes his ways of doing things and he'd like you to like his ways. And practice them to the letter. Penny Leitner, his secretary, stopped me one day and said, "Theresa, want a tip? Ask Doctor Waltzman for his advice."

"On what?"

"Anything."

I should have done that, I think.

Superintendent Dalton Prevell had not been totally accurate in describing my duties. My three classes are an odd mixture ranging from "I-can't-believe-I'm-doing-this" to the kind of delight the enthusiastic Superintendent had promised.

The "I-can't-believe-I'm-doing-this" class is something called "English for Business." The textbook is titled "Market Leadership," written by seven people, most of them with MBAs and various corporate credentials. I am taking the class through chapters on "the vocabulary and grammar you will need to impact your job interview," "the art of impactful self-presentation," and "how to say what you mean." Apparently some of the local politicians got this class incorporated into the high school curriculum in order to "make our education more relevant and responsive to real world needs." Doctor Waltzman is all in favor of the course, so I have been careful to adhere to the unbelievably uninteresting textbook. Business has never been my passion, but I am trying to put my heart into instructing the mostly senior students in what will no doubt be the lucrative art of "writing proactive facsimiles and memos for maximum impact."

"Impact" is the textbook authors' favorite word.

Sophomore English class is also something of a chore. In particular, some of the girls drive me crazy with the constant primping of their hair and make-up. They're only sophomores, I know, but it has been well nigh impossible for me to connect with them on a good share of the material or on a personal level. For example, I'm truly disappointed in my total failure to adequately portray Portia—one of the best roles for a woman in all of literature—with so little (if I may borrow the word from Business English) "impact" on them. You would think they might find some way to admire Portia, even just a little bit. After all, Portia is practically a Miss America candidate—charming, intelligent, funny. Portia's speech on mercy is too wonderful.

It impressed them about as much as a toothpaste commercial. I know they come from well-off families and will no doubt eventually find some college that will welcome them. But I've yet to find a way to elicit more than bored, adenoidal expressions from these young women. Their bodies are in class, but I have no idea where their minds are. I also must confess that from the very first day I sensed that two or three of those girls were actually predisposed to resent me. Their dislike, I suspect, was intensified by the penny-pitching incident with Chuck, the boy with Down Syndrome. I was appalled by that.

However, my advanced English and Drama class is a genuine pleasure. I know that some people and, indeed, some teachers such as Miss O'Malley, dismiss the entire younger generation as empty-headed and as incurious as my sophomore girls seem to be. But my AP kids are just plain fun for me.

Most of them seem to get right into the spirit of whatever we are covering, sometimes so exuberantly that they disturb Miss O'Malley, who is always hovering right next door. They ask more questions than I can answer. They speculate on and disagree over meanings and literary intentions and worth. Friendly disagreements are not unusual. ("The Natural?" "The movie was a lot better than the short story," says one student. "No it wasn't. The movie distorted Malamud's meaning," says another. Etc.)

After class I can usually count on a couple of them stopping to wave a book in my face, saying, "Miss Austin, have you read this?" Yesterday it was *The Giver*, which, of course, I now have to hurry up and read. If I'm ever fortunate enough to have children, I hope they might have some of the qualities of these.

Students vary all across the board, of course. Three of them are, it seems, quite religious and literal, and most unfortunately without a scintilla of a sense of humor. I know that, for them, sometimes I'm not as sensitive as I should be. When we were trying to deal with Chaucer I probably was too offhand in my mention of the Wife of Bath's talk of whipping her five husbands. Discussing Shakespeare's theater and Queen Elizabeth also got us into a thicket of issues regarding her father's six wives and the constant bickering over church matters in England at the time, not to mention the question of which parent is responsible for the sex of a baby, the king or the queen. I was into eggs and sperm and X and Y chromosomes before I knew it. Lord knows, I've probably been offensive in uncountable ways that I wasn't even conscious of. I horrified myself when I thoughtlessly blurted out that religion and ethnicity have been the major causes of most wars. I don't know what got into me, but I backpedaled and modified myself to such a degree that I was effectively refuting my own assertion. Thank the gods for the bell.

One girl, Keri Quinn, stands out because she is so earnest and literal that it's painful. School is very, very serious for Keri. I don't fault her. She is in my class because she was convinced by some counselor— probably Trisha Whitestone—that even if she hates this course, she has to get that particular AP ticket punched in order to get into a "really good" college. She's smart and very hard working. But I do wish she could lighten up a bit now and then because, Lord knows, there ought to be some times in the course of growing up that a sixteen-year-old girl can just be...well...*young.*

I have two students who are not young. They are incredibly young. Amy Fowler is thirteen and, when the fall term started, little Christopher Mullins had not yet turned thirteen. They both look even younger than they are. And they both are very bright. Christopher in particular is off the charts. He's the one who brought me *The Giver*.

My heart aches for these two, surrounded as they are by all these older students. I have mixed emotions on the wisdom of dropping such very young children into this environment. They certainly can handle all the work, and then some. But I wonder if this is healthy for them.

At any rate, I adore both of them. I want to protect them. In retrospect I should have been much more cautious. But Christopher was having a rough time. For a short while it was thought that his mother was missing and that his father might somehow be implicated. It turned out to be some kind of mix-up, but was understandably difficult for Christopher.

Amy Fowler confided in me during that period that Christopher's mother seemed a little unbalanced at times. She apparently even threw things at the boy.

During the period when Christopher's mother was missing I really wanted to try to comfort him. He was tearful at times, and I imagined that he must feel forlorn. It was not a mistake to want to help Christopher. It was a mistake to have him and his charming father over for dinner.

How could I have known that my bewitching cousin was bewitching this boy's father? Adalicia was disgracefully brazen. I'm sure Christopher was aware of the situation. Then, to top it off, she got the boy drunk.

And we got snowed in.

CHRISTOPHER

I got home from school. Dad wasn't there, but he'd left a note. "Took your mother to ER as precaution. Stay at Amy's. Will call. Love, Dad."

I fully recognize that most of humanity is suffering awfulsome horribilis fates at this very moment. Some innocent Indian is casually bathing in some soothing river in India and, bingo, there's a snail and he's got incurable schistosomiasis. There's elephantiasis—lots of people must be consigned to freakdom like John Merrick in that play Miss Austin assigned. Hundreds of children disappear into jungle-size sinkholes that swallow whole houses in seconds. And some tribes still eat human flesh as a high protein diet. I recognize all these ghastly situations and many more are far, far worse than my own. Diresomeness is everywhere.

Therefore, even though as I've said before, my own problems are the most important on earth to me, I've managed to develop an unruffled, almost serene outlook, and upon reading Dad's note I do not beat my head against the wall.

I am chillsomely poised. Nonchalant.

I saunter over to Amy's as instructed.

Maria is not happy. She'd had a call from the school informing her that Amy had broken some boy's nose.

"He's an asshole," Amy says.

Josephus laughs.

"You're encouraging her to use language like that?"

I entered into the conversation.

"He *IS* an asshole."

"Who started it?"

"I did."

"You? Then why did Amy break the asshole's nose?"

We explain.

Josephus says, "Man is born into trouble as the sparks fly upward."

Maria: "What is that?"

"Job."

Calmly: "Mom's in the hospital."

Josephus says this weather is what the Scots call a "dreich" night—cold, rainy, with a howling wind that rattles the Fowler's doublewide. Amy and I are huddled on their couch watching the X-Files.

243

Mulder strikes me as a bit dense. Amy thinks that's pretty logical because if you're exposed to lots of paranormals who are smarter than you, you're bound to begin to believe in their superiority and act inferior. It's true in education, she says, where what teachers expect from students is what they get. Low expectations, low performance. Mr. Spurling's class is proof, she says. Everyone in it except us is a classic case of walking low self-esteem.

I think Amy has been watching too much Public Television. Josephus agrees.

I practice my magic on Amy. Dad got me Penn & Teller's *How To Play With Your Food,* which is really funny and has helped me with some tricks. However, I am trying to master the art of forcing a card and failing. Either the cards are too sticky or Amy just won't cooperate because I never get her to pick the card I want her to pick.

Maria has popped popcorn and brings in a bowl of it. She asks me again for the ninth time what time Dad took Mom to the hospital. I tell her again that I don't know.

The phone rings. Everybody looks at the phone like if we stare hard enough it will begin to tell us something.

Josephus: "Is everybody deaf?"

Maria answers the phone. Now all we hear is a series of "ohs" and "I sees" from Maria.

"For God's sake, Maria. What's going on?" says Josephus.

Finally she hands the phone to me, "It's your father."

Even people I really like, like Maria, are beginning to frazzle me.

MARY

I'm not going to spend the night in this goddamned hospital, no matter what they say. I haven't been in a hospital since that awful experience giving birth to Chris, and I'm not going to start now. We've been here all day and half the night! They needlessly pumped my stomach, which was not a walk in the park, let me tell you. And then they just left us in this corner of the Emergency Room, surrounded by a blue curtain, and me in this itchy paper gown. It's pretty clear, they're taking care of everyone but me. I told Jeff to go let them know that I'm still here and need attention as soon as possible.

This whole incident is just another example of Jeffrey's overreacting. Yes, I woke up feeling a little sick to my stomach and he may have thought I was not making sense, but I knew what I was saying. There was no reason to go speeding off in all directions at once.

I'm fine now. There is a Hispanic man whose name tag says "Maximiliano," which I can't easily pronounce, so I don't. I later learned he was only a Physician's Assistant, but he seemed fairly competent. He confirmed exactly what I knew was wrong. He said I was just experiencing some bad side effects from the lithium and the other stuff and my doctor should adjust the dosages. I didn't tell him that I was not going back to that doctor or that I had probably taken more than I should have because I was upset over my son's being abused by a black Arab teacher.

The Physician's Assistant told me I was certainly looking good for someone who had just had her stomach pumped. I asked him for a mirror and my purse so I could at least put on a little make-up, but he said I probably shouldn't bother with that just yet, and besides, he said, I didn't need any. What a beautiful smile Maximiliano has.

He explained that they still had to take an X-ray as a precaution. So, okay. But does everything they do have to take so long? We've done nothing but wait, wait, wait! Meanwhile we are surrounded by all these flu-infected, coughing and moaning people—all in shorts—hairy-legged and fat.

Finally, a man with a face the color of coffee grounds comes in and introduces himself as Doctor Balakrishnan. It's amazing that the name fits on that little tag. (Is no one in this place named Smith or

247

Johnson?) Balakrishnan smiles and talks just like the taxi driver in New York. He's very difficult to understand. He says that Radiology wants to study the X-ray and possibly take a few more. He asks if we have a neurologist where he can send my records.

Now pardon me, but who in hell has a neurologist they can just pick up and call? We don't have one and furthermore we don't need one.

Bala-christmas-whoever is not terribly concerned, but he really thinks we should see a neurologist. Jeffrey says we will do that right away. Doctor Bala mentions a couple of names which Jeffrey dutifully writes down.

I speak up.

"I need to go home now."

Well, this quack doesn't think that's wise. They would like to observe me—mini ischemic this—carotid arteries that—blah, blah, blah. I just couldn't listen anymore.

"I have urgent things to do. My son is in trouble."

Jeffrey, the biggest fool on this planet, contradicts me.

"Jeffrey, Sweetheart," I counter, "you didn't get the call to come to the school. I DID! And we can't waste time here. Thank you very much, Doctor. We will take your advice and see one of your neurologists as soon as we can. Meanwhile, my son is in danger."

So, he reluctantly lets us check out, explaining that our insurance may not apply if we leave without the radiologist's sign off. Is that my concern?

Jeff and I argue all the way home. Jeff does not agree that Chris is in some sort of danger from the Auttenberg teacher. He even has the gall to say that he's met this Miss Austin and she's not black and she seems like a good teacher and Chris likes her.

Well, of course, Chris likes her! If Jeff knew anything he'd know that people often like their abusers. It's on TV all the time. Of course, he hardly watches what the rest of the world is watching. Old head-in-a-non-best-selling-book-no-one-ever-heard-of-Jeffrey-Mullins. God!

Furthermore, Jeff can't possibly have any perspective on the issue since everyone knows that he is fucking around with that whore, Adalicia. Everyone in town is laughing at me for being—what do they call it? A "cuck-hold." I know, I know—cuckold refers to a *man* who has an adulterous wife. Well, I'm beginning to think a little adultery on my part might not be a bad thing.

We arrived home near midnight. I went to bed without taking either of the medications that Kandelman had prescribed. It was such a mistake going to him. I found my old pills, Ambien, and took just three of those. I should have been doing my own prescribing all along. "Who knows you better than YOU?" is my new motto. And sure enough, this morning I awoke "refreshed," as they say.

I know exactly what I'm going to do. I'm going to call Polly Findley. She's on the School Board, and I'm going to INSIST that she get that black Arab teacher fired!

Thank God I'm thinking clearly. I suddenly feel that I really do know what I'm doing. I've tiptoed around the issue long enough.

Polly seemed pleased to hear from me, particularly when I mentioned my concern over our luncheon conversation about the black teacher. I felt we needed to act. She agreed.

She and Louise and I made an appointment to see Doctor Waltzman. Did we want to bring Franny in also? Franny certainly had some firsthand information through her darling daughter Kimberly, but perhaps, in terms of making the best impression this time around—well, Franny had let herself go a little and four of us might be too many.

I felt the three of us would be best. Louise agreed. She also noted, confidentially, that Franny could be a bit of a gossip and this entire situation required extreme discretion.

I had to wear the tweed suit again. I couldn't think of anything else. Maybe if I unbuttoned the top button and folded in that scarf I had borrowed from Martha when I was in New York, it would look better.

I told Polly and Louise that I had already spoken to Doctor Waltzman, and he said he had listened to "Mrs. Findley's and Mrs. Schaller's concerns" over this teacher *AND* he shared their concern. I could tell they were pleased. I said I thought we should do more than talk this time. I thought we should insist that they get rid of this woman who was "bothering" Chris. Based on what Louise had seen, and what Stephanie, Kimberly, and Nicole had seen, they agreed.

Doctor Waltzman seemed delighted to see us.

As Chris's mother, I felt obligated to be the most assertive of the group. I began by saying that I could tell something was odd about Chris ever since he began that class with that Auttenberg woman.

While I had not actually talked with Chris about that teacher, I was well aware of a change in his behavior. Although both Jeff and Martha had pooh-poohed my worry, Chris certainly was more devious than he had been in the past. And while I had in truth thumbed through only that one book about the Madame that Chris was reading, I could honestly infer—yes, infer—an influence of unhealthy, foreign ideas in Chris's whole attitude. Not just the kind of crap he picked up from Jeff and his uncle, but more corrupting. As Doctor Waltzman himself had pointed out, nobody knows a boy like his mother.

So I thought it would add weight to what we mothers were saying—and impress Polly and Louise—if I indicated to Doctor Waltzman that I had looked over some—many—of the class materials and I wasn't at all sure everything was *appropriate* for any high school student, much less one who was only twelve-years-old. I said I couldn't be specific, but it seemed that some of the class readings contained strong sexual—what would you call it—?

"Overtones," Polly said eagerly.

"And undertones," Louise added.

Doctor Waltzman nodded. I was gratified to hear him say that, yes, some others had voiced concerns over the readings and discussions in that class.

Louise chimed in that Stephanie heard from Lisa James that this Miss Auttenberg—*Austin*, Polly corrected—had spoken at length about the Christian religion as a cause of war.

Doctor Waltzman nodded and made a note.

Louise beamed.

I didn't care about war, but I said I had heard that, too.

"However," I continued, "I'm not worried so much about what this woman is saying to her class, bad as it might be. It's what she's doing to Chris! MY SON CHRIS! THAT'S WHY I'M HERE!"

I shouldn't have raised my voice. I realized it immediately.

Waltzman was taken aback for a second. Then he asked, "Have you asked Chris directly about any of this?"

Calm now. Sweetly, "You told me not to."

"That's true, but I just wondered if you had."

"No. And I don't have to. I told you, he's different. He always used to talk to me, confide in me. He was always eager to tell me everything. *Everything.* Ever since he was a little boy he was so anxious to do the right thing and to please me. Even when we'd play hide and seek and I'd say where are you, he couldn't stand to deceive me. He'd jump out immediately and say, 'Here I am! Here I am!' Now, just this fall since he started in this class, even though he's only twelve, suddenly he's become devious and secretive. I couldn't confront him."

"I doubt that he'd admit anything," said Polly. "Based on my work with the church youth, I would imagine he'd be too ashamed."

"HE has nothing to be ashamed of," I declared.

Polly quickly agreed, "Chris is not the issue."

Doctor Waltzman agreed.

Louise said she thought Chris simply had something of a childish crush on this teacher. Polly said such a thing would not be unusual. It happens all the time. Doctor Waltzman agreed.

Louise said that Stephanie said that this Miss Austin person seemed to cast a spell over some students, not unlike a witch. Louise was going to say more about this mystical quality, when I interrupted. I was tired of hearing all this pointless chatter.

"I think we should leave Chris completely out of the matter," I interjected. "What we're dealing with is a predator taking advantage of a little boy's crush on her. We have all read or heard about predatory women, haven't we? I don't want to use the term 'rape,' but isn't that the possibility we're talking about?"

"While 'rape' might seem a bit extreme, and it seems like an almost impossible consideration, we should not rule it out because there could be other victims," Polly seconded.

"I want to emphasize," I reminded them, "that the victim in this case is MY SON!"

Doctor Waltzman quickly jumped in, "I understand. You are right not to raise the subject with Chris. We don't want to upset him. Let us carefully work through the process in order to ascertain the truth and minimize publicity that would be detrimental for everyone."

"Who cares about publicity?" I said.

Well, Doctor Waltzman and Polly and Louise all said nobody wanted any names in the Courier—or anywhere else. Louise said something about doing our own dirty laundry in private. Polly emphasized the great reputation of the school.

I had had it!
I said, loudly, "THE REPUTATION OF THE SCHOOL IS A DAMN GOOD REASON TO FIRE THIS FUCKING WITCH OF A WOMAN NOW!"

Polly and Louise jumped.

Doctor Waltzman quickly asked his secretary, "Mrs. Leitner, would you bring Mrs. Mullins a glass of water, please?" Then he took my hand.

"That is what everyone wants," he soothed, "but we have to do it properly. Very properly. After all, if this is played up, think of the harm it will do your son. His name. His future. We don't want the boy so noticeably upset that he attracts attention."

All right. Okay. Namby-pamby people. You can go back years and I'll tell you that not doing what *I THINK* should be done never works out. *NEVER!*

Mrs. Leitner brought in a bottle of Polar Spring water and a paper cup. I thanked her. (We should start drinking this purer water at home. Who knows what's in the water on Shit House Road?)

Okay. It would be better for Chris to keep his name out of it. Isn't that what I've been saying all along? The black teacher had to go quietly without involving Chris at all.

Doctor Waltzman said I was absolutely right. He would handle this whole thing with kid gloves.

Louise and Polly said that they—and we'd have to talk to Franny, too—they all would quietly inform their daughters that their suspicions were probably unfounded, but as a *precaution* there would be a new teacher in that AP class, and, of course, in their sophomore English class.

Louise said that Stephanie said that from the first day this teacher seemed inexplicably irritated with the class. Thank heavens their daughters were perceptive enough to sense this potential problem before others in the school took notice. They were all sensitive girls, mature for their age and could be trusted to be very discreet.

Chris need never know anything.

We were all in accord. Doctor Waltzman assured us that he had had a similar experience a number of years ago when a parent suspected that the drama teacher at the renowned Palmer High School could be undesirable. After a discreet investigation, the man turned out to have been seen with other, shall we say, peculiar men, and Doctor Waltzman did as he was going to do here at Watson. He created an Ethics Committee, and they were able to deal with the issue with hardly anyone suspecting a thing. The man was there one day and gone the next.

Doctor Waltzman would be in touch with all of us. We needn't worry. This was, after all, a Waltzman school.

Polly and Louise drove me home, assuring me that Doctor Waltzman knew what he was doing and that our cooperation with him and support for him was just the right thing at this time, blah, blah. By now I had a slight headache.

I couldn't invite them in. Jeff or Chris might have left dishes in the sink. Or something else might be amiss in our crappy little trailer. What if they had to use the bathroom? Everything in there was plastic.

So, I told them goodbye and went in. I swore I wasn't going to, but I decided to take Kandleman's pills anyway. Even though they might not work. Probably wouldn't work. I'd be careful to take only the one pill of each. Well, two of the lithium.

Then I rearranged the furniture.

"People don't see what is. They see what they want to see."

-Uncle Bill

MISS THERESA AUSTIN

I've got to get another even louder alarm clock. One is not enough. I overslept, again. Adalicia had to waken me, again. I hate morning.

"The neighborhood is alive and watching," says Adalicia. "I'm thinking maybe you need a slightly less flashy car and a wig."

"You should talk."

"I've definitely lowered my profile of late, you'll be pleased to know."

On my way up the school stairs, Penny Leitner stopped to tell me that Christopher's mother and Mrs. Findley from the school board along with Mrs. Schaller had been in to see Waltzman yesterday. He also had called their daughters into his office. And he'd scheduled a meeting with some of the faculty after school today.

"Be alert, kid."

"Thanks, Penny."

There was a cryptic note on my desk in Walzman's handwriting over his dramatic Spencerian signature. "Please make yourself available for a meeting in our office at 4PM today." Who put it there? No need to guess.

Miss O'Malley tapped on the doorframe.

"There you are. I got in early as usual and picked up that note for you."

"Why didn't he just put it in my mailbox?"

"He did. I just know you don't always bother to check your mailbox, Dear."

She was right, of course.

"Thank you."

"See you later, Dear."

DOCTOR WALTZMAN

I asked them to assemble in my office. As always for my important meetings, Mrs. Leitner had laid out a small smorgasbord of cookies, nuts, soft drinks, and bottled water.

When I got there, Beverly Beatrice Spurling, Trisha Whitestone, Miss O'Malley, Ivan Stetlik and Acting Vice Principal Himoski were already arrayed around the conference table. Mrs. Leitner had set in front of each participant a yellow pad of paper, a pencil, and a three-page Situation Review. I sat down at one end of the table. Mrs. Leitner sat on my right, taking notes of the meeting. Himoski moved to sit on my left. He picked up the Situation Review. I lifted my hand.

"We'll get into that in a moment, P.B." He put it down, and I went on.

"Thank you all for coming. I know the last thing you need after a long and never-ever-easy day (they all chuckled) is an added duty. But we have an unusual potential problem in our school, and our community, and I'm asking for your advice and consent in helping me to resolve it."

As I expected, they all gave each other questioning looks. I heard a nervous cough or two.

Himoski, always eager to show that he is more-than-on-top-of-whatever-it-is-he-should-be-on-top-of, begins writing down a few immediate thoughts on his yellow pad. PB is basically a good man to have covering your back, but he's not the brightest jelly bean in the jar, so to speak.

I continued, "Last year our new Superintendent —young *Princeton-educated* Superintendent Prevell —as well as some members of the School Board, felt—and rightfully so—that more diversity in our faculty might be a good thing. I heartily agreed—in principle.

However, the trouble with diversity is, diversity can cause trouble."

All of them nodded.

"We live in a very litigious age. Many diversity people are exceedingly sensitive and, unfortunately, quite a number of suits have been filed by diversity people against various School Boards around the country.

You have all been with us all these years since we first came to this school. The spirit of Watson is in your blood. We understand that you understand our delicate position."

I picked up the Situation Review. They all did likewise. Miss O'Malley smiled, obviously pleased by what she saw on the first page.

"You all know Miss Austin, Theresa Austin. She has an excellent background and comes to us with the strong recommendation of young *Princeton-educated* Superintendent Prevell. Unfortunately, the Situation in Review is that we have received a number of complaints of varying degrees of gravity regarding Miss Theresa Austin."

Uncomfortable shifting, examination of papers, scribbling. I continued.

"Miss Austin is, as you all know, our newest teacher and the youngest teacher I have ever had on my faculty either at St. John's or here at Watson, or years ago when I was quite young myself—though certainly not as young as Miss Austin—beginning my career at the renowned Palmer High School in the city. Each of these institutions was and remains an excellent example of a Waltzman school."

I paused to take a strategic sip of water and gauge the effect of my rhetoric. Spurling looked puzzled. Stetlik looked—as I expected he would—concerned. The rest looked rather pleased, certainly in agreement with me.

"What do I feel characterizes a Waltzman school? You've all heard me spell this out many times. In a nutshell, we adhere to the highest academic and *ethical* standards and do everything necessary to maintain a reputation as unblemished as this tabletop. Needless to say, I want that record to continue. I'll be honest. I may suffer a tad from the fourth sin (Stetlik definitely frowned)—the sin of pride. However, I *AM* proud. When I retire, I want people to say, 'Doctor Harold Waltzman was a great *EDUCATOR* with a capital *E!*'"

Miss O'Malley clapped her hands. Himoski said, "Hear, hear." I went on.

"I'm not going to let an inexperienced person who doesn't seem to want advice ruin this tabletop, metaphorically speaking."

Himoski busily made a note. I fleetingly wondered what he could possibly be scribbling. I flipped through the Situation Review.

"Now, if you'll flip through your sheets, you'll see the name of one of our mothers, Mrs. Quinn. Most of you probably know her because she helps a great deal in putting together our entrance hall exhibits. You've all seen the interesting one we have now on aviation."

Mrs. Leitner, who knows how busy I am, and I must say is always rather maternally protective when weighty matters preoccupy me and cause me to be less observant that I should be, said, "Doctor Waltzman, our exhibit has just been updated from National Aviation Month to Native American Heritage Month."

"Ah, and I've walked right by it. Native American Month it is! And I'm sure Mrs. Quinn helped get the Native American things that are in it.

She also has brought us several concerns that her daughter, Keri, has expressed regarding the assigned readings and class discussions in Miss Theresa Austin's class."

Miss O'Malley said, "Her class doesn't have discussions. They have boisterous disturbances of the peace. I'm right next door, you know. They might as well be having some of these rock and roll concerts over there."

I acknowledged this with a nod and continued, "Lisa James and two other students also objected to some of the readings, and comments Miss Austin has made, on religious grounds."

Stetlik said, "Excuse me, but what readings? What comments?"

Trisha Whitestone pointed out "They're on page two, Ivan."

Stetlik acted exasperated and he waved the Situation Review at everyone, "Okay, fine. But look (he pointed), here it says 'teacher seems to advocate dissipation by staying up all night burning candles.' That makes no sense. Shouldn't we ask Theresa herself about this stuff?"

I have respect for Ivan's knowledge and his teaching ability, but he has always been troublesome. He is not a team player. But I need him on my committee in order to appear completely fair, should anyone care to ask. He will argue, but we will outnumber him.

I assured him, "Miss Austin should be here at four. However...however...."

I paused to let my "howevers" sink in. You could have heard a pin drop. The battery-powered Regulator clock ticking softly was the only sound. From my perspective, the air in the room actually felt like a storm was gathering. Which is exactly the mood I wanted.
I got up and went to get a jelly bean.

"Jelly bean, anyone?"
All declined.

"However," I went on, "the most serious complaints pertain to her *alleged behavior.*"

Now I had everyone thoroughly engaged. I've always had a good ability to read people. For

Himoski and O'Malley this was wonderful news, as I instinctively felt it would be. Spurling, and— surprisingly for someone steeped in psychology— Whitestone, seemed puzzled. Stetlik was irritated.

Stetlik: "What alleged behavior?"

I told him: "Alleged inappropriate behavior, according to some of the mothers, including Mrs. Findley, who is on the Board as you know and Mrs. Schaller, who supervises the cheerleaders and pep squad. They've each talked to me about what they've seen and what they've heard from their daughters. They want us to deal with this situation and render a satisfactory disposition."

Stetlik: "This isn't a court of law, Harold."

Now, I had to be firm with him. "For this school at this time, it is, Ivan. I'm recusing myself because I have my own opinions and don't want to influence your decision."

Spurling: "Just what are we deciding here?"

Then I said it, very simply and bluntly. "How best to rid ourselves of the Theresa Austin problem."

They murmured, doodled. Himoski scribbled several sentences on his yellow pad. I'd love to know what they were. Nonsense probably. O'Malley made notes on her pad, too. Following their example,

Whitestone and Spurling did likewise. Stetlik made no notes. He stood up.

> Stetlik: "Oh, for God's sake, Harold."
> Spurling: "You mean firing?"
> O'Malley: "I said right from the beginning that she was too green behind the ears."
> Stetlik: "When did you look behind her ears?"
> Himoski: "This is no joke, Ivan."
> Stetlik: "Right, Chief. I'm sorry, but I want no part of this. Theresa has a contract, people."

"I know that, Ivan," I countered, "but you're going to help us work around that."

I may be proud, but I am justifiably proud. I've kissed the asses of too many School Board members and tussled with too many changes in school Superintendents (like young *Princeton-educated* Prevell who wanted this Austin woman over my experienced, State-educated objection) and I've coped with too many asinine state and federal requirements and too many nettlesome union demands and fractious teachers—to find myself just six years away from my hard-earned pension faced with something that could actually attract the attention of *The Courier*—or God forbid *OTHER MEDIA*—and turn my lifetime of effort into contentious shit with stinking fumes that would blacken and *totally tarnish my sterling reputation forever!!* Watson is a model school! A Waltzman school! Even Himoski's football team has managed to have a winning season!

Yes, sir. They're all going to do their duty because *it's in everybody's best interest.*

I said, "Sit down, Ivan. Listen to me. Scandal taints *ALL* of you. Our profession is under enough fire these days. There has never been a scandal at a Waltzman school. We won't have one now. But we want to be able to say that we have been absolutely fair. We are not going to be sued. We are going to satisfy these mothers. Some of them are impatient, particularly Mrs. Mullins, which is understandable."

Whitestone: "Christopher's mother?
"Yes," I said.
Spurling: "Why?"
"The rumors are that Miss Austin is bothering her son," I said.

If a collective gasp could have been rehearsed, the group reaction could not have been more chorus-like, though in different keys ranging from puzzled to pleased. Everything up to this point had merely been a preamble to the real manure pile of this meeting. Frankly, this meeting had been one of the better meetings I've conducted so far this year, in terms of reactions.

Himoski beamed.
O'Malley smirked.

Whitestone shook her head: "God, I should have known."

Spurling: "I'm not sure I understand."

I got up. "I'll leave you all now. But you are all witnesses to the fact that Miss Theresa Austin was not judged by this administration—not by me—but by *YOU*—her fellow teachers and union members. I've said it before—in a Waltzman school we think the best judges of peers are other peers. *YOU* are now officially our Ethics Committee and *YOU* are going to see to it that I do not have to go through the interminable complexity of dealing with her. No fuss. No publicity. She is going to *RESIGN!* See to it. Mrs. Leitner is here to take notes."

And I left.

EXCERPT
from
MRS. LEITNER'S MEETING NOTES

Stetlik: Harold is totally mashugana. Look at him. He's gone mad. We can't do this.

Spurling: What rumors?

Himoski: Sex, you idiot.

O' Malley: Stephanie Schaller and her mother—they say the boy spent the night at Theresa's house. Isn't that true, Penny?

Stetlik: How would they know that?

O'Malley: They live across the street.

According to Mrs. Schaller, they saw them both get into that fancy car and leave the morning after the snow. Stephanie Schaller and Kimberly Wellborn and Nicole Findley, plus that boy who got his nose broken by Amy Fowler, all saw them arrive at the school. They said the boy, Chris, was unsteady getting out of the car.

All present, except for Mr. Stetlik, agreed that the evidence was incontrovertible.

"Oh, woe, the gandlin ormit
that swinges across myne brow,
the hedges sward lord Wynstayne,
before him I would bow.
Eyoe witches, in your blind eyens,
So morbic, cupidic, bestow,
Eyoe ken venom, fool fiends,
Eye promise, eyoe will die in pain."
                              --Dame Therasia Awstin c. 1380

MISS THERESA AUSTIN

I dug around in my desk and did manage to come up with a copy of the lesson plan that I probably filed before school started. It bore no resemblance to what I was teaching, but I thought I'd better bring it along. If the reading materials were really the issue, this would be a starting place. I could justify modifications on the basis of an evolution in class interests, current events, the price of cheese in China, something.

Penny was not at her desk, but the door to Doctor Waltzman's office was open partway. I'm feeling very nervous.

I knocked tentatively.

To my surprise, Mr. Himoski came to the door. Doctor Waltzman was nowhere to be seen, but seated at the conference table were Miss O'Malley, Trisha Whitestone, Bev Spurling, and Ivan. Mr. Himoski invited me to sit at one end of the table, then seated himself imperiously at the other.

"Harold asked me to chair this meeting."

"What meeting? No one told me there was a *meeting.* I'm here to see Doctor Waltzman at his request."

Silence. Everyone looked down at papers and pads on the table. No one looked at me.

"We'd like to clear up a few things, Theresa."

"Wait, wait. Who is 'we' and what is going on?"

"Doctor Waltzman has asked us to form this Ethics Committee."

"An 'ethics' committee' regarding—?"

"First some small things. In your class did you say that women want to whip their husbands?"

Ivan: "Jesus, people. This is bullshit."

I knew that I had not been cautious enough in how I approached or presented certain subjects. It does not pay to be flip when not all little ears hear exactly what you intended them to hear. However, rather than docilely permit this man to interrogate me I immediately lost my temper.

"This is outrageous! I don't have to answer to any of you about what I teach or how I teach! Chaucer or anything else!"

"We're the only friends you've got, Dear."

That's chilling. I am disturbed and a bit frightened. I don't know what's happening to me here, but I'm beginning to realize that these are the peers Waltzman referred to—the peers who will judge me. For some reason he has cast me in the role of Anne Boleyn. And Himoski is my Cromwell. I feel my head rests uneasily on my shoulders.

Mr. Himoski offers a big smile and goes on. "Another thing on the list here—are you teaching a book about a madam who runs a brothel in France? Did you also say that it's not a sin to sleep with your mother and some stupid woman named Bennet reminds everyone of their mothers? And—and—and one of the girls complained that you talked about sperm."

"Moby Dick," said Ivan. "We're talking whales, you idiot."

"Sperm and dick—wow—I wish I'd had this class when I was a kid!"

"Pardon me, Mr. Himoski, but if I didn't know better, I'd say that you seem to be somewhat illiterate."

"Could be, Sweetheart. There's just two more things."

"What exactly do you people think you're doing?"

"Did you say that the Christian religion has been one of the main causes of war?"

"All religions have caused war. Religion and ethnicity."

"And *what*, Sweetie?"

"Ethnicity."

"You apparently haven't heard of the commies, Sweetie. Before your time. And this here—you had some students talk about 'kissing a hole.' I don't want to say anything, but I think we've got an X-rated class in our school," says Mr. Himoski, with obvious delight.

Ivan laughs. "I can't believe this."

I said nothing. I got up and started to leave.

"There's something else."

"What?"

"Mrs. Mullins says you are bothering her son."

"Bothering? Mrs. Mullins? Little Christopher Mullins' mother? I'm puzzled by—"

"You know exactly what we're talking about, Sweetie."

Suddenly, I did know. I was utterly and completely unprepared for this. Adalicia warned me about being a new teacher in a small, conservative, religious community, but this implication staggered me. I couldn't speak. I'd heard of things like this, but

it never dawned on me that I would be accused—
accused—

I felt sick—I bent over to stifle a cry.

Ivan came to me, put his arm around me, a hand on my elbow. "Goddamn it, Paul, you all can't do this. If somebody has evidence of something, anything, then let's get the law involved."

"Good idea, Ivan. You'll have TV cameras all over this place in fifteen minutes. You want to be on TV, Sweetheart, fine, and probably that little boy, too. Sex is news, in case you hadn't noticed."

"Has anyone talked to Chris?" said Spurling.

"He's been hurt enough, Bev," said Trisha Whitestone in her finest grief-counselor tone.

"Hell, it's his mother who's making the accusation," said Mr. Himoski.

"It will be best if you resign, Dear."

I straightened myself and glared at the assembly. "Penny, please tell Doctor Waltzman that I made myself available for a meeting at four o'clock today, but he wasn't here."

I then left and headed toward my car. Among a group watching I saw those girls from my sophomore class, Stephanie, Kimberly, and Nicole. Stephanie stepped in front of me.

"Excuse me, Miss Austin. Have you seen Chris? You know, the little Mullins boy?" She giggled as I brushed past her.

*"If you fall in a hole,
stand on your tippy toes
and yell help as loud as
you can. Sometimes
someone will come."*
                    -Uncle Bill

CHRISTOPHER

Let me state this in an as unhystericalsome way as I can. School, Jason Willard Watson High School, has become more, shall we say, *Off-Putting* than usual. "Off-Putting" as in *"I am putting off throwing up until I can get home."* Or almost home. I'm unbalanced, feeling disturbing tremors wherever I walk. Monsters are under the floors. I'm sick all the time.

Today going to school on the bus when I told Amy how I felt, she had the nerve to say, "Chris, come on. It's bad, but you know what my dad says, 'Nothing is so bad that it couldn't be worse.'"

That is just plain stupid, and I told her so. She then said that I was getting to be a whiny pain in the ass. I told her to go take a flying flip. Now, we aren't talking.

I don't care.

God, I'm beginning to sound like Mom.

The lewd laughing of the crude hall-and-lunchroom crowd, the Witches and Chief Broken Nose Todd (formerly The Man Todd) are pretty much what they've always been, only more so, more obscene. I don't even hear them now. I try not to anyway. They're all talking about me, though—I know that. I'm not paranoid. They want me to hear them, and I do, that's all.

However, there's a *new* tension with both Spurling and Miss O'Malley. Spurling acts like he'd like to ask me some question, finger in the air, mouth slightly open, then nothing, a "never-mind" shrug. This has happened each of the last two days.

Miss O'Malley does something similar. She acts like she wants to tell me something, give me a piece of advice. Then nothing. In gym I find P.B. just leering at me, a big grin on his face—a big, as Uncle Bill says, "shit-eating grin!"

God, I'd love to see him trip on his jock strap and knock those teeth of his into his throat! I frankly don't think that would be nearly cruel and unusual enough punishment.

Miss Austin has been out sick for two days now.

I asked Mrs. Leitner if she knew what was wrong with Miss Austin. She said, "Flu." But she seemed evasive. Normally Mrs. Leitner is quite nice to me. Nicer than she is to lots of people. Now she looks away from me.

I'd like to know what's wrong with Miss Austin, but it wouldn't be smart to ask anyone else to try to find out. I'd just make more trouble.

The substitute for her class is Shirley Ann Binley. She's from South Carolina, has a voice like a banjo, and knits during class. We were supposed to be reading *The Metamorphosis*, but she switched our assignment to *Little Women*. Yesterday, when we still were talking, Amy said Shirley Ann is knitting a *church*! Amy does have some funny lines.

Mr. Stetlik has become quite solicitous, asking how things are going almost every day.

I haven't seen my counselor, Mrs. Whitestone, except to pass her once on my way to a class. She stopped me and said, "I want you to know that you are in my prayers." I have to say, it's a nice thought, even though it does seem a peculiar sort of thing to say.

I've been very, very worried.
Amy had told me Mom had been at school with Mrs. Findley and Mrs. Schaller. They met with Waltzman. Waltzman had also been talking earlier with the Witches.

Mom at school. Again. This was not good. This is worse than when Mom was missing. I hate to say it, but I wish she was missing again. I wish— damn, fucking, damn, I can't talk to anybody.

No. I don't wish she was missing again. I didn't mean that, God.

The furniture is all over the place and Mom is asleep. She was at school and now Miss Austin has been sick for two days.

"SUICIDE IDEATION AMONG EARLY ADOLESCENTS IS SO COMMON THAT SUICIDE IS THE FOURTH LEADING CAUSE OF DEATH AMONG TWELVE-YEAR-OLDS. SCHOOL COUNSELORS NEED TO BE ESPECIALLY ALERT TO THE ELEVEN SIGNS, OUTLINED IN *STOLLER AND BRICKLAND*." -DOCTOR H.

Mom's right. I should never have been born. If I were the one missing, then everything would settle down.

But as you know, I'm not comfortable getting even little vaccinations or blood tests, so if I killed myself, it would have to be painless. That one poet, Sylvia Plath, put her head in a gas stove. Unfortunately we have an electric stove. Baking yourself to death seems impractical.

I'm finishing the Kafka even though it's no longer assigned. How did Kafka die? He would seem like a good candidate for suicide. I must look this up.

Amy knocked on the door, and then opened it. Like her door, it's never locked.

"Come over. Mom's making sfogliatelle."

"What's that?"

"It's good. Come on." She took my hand.

I love Amy Fowler.

"Divorce is like a colonoscopy. Unpleasant, but such a healthy thing to do you'd gladly do it again."

—Uncle Bill

JEFF

Bill and I were sitting talking in my little office at Bigley after we'd been walking around looking at the recent truck trade-ins just to see if there were any bargains. We didn't expect there to be any and, true to the wisdom of any good self-fulfilling prophecy, there weren't. But we weren't wasting time with idle chatter. We were in the midst of a deeply satisfying discussion about the performance of the new Pontiac Firebird with its killer 400-cubic-inch V8, and had not touched at all on the situation on the home front, when Adalicia called.

It was good to hear her voice. What a strange and wonderful woman. I've missed her greatly. I guess I was rationalizing my errant behavior, but for a short period I had told myself that Adalicia, even with all of her outlandish proclivities, would be a better mother for Chris as he grew older than Mary would be. You wouldn't think it, given Adalicia's flamboyant personality, but the same as with Martha, I found great comfort in this woman's company.

Nevertheless after mutually acknowledging our foolishness and the futility of that foolishness, Adalicia and I thought it would be best for everyone if we didn't see each other. I reluctantly agreed.

Bill shakes his head whenever we touch on my women problems. He can't understand why I don't find some way to divorce Mary.

But I could never abandon her. I don't know what would happen to her. Or Chris, God save him.

Not that I'm much good for either of them, but maybe something can be done. I'm trying—or maybe I just tell myself I'm trying. I was encouraged when we had Kandleman. I called him and he was willing to see her again. But Mary was adamantly opposed. I talked to Doctor Shore. He said he would have to defer to Kandleman. I am so weary. There's no doubt that Mary is increasingly disturbed, loading up on medication which seems to make her more erratic than ever.

Which was why Adalicia had broken our silence and was calling me. Her cousin, Theresa Austin, was in trouble. And...

"One of the reasons she's in trouble, Jeff, is that your wife has been talking to the principal at the high school. She's accusing Theresa of quote 'bothering' unquote your boy, Christopher."

"I'm not sure I've got this straight."

"Yes, you do. And it's just plain *awful.*"

Over all these progressively difficult years I've certainly learned not to be surprised by anything Mary does. This however was a chilling jolt, a jolt that I couldn't believe, and yet the simple truth was that I knew it was true. It was true and terrible. The pretty young teacher who had been so kind to Chris, the teacher who had had the truly nice idea of having Chris and me to dinner when half the town thought I was a murderer—this lovely woman was in deep trouble because Mary is crazy as a loon. And I don't know what to do about it.

MISS THERESA AUSTIN

After my meeting with the so-called "Ethics Committee" I felt physically ill and dirty. Everything about me was stained. I had done nothing. Yet, I had carelessly done everything. I had made that sweet, brilliant boy a victim of the worst kind of filthy innuendo.

Now I was holed up with Adalicia and Aunt Elissa in an unfriendly town. We sat at the kitchen table playing with our food, whispering to each other as if one of the neighbors might be listening. And they probably were.

I'd called in sick two days in a row. We didn't know how much longer I could hide without taking some action—deciding either to run or fight. My inclination was toward the latter course.

"I know this is my own fault."

"I didn't help," said Adalicia. She looked at me with the sad eyes of someone who knew that they had been complicit in inadvertently hurting someone else.

I said, "This could ruin Christopher's life. Don't you think I've got to fight this?"

"That would probably make things worse for him."

Aunt Elissa, who hadn't participated in any of our discussions of my problem, had a question: "Who was it who hired you, Theresa?"

"The Superintendent. Dalton Prevell, why?"

"That young man you said was so smart and good-looking?"

"Yes."

"Call him."

Dalton Prevell would be happy to see me. I'd been at the school, what, about four months now and he'd been wondering how I was getting along. I could drop by his office, oh, let's see—how about next Monday? I really wanted to see him sooner, if possible. I had a problem. Oh, had I talked with Harold about it? Yes, I'd talked with Doctor Waltzman and frankly Doctor Waltzman was the problem.

The next morning at eight I was in the young Superintendent's office. He listened to the story. Of course, he was disturbed. Said he was terribly sorry. This must be a misunderstanding of some kind. He called Doctor Waltzman's office. I sat listening to his

"Ohs" and "I sees" for what seemed like at least twenty minutes, but probably was only three.

He picked up a pencil, tapped it.

"I've never had a problem like this, Theresa. According to Harold, he's not your problem at all. The problem is some of the mothers. In particular, Mrs. Mullins is accusing you."

"Yes, I know that. But they have no reason, especially Mrs. Mullins."

"Perception, Theresa. Perception is reality. People have seen you taking him for rides. They say he spent the night at your house. Maybe the boy himself has said something."

"He wouldn't have."

"You don't know."

Oh, ye gods of controlled comportment, let there be not moisture in mine eyes! I stood up to go. I told him how sorry I was to have taken his time.

"Wait. What do you want to do?"

I said I was inclined to want to sue for defamation of character, slander.

"Who would you sue?"

"Waltzman—O'Malley—Himoski—"

"The boy's mother, too? The whole school district?"

"No."

No. Not at all.

"Theresa, I'm so sorry this has happened. I know you don't want to, but I suggest you do resign—for health reasons—family reasons. I'll see to it that your resume does not reflect any of this. Meanwhile, consider this option—I will recommend you to a friend of mine who's in charge of the American Embassy school in Manila. I think they call it the International School. It's a fairly small, private school. Classes in English. The pay is good and it's a good chance for foreign travel. Go new places. See new things. Meantime, this whole ugly incident will eventually fade away."

"What about the boy? Christopher?"

"He needn't know why you resigned."

"You're kidding?"

"I really don't know. What about referring him to the counselors?"

"At school? Mrs. Whitestone?

"I guess."

"You're still not serious?"

"I'm sorry, Theresa. I really don't have any suggestions regarding him. Do consider the Manila school."

"Every family tree has its sap."
-Uncle Bill

JEFF

After Adalicia's phone call, I left Bigley early. When I got home, I found a too familiar sight—Mary lying on the couch with a wet cloth on her forehead. Even after several days, I still hadn't gotten used to having the couch on the opposite wall from where it had been. Mary was not asleep. She eyed me warily.

I pulled up the ottoman next to her and reached for her hand. She started to pull away, then let me hold it.

"Mary—"

"I have a headache."

"I know. But there's something I need to know. You went to Chris's school the other day."

"What of it?" She pulled her hand back. I could see that she was irritated by my attempt to get on her good side, but I pressed ahead.

"Did you accuse Theresa Austin of hurting Chris?"

"Who?"

"Chris's English teacher."

"No."

"What have you said to Chris?"

"He's your wonderful son. You talk to him."

I got up, went to the refrigerator, opened it, looked in, closed it. "Is Chris at Amy's?"

"I suppose."

I picked up the copy of *The Metamorphosis* that Chris had left on an end table that was still beside its original wall, but was now no longer flanking the couch. I opened it and read the first line softly to myself: *"One morning, as Gregor Samsa was waking up from troubled dreams, he discovered that in bed he had been changed into a monstrous verminous bug."* Right now, I don't think I'd mind being a verminous bug.

Mary sat up. "What bug?"

"Verminous."

"You don't make any sense, Jeff. No wonder I have a headache."

"Why were you at the school, Mary?"

"Louise and Polly and I were there together! We decided something had to be done!"

"About what?"

"About that black Arab teacher."

"Why?"

"You dumb-headed, complete fool, Jeffrey. What fucking planet do you live on? I TOLD YOU Chris was in danger from that woman! It turned out he was! So, they're going to get rid of her. Go away."

I walked to the sink and stood there, holding my head in my hands.

MISS THERESA AUSTIN

I arrived at school just after the buses. Those vapid sophomore girls were, as usual, talking on the steps with the slouching boy who smokes. They are apparently there in all weather.

I walked past the little group, and they sing-songed, "Hello, Miss Austin."

I nodded and went into the school, up the stairs to Waltzman's office, past Penny, opened the door and stepped into his inner office. He was at his desk with a stapled document in his hands.

He looked up, quite startled. I opened my shoulder bag and reached inside. Waltzman dropped the document and actually ducked.

I pulled out my contract and walked to the edge of his giant desk. The little man was cringing. I tore the contract into six pieces and dropped them on his desk.

I walked out, nodded to Penny, and marched up to Miss O'Malley's room. She was at the door as students were filing in. I said, "Good morning, Dear," walked past her and left the T-Shirt on her desk. It was colorfully lettered: "Be Great—Celebrate—Black History Month—February."

I went down to the gym. Himoski was out on the floor berating his hapless captives. I went to his office and put the paperback on his desk: *Erasing Sexual Harassment From Our Schools.* I inscribed the fly-leaf: "Hope this is helpful, Theresa Austin."

I passed Spurling at the door to his room and blew him a kiss.

I went down to Trisha Whitestone's office. She was not there, as usual. I left the paperback on her desk: *Understanding Teens.* I wrote in the same inscription as Himoski's book, "Hope this is helpful, Theresa Austin."

Finally I went up to Ivan's classroom. His students were all in their seats by the time I got there, but he was still looking over some notes at his desk. As I walked in, there was a slight murmur from the class. He looked up, wildly red-eyed as usual.

"Theresa?"

I put an apple on his desk. "An apple for the teacher. Thank you, Ivan."

I left. I couldn't bear to talk to anyone, not even Ivan. I had to get out of Jason Willard Watson High School and get home to fill out my application to the International School of Manila on University Parkway, Fort Bonifacio, Taguig City, Philippines.

CHRISTOPHER

It's official. I asked Mrs. Leitner and she said, sorry to say, yes, Miss Austin had resigned.

I went to her classroom and saw that she had cleared out her desk. The *New Yorker* is gone. Persephone is gone. The old homecoming poster is all that remains on the otherwise unused bulletin board.

Shirley Ann Binley is now our teacher. A knitting ninny for a teacher. Depressingsome. *No. Enough of this affectation.* I no longer feel like making up words. It's just plain depressing. The empty feeling of this joyless place is now permanent. Without Miss Austin the light at the end of the day is gone for me.

Teachers come and go, of course. Amy says we have to get used to that fact.

But still—it is so empty here.

Dad was home early when I got there. He was just standing by the sink, holding his head. Mom was on the couch with a cloth on her forehead. Apparently Dad had caught Mom's headache. Dad said, "Hi." I said, "Hi," and went to the refrigerator.

"We're out of milk."

Dad said, "I know."

"Miss Austin is gone. She resigned," I said. "Let's go get some milk."

Dad and I hopped in the car and went to the 7/11. We picked up a frozen pizza, thin crust, imported from Canada.

"Did Mom get them to force her to resign?"

"I'm not sure exactly what she did, but she and a couple of the Ditzy-Dip women went to see Principal Waltzman, so yes, I guess they were probably instrumental in her resignation."

"Aww, Dad, face it. She did."

When we got home the couch was back in its original place. Mom was sitting on it, smoking a cigarette, reading *The Metamorphosis*. I had never in my life seen Mom smoke. Or seen her read much of anything besides magazines.

Dad said, "Mary, when did you start smoking?"

"I've always smoked. I just quit when we had the trouble, but I decided to start again yesterday. Nicotine, I read, is very soothing. This is an awful book. I can't imagine anyone wanting to read it, much less assigning it to children."

"It's a classic," I said.

"Who says?" Mom said.

"Everybody," Dad said.

"That black Arab teacher, I suppose. Come here, Chrissy. I'm so sorry for what she did to you, but in a short time you'll forget the whole thing. Your father refused to protect you, but I did."

294

I have been afraid of my mother. But at that moment I was not. I stood over her and shouted at her—

"YOU AWFUL, AWFUL WOMAN! YOU DID THIS TO MISS AUSTIN!"

Mom pulled back, cowering into the couch. Dad tried to hold me back. I stuck my face right into her face and screamed. *"She's gone because of you! You ruined everything! I could kill you, you bitch, you fucking, horrible creature!"*

I turned and went to the door. *"I don't love you at all! I HOPE YOU GO TO HELL!"*

I ran out the door. I had no idea where I was going. I just ran into the woods. Dad was coming behind me, calling my name. I ran faster, stumbling, tearing through the blackberry bushes, tripping on the honeysuckle vines. I heard Dad still calling. My face and hands were cut and I didn't care. I wanted away from both of them. My lily-livered, coward of a father. My horrible mother. I ran until I was out of breath, exhausted, crying. There were still small remnants of the last snow piled here and there. I tripped on some rotten logs and fell down into damp, mucky dirt and thorny weeds. I hoped a rattlesnake would crawl out and sink his fangs into me and I would die. When they found me, rigor mortis would already be setting in. I would be cold, stiff, my eyes lifeless, unseeing. Dead. Dead. *Dead!*

I was lying there for I don't know how long. I was very cold now, shivering. I heard my dad crunching through the woods, still calling my name. I didn't move until I felt bugs of some kind on my arm. I'd read that if you disturbed fire ants they would attack you, even in winter. Whatever these were, I shook them off and moved several feet away to a dryer, flatter place. I was worried now that they might not find me, and it was getting colder, so I got up and started to walk toward where I thought the main road was. I would hitchhike back to the 7/11, borrow some change from Mr. Patel, and call Uncle Bill, if I could remember his number. I never had dialed it. I'd only seen it—was it 679-252-0914 or 041? One way or another I would ask him to come get me, then from his house I would call Aunt Martha. That was my plan.

I was walking along the side of the highway when I heard the fire truck. It was coming in the opposite direction from the 7/11. I turned and watched it.

MARY

Jeff had run out chasing after Chris. It seemed like a good idea to get rid of the verminous bug book. No one should read such repulsive things. Certainly not Chris. I went into the kitchen and dropped the filthy thing into the sink. I lit some of the pages with a match and watched as it slowly began to smolder, then burn. It made the room smoky. I opened the window and went back into the living room

I knew I had been so absolutely right, and Chris's behavior confirmed it. "Acting out" like he did would never have happened if Chris had not been involved with that teacher. It was so clear.

But they wouldn't see it that way, would they? They'd think it was somehow *my* fault. The crazy-acting mother is to blame for her crazy-acting son. That's what they would say.

All these years. People not listening to me, treating me like that Kandleman did. Mental! That's the word all those fucking people use. I know that. Well, now I'm crying. Chrissy said such hateful things. I never knew he even knew such hateful words. I suppose that girl, Amy, uses rough language. She probably would with her background, but I never thought that Chris would.

He says he doesn't love me.

He wouldn't say that if Martha were here. Once again, she is not here.

I walked around as I thought. Like before, they just *had* to see that my point of view was sensible. Sometimes you just have to *make* people pay attention.

I got out the scrapbooks, the pictures and souvenirs of Martha, the pictures of Chris as a sweet child, the Christmas cards. I took all of those things and piled them in the center of Chris's little bedroom off the narrow hall of that crappy house. I went to the kitchen and found that vegetable oil spray that Jeff had bought for his sautéed garden vegetable experiments. Tasteless messes of health food garbage.

I went back to Chris's room and lit a few old Christmas cards. I placed the scrapbooks on the flames, and then sprayed the pile with the oil spray. The flames shot back toward me. I threw the can into the burning pile and went back to the kitchen. I took four pills, lit a cigarette and went out, intending to sit on the steps until Jeff and Chris got back and would see what they had made me do. But on the top step something happened. The sky spun and I felt myself falling down off the steps to the ground.

CHRISTOPHER

When I saw the fire truck and turned to watch, it turned in just beyond the woods. That would be Frog Pond Lane, our road. Our house? Amy's? I ran to follow the truck.

As I was running toward Frog Pond, an ambulance came down the highway, following the fire truck into our road.

By the time I got back to the yard outside our house there was a lot of smoke pouring out of the windows and flames shooting up here and there across the roof of the doublewide. Amy and Maria were standing bundled up together, watching while the EMT crew was strapping Mom to a stretcher, preparing to load her into the ambulance. Dad was talking to her. I ran over to him. He grabbed me and hugged me tightly, kissing my cheek and forehead.

"There you are! I couldn't find you! You're frozen!" He held me.

"What happened?"

"She tried to burn the place down."

Mom was looking at me. I don't know if she really saw me. I touched her face and kissed her hair.

"I'm sorry, Mom! I'm really sorry! I didn't mean anything I said!"

She continued to stare. There were tears in her eyes.

She said, quite clearly, "I'm really sorry——." She seemed to be repeating what I had just said to her, but I felt she was far away, lost in some unhappy memory.

I heard her mumble something like "——just Florida——" and then she shut her eyes and turned away. The EMT crew hoisted her into the ambulance and shut the doors.

"She set the fire?"

"I'm afraid so."

I started to cry. *I brought this on. I yelled at her. I said terrible things.*

"I DID THIS!"

"No, Chris. No, son."

"Was she burned?"

"Not at all. She was on the ground over there. She wasn't in the house at all."

"What happened to her?"

"They can't tell. Could be a stroke. We don't know. I'm going to follow them to the hospital."

We borrowed coats from the Fowlers and hurried after the ambulance.

****

CHRISTOPHER

2003

After Mom's funeral, Aunt Martha went back to New York. Dad, Uncle Bill, and I went up to Bill's place. His house is just over the county line inside Leistermont County. Dad and Uncle Bill decided that, with a little patchwork and a new roof we three could live there in shabby comfort and I would go to Leistermont High School.

Leistermont had only 480 students and the most active organization in the school was the Future Farmers of America. Most of the kids had to hurry home to their chores, so the school's athletic teams were greatly underhanded. As a result, I became the catcher on the softball team! I can't explain it, but baseball began to fascinate me.

As it turned out, I did get to Harvard. After graduating with a useful major in (wait for it—like father like son) PHILOSOPHY. Aunt Martha had a connection that landed me a job teaching English at Rye Country Day School.

Yes, dear Reader, I am in *EDUCATION!*

Worse than that, I am in *EDUCATION* teaching *RICH KIDS* who would probably not even speak to me if I were not six-foot-three and the baseball coach. I grew. I grew in high school. And I continued to grow in college. And, thank you God, I look a little like my dad.

I live in a studio apartment over the garage of a charming guest house on Grace Church Street. I have a dog of my own, finally—a something artfully mixed with several other things, named, in honor of Miss Austin, "Thisbe." Thisbe is allowed to come to school with me and stay in the corner of my classroom. The school is really quite progressive and quite a few of the kids—well, I like them in spite of the fact that their fathers all run hedge funds.

I also have a friend, Carrie Witte.

> "Carrie Witte says she is looking forward to the challenge of playing the controversial opening solo in the orchestra's forthcoming performance of Stravinsky's *The Rite of Spring.* She says, "Bassoon lore is full of stories about bassoonists driven half mad by the piece ever since its premiere in 1913. Some say it should be placid. Others contend it should be primitively wild. Since it's actually beyond the range of the instrument, I'm on the wild side."
> --Rye Community News

Carrie works in an organic coffee house and plays bassoon in the community orchestra. I love to watch her wildly play her bassoon. It is a perverse pleasure. She looks like any minute her head will explode. She is a clown. A feral bassoonist!

She has what she calls "a degree in non-profit theater," and a delicious laugh that sounds like bells. As it just so happens, she has beautiful Prussian blue-black hair, short, with little bangs.

Amy Fowler went to Penn, majored in finance, and is now a social worker in Philadelphia. She says she was torn between social work and going to work for Goldman Sachs, but her dad said she would meet a much more refined and intelligent group of people in social work, especially among the homeless. We keep in close touch.

Much as one would wish it weren't so, as far as I know, nothing bad happened to the Ditzy Dips or the young Witches of Watson. P.B. Himoski went on to win a state championship, and for his work with crippled children he was given the Humanitarian of the Year Award by the Jason Watson VFW Post 5357. Waltzman, I'm sure, went on to a quiet retirement in some place warm. I visualize him wearing peach Bermuda shorts, black socks, and a lime Izod shirt with his flaccid old-man breasts protruding while he ogles teenage girls in bikinis.

Beverly Beatrice Spurling married one of the nice lunch ladies who, ironically, is also named Beverly. I heard that Mrs. Whitestone published a

303

book called *Putting Jesus Back in the Classroom*. And Miss O'Malley is probably embalmed but still teaching.

Todd London, Chief Broken Nose, was killed in a motorcycle accident.

My dad—the lovable, comfort-seeking rogue of Bigley Buick commercials—manages somehow to split his time between two women. He, who had never been skiing in his life, went skiing at Chamonix with Adalicia Auttenberg. He went on a cruise to the Galapagos with Aunt Martha. My father has always been wonderful company, especially for women it seems. I wish Mom had been able to enjoy him.

Every time Dad and I are together we talk about her. The conversation begins with "we should have" and we go on to share great regrets about all that we had left undone in her care.

I see Aunt Martha in the city quite often. She's very open about the fact that she was once madly in love with Dad. Now she says, "I love being with him, but when I'm not, I don't miss him."

I've come to realize that not understanding much about people who were older when you were young is just a fact you have to accept. The puzzle never comes together.

Dad and Bill and I went back to the burned out trailer three times to see if we could salvage some of the things we really wanted. Most stuff was badly damaged or so smoky-smelling that it was unusable. One item, however, was the book of Philip Larkin's poetry that Aunt Elissa had given me. A poem that provided a delightfully shocking bit of secret pleasure for Amy and me when we discovered it was this:

This Be The Verse

"They fuck you up, your mum and dad.
They may not mean to, but they do.
They fill you with the faults they had
And add some extra, just for you.

But they were fucked up in their turn
By fools in old-style hats and coats,
Who half the time were soppy-stern
And half at one another's throats.

Man hands on misery to man.
It deepens like a coastal shelf.
Get out as early as you can,
And don't have any kids yourself."

--Philip Larkin

At the time we read it Amy and I agreed that we definitely wouldn't have any kids. Not because they would perpetuate misery, but because we thought it was just plain unfair to bring them into a world like this. Amy and I agreed that everyone, everywhere, has pretty much made a fucked up mess of everything.

Now, I'm not so sure. I know Amy doesn't feel quite the same. She just had a little boy. Named him Josephus after her father.

I may be in love with Carrie. I really don't know. The whole settling-down thing is troublesome to think about. There are so many potential disasters lurking out there. You could be married to someone who turns out not to be at all what you thought she was. The probability of that happening must be rather high.

However, one can't spend a lifetime of total avoidance.

Uncle Bill said his wife, Miyako, wanted a dog desperately but would never get one because, she said, the dog will get old and die. Bill insisted anyway and got her an Akita because she was Japanese and the breed has a kind of "mythic aura" that complimented Miyako's personality, he said.

The dog didn't die. She did. Cancer took Miyako many years before the dog went on to join its ancestors.

What of Miss Austin?

Very curious. She went to Manila, then to another embassy school in Bishkek, then she was never heard from again. Adalicia told Dad that her cousin just fell off the face of the earth. She didn't return for holidays nor for Aunt Elissa's funeral. They don't even know if she is alive.

Perhaps she wasn't real. Like one of those moments in the past that I didn't know if I'd really remembered or I'd just heard about so many times I believed I was there.

No, Miss Austin was there all right. For just a few months when I was twelve years old, there was this perfect creature in an imperfect place.

Those who condemned her were right about one thing. I did love Miss Austin. None of them could ever ruin the purity of that love—a kind of love you can't ever equal again in your life. I loved the way she pronounced my name—"Chris-to-pher"—stretching it out musically, like the chimes of a Westminster clock.

I loved her catching herself talking in circles to avoid offending the religious members of the class, knowing full well that she had already offended them.

I loved her blazing eyes, her smile, her dramatic gestures to the gods of literature, the nimbus around her shining hair.

Yes, I did love Miss Austin.

ABOUT THE AUTHOR

Connor Marshall is a freelance writer
who has written for various media,
publications, and productions, including
plays produced in Chicago, New York, and
Europe. Connor lives in Frederick,
Maryland, and may be contacted at
cnnor.mrshll@gmail.com